CAGED BY HER DRAGONS

CAGED BY HER DRAGONS

FATED MATE OF THE DRAGON CLANS, BOOK ONE

by

GINNA MORAN

Copyright © 2020 by Ginna Moran
All Rights Reserved.

All rights reserved under International and Pan-American Copyright Conventions, including the right of reproduction in whole or in part in any form or by any electronic or mechanical means including information storage and retrieval systems, without written permission, except in the case of brief quotations embodied in critical articles and reviews.

ISBN 978-1-951314-54-5 (soft cover)
ISBN: 978-1-951314-55-2 (hard cover)

This is a work of fiction. All of the characters, organizations, and events portrayed in this novel are either products of the author's imagination or are used fictitiously.

Cover design by Silver Starlight Designs
Cover images copyright Depositphotos

For Inquiries Contact:
Sunny Palms Press
9663 Santa Monica Blvd Suite 1158
Beverly Hills, CA 90210, USA
www.sunnypalmspress.com
www.GinnaMoran.com

For Mom,
I wish you could've been here for this.
Love you forever and always.

CHAPTER 1

Sky Dancers

"IF YOU DROP me, you're dead." Galaxy Gold puffs out his bare chest, standing beside me on the platform only big enough for the two of us.

Music blares from the speaker below, muffling the soft commotion from our audience. A spotlight shoots a beam from below, setting the sequins on my costume sparkling. My chest heaves with my breath, the anticipation of our routine humming through my muscles. I don't usually get nervous, but Galaxy threw off my mojo an hour before we were to step on stage.

"Maybe you should've thought about that before changing the routine tonight," I say, faking my biggest smile. The glitter from my makeup sparkles on my eyelashes, distracting me just a bit. Luckily for me, I can do most of my routines with my eyes closed, even with last-minute changes. "Plus, if I drop you, you'll be the dead one. So say a prayer, babycakes. Thirty seconds."

The spotlight illuminates the world, shadowing the crowd fifty feet below. We have zero permits for our setup, but that doesn't matter to Galaxy. We'll be on the road before any of the county law enforcement comes patrolling.

Galaxy clenches his jaw, trying to get his smile to outshine mine. "Twenty seconds. Don't fuck up. You fuck up, and no one will tell their friends. We'll be out of business by the next town."

Star Slater claps her hands to the beat of the music, screaming for the audience to cheer us on. According to her, silence during a performance is deadly. I think it's more relaxing than anything. It's far better to have someone silently hope for the worst, keeping their morbid thoughts to themselves, rather than having a bunch of asshole teenage boys chanting for us to fall. Fifty feet is a long way down with only asphalt to splat on.

CAGED BY HER DRAGONS

"Yeah, right. If I drop you, more people will come to see," I tease.

Galaxy groans and tightens his fingers through mine. He stretches out his other arm and straightens his back. I stare at him in my peripheral vision, awaiting his cue. Pointing his finger, he motions to Orion O'Brian below. I bounce on the balls of my feet and mirror Galaxy's pose, waving my arm out on the opposite side.

"Ten seconds, sugar pie," he mutters through his clenched jaw, his mouth never breaking from his performance-ready grin. He flexes his muscles and watches Orion dance across the stage below to give Star the ends of the silk ropes.

She twirls them in her hands and swings across the stage to position herself beneath us. Tipping her head back, she greets me with a dazzling smile. "Let's hear some noise for the brilliant sky dancer, Nova!" Star claps her hands and shouts my name over and over, cheering me on.

I chuckle and blow a kiss at her, the fact that she doesn't get the audience to chant for Galaxy not going unnoticed. She's still pissed off that he cut her act in half and made her the emcee for tonight's show because Mars missed our departure time and got himself stranded in Bay Port until tomorrow. The dumb fuck. He knew better than to keep Galaxy waiting. If Galaxy is one thing, it's punctual. And stubborn.

Galaxy squeezes my hand, drawing my attention to him. "Get ready, Nova. If you don't screw this up, I'll give you the closing act tomorrow night," he says, snatching the silk rope Star swings at him from below. He quickly twines it around his bulging muscular arm and prepares to jump.

"What?" I ask, excitement rushing through me. The closing act? He's never allowed anyone to close with a solo apart from himself.

"Now!" Galaxy launches me through the air before I'm ready.

The world whirls around me as I flip midair, my brain screaming to get my shit together. I should've expected a low blow move from Galaxy. He loves testing me and freaking out the crowd. I miss my mark, my fingers an inch from the bar I'm supposed to swing around to land on the next platform.

The crowd gasps and screams as I freefall a dozen feet. I snatch the rung of the metal ladder on the backup platform and jerk myself to a stop. My fingers scream in pain, and my arms stretch with the force, but I manage to save my ass.

Erupting in loud cheers, the audience continues to yell and chant my name. I flick my hand out and wave, acting as if missing my mark is all part of the show. With a breath, I climb the ladder halfway up and stretch my legs open and out to do the splits in the air just to piss Galaxy off. I bet he didn't expect me to recover so gracefully. But hell, I'll be

CAGED BY HER DRAGONS

sore tomorrow.

I reach the platform and blow a kiss to Galaxy, letting him know I'm ready. He wraps the silk rope around his waist and jumps from his platform, spinning a few times. Orion adjusts the length from behind the flimsy curtain of our make-shift stage, sending Galaxy another ten feet into the air. As much as Galaxy gets on my nerves, I can't help myself from admiring his lean, muscular frame. His arms flex and his abs tighten as he performs his aerial acrobatics, twisting and untwisting himself far more skillfully than I ever could.

The crowd cheers with his quick spins, and I rub my hands together and count silently through the last twenty seconds of his performance. Galaxy climbs all the way to the top of the scaffolding of our stage and hangs by one arm to show off his strength.

He blows a kiss at the audience to signal my cue. Swinging by his arm, he jerks his body to fall toward the other platform. He purposefully misses and yells out, flailing his arms. Bending my knees, I jump into the air and grab onto the silk rope.

Right on cue, Galaxy catches my leg and stops his freefall. I jerk a foot down with his weight, burning my hands on the ropes. I nearly let go in the process. Our roles should've been reversed considering he's a good seventy pounds heavier than I am, but he controls the act and spotlight. It's his name on the marquee. *Galaxy Gold and the Sky Dancers*. Funny, I know. But I love performing, and I can't beat free travel and a place to sleep in the RV, even if I do have to share the bed with Star.

"Let's give it up for Galaxy and Nova!" Star yells, clapping her hands.

Galaxy slides down the rope and stops a few inches from the ground. He tips his head back to look up at me. I release the rope and somersault through the air, silently begging for Galaxy to catch me. His strong arms engulf me, and he swings me back into the air to flip once more to land on my feet.

I fling my arms out with my smile, listening to the roar of the crowd. Galaxy grabs my hand and twirls me to him, where he locks me into a hug and kisses me right on the lips. I tug myself away and narrow my eyes at him but keep smiling. We bow to the audience, and Star reminds them that we live on their generosity and wouldn't be able to entertain them otherwise in her polite way of asking for donations.

Skipping behind the curtain, I duck through it and grab my water from the folding table. Orion jogs to me and scoops me up. I laugh and pat his cheeks, squirming until he sets me down. This is my favorite part of the show. The finish. Not because it's over but because we're all high on adrenaline, and Galaxy sheds his hard-ass attitude for a few

CAGED BY HER DRAGONS

hours.

Star whistles through her fingers, bolting toward us. "That was fucking brilliant, Nova. You were a rock star." Hugging me, Star kisses each of my cheeks. "Maybe we can work on an act. I had some ideas—"

"All right, everyone. Listen up," Galaxy says, stepping backstage while cutting Star off.

A tall man in a suit follows behind him, staying close to his side. His blue eyes search around the room before landing on me. Starting from my feet, he works his way up the length of my body to drink me in. Galaxy notices the man's attention on me, and gives me what I can only describe as The Look. Galaxy must want something he thinks I can get with my charm. Or my ass. Whichever works. Fucker

"This is Mr. Lioht. He's kindly invited us to his bar for drinks on him. Get changed and hustle. We leave in five." Galaxy smirks at me, daring me to argue. It's not that I care—because it wouldn't be the first time one of us, including Galaxy, has used their assets for something. Maybe Mr. Lioht is a rich bastard who wants to book us for entertainment.

Star squeals and claps her hands, rushing toward Mr. Lioht. She curtseys in front of him, stretching her long legs. I silently beg for Mr. Lioht to turn his interest to her, because she's pretty, bubbly, and a lot of fun, but his attention remains glued to me.

"Thank you, Mr. Lioht," she says. "Nova and I love a good bar scene." She's not wrong about that.

Mr. Lioht remains utterly silent and only responds to Star with a nod. I run my fingers over my head and tug my hair from its bun. The red tendrils cascade over my shoulders and down my back, tickling my waist. I stroll the few feet to where I left my boots, not giving Mr. Lioht my attention but remaining aware of him.

I don't rush to change with Star or touch up my heavy makeup. Wasting clean clothes on some bar is the last thing I want to do, but I know pajamas wouldn't fly with Galaxy. My glittery black and sequin costume will do. It's not like the costume is too far out there. The soft material hugs my curves, my long legs on display from the shorts of my one-piece and rhinestones decorate the collar of my halter top. I love this particular costume the most. Galaxy prefers we get attention anyway. It helps bring people to our show.

"Your performance tonight was splendid." The deep, sultry voice draws my attention to Mr. Lioht. His shadow casts across the floor as I tie my heeled boots. "It was unlike anything I've seen. You're a natural in the air. Elegant and graceful." This guy. He's sure laying it on thick.

I stand up and straighten my bodice, keeping my voice soft to sound sweet. "My aunt put me in gymnastics when I was a child. I've spent most of my life in a gymnasium and being a daredevil on anything I could climb and balance on.

CAGED BY HER DRAGONS

I've always loved the feeling of flying through the air. Galaxy helped hone my performance skills," I comment, turning my head slightly to meet his gaze. I bite my lip with a smile as he pretends to be engrossed with what I have to say. "And thank you, Mr. Lioht. I'm happy you enjoyed the show. It's why I do what I do."

"I must admit that the whole performance was enchanting. I'd have never guessed you to be...what do you call it? A sky dancer?"

I try not to let my smile falter. His comment rubs me the wrong way. What does he mean by it? I decide not to overthink it and say, "Aerial acrobat. But I love being called a sky dancer. It feels more fitting in my soul. I love what I do. I mean, look at you. I'd have never been treated for a night out by a gentleman otherwise. I know Star feels the same. It's so nice of you."

I can already see his interest in me building. He's a little older than I prefer, but he does seem nice. Maybe Galaxy will hold true to his word if I manage to get whatever he wants from Mr. Lioht. And hopefully it is a paying gig. It would benefit all of us.

"It's my honor, and please, call me Rhett." He offers his hand out to me, and I automatically shake it.

Static shocks the both of us, making me laugh. Energy always seems to cling to me after a performance with the ropes. I tilt my head up to glance at Rhett. He graces me

~15~

with a smile that crinkles the corners of his startling light blue eyes. It's not seductive or leering, purely friendly, and I wonder if I misjudged him. I'm just not used to men offering me compliments just to be nice. I guess I'll find out.

I study his features for a moment, trailing my gaze over his sharp cheekbones and to his angular, clean-shaven jaw. His brisk, floral scent wafts with the breeze. My hair blows around my shoulders, and I realize we're both staring at each other far longer than we should.

"I hope this isn't too forward," Rhett says, breaking the silence. "But have you considered trading in your profession with a traveling show to something more permanent? I've been thinking about having a nightly act."

I shift my gaze, watching Star and Orion exit the RV. "That's an interesting proposition. I've never done something completely solo, and well, this is my family."

He hums under his breath. "Perhaps you'd consider the idea if I extended the offer to your companions. I just, there is something about you. I'd like to get to know you." Well, if that isn't a bit much, offering me a gig just to get me to stay longer.

If Galaxy didn't saunter from his trailer and smack his hands together for attention, I bet Rhett's next words would have been asking if he could take me to dinner. It's not the first time I've been hit on after a performance...just not by anyone quite like Rhett. I mean, who the hell wears a suit to

CAGED BY HER DRAGONS

a popup sideshow? Or try to extend my stay with crazy propositions?

I don't get the chance to ask because Star and Orion join our group. Rhett doesn't persist with his conversation and allows Galaxy to lead him toward the parking lot. Galaxy automatically starts inquiring more about the area and which towns are better to stop in. He even suggests a performance at Rhett's bar tomorrow night. A blip of concern washes through me. What the hell would I do if Rhett offered Galaxy the gig as a way to get me to stay? Would I? I'm not even sure if I'd have a choice. This is my life. The only thing I can count on is that Galaxy doesn't like to stay anywhere for long.

"Nova, damn it. Did you hear me?" Galaxy asks, drawing my attention from the shiny convertible parked next to the junk jeep we tow behind the RV.

I purse my lips without comment.

"Mr. Lioht wants you to ride with him. You cool with that?" Galaxy glares, daring me to tell him no. I don't have to read his mind to know he wants me to take advantage of the situation to find out how much we can get out of this man.

I bob my head. "Yeah, that's fine." I only agree because I know Galaxy will be following. Also, I can't resist wanting to climb into the convertible. I don't recall ever riding in a luxury car, and I'm down to experience things at least once.

I doubt Rhett will do anything crazy. He wants me to hang around and not flee.

Rhett smiles and waits at his black two-seater Porsche with the passenger's door open. I look at the pristine leather and then down to my glittering ensemble.

I hesitate. "Maybe I should ride with my friends. My costume might get glitter everywhere."

Rhett motions to me to get in. "Then it'll just be another way for me to remember you, sky dancer."

I giggle at his flirting and slide into the cool seat. Before I know it, Rhett's speeding down the dark road with tall trees on both sides. I keep an eye on Galaxy's Jeep in the side mirror. It's a good thing he drives like a maniac or he'd never be able to keep up.

"Nova? I'm assuming that's not your real name, is it?" Rhett asks, adjusting the volume on the stereo until it reaches a background level pitch.

I swivel to glance at the side of his face. "It is now. I legally changed it. Nova Noble, Sky Dancer for Galaxy Gold. I think it has a nice ring to it, don't you think?"

"It does," he says, his features softening. "Nova Noble." My name sounds softly on his voice as he says it to himself like he wants to imprint it on his brain forever. "May I once again be forward with you?"

Ah, hell. Here it comes. He's going to ask me out. I wish he would've waited until the end of the night.

CAGED BY HER DRAGONS

I flick my attention to the Jeep behind us again. "It depends. I'm not going to go out with you so that you can fuck me if that's currently what's on your mind." Crass? Maybe. Worth seeing his surprise? Absolutely.

He laughs in exasperation, the husky tone of his voice lingering in my mind. "I suppose I should've chosen my words more carefully. I can imagine you get propositioned a lot in your profession."

I crinkle my nose. "Asked out, yes. Propositioned? I'm a performer. Nothing more."

He groans, shaking his head. "My apologies. I didn't mean to insinuate anything."

I slouch in the seat as awkward silence falls between us. Staring out the windshield, I keep my attention on the road. I can feel Rhett's eyes penetrating the side of my face, but I don't want to look at him. I just hope this car ride ends soon.

"Where the hell is your bar anyway?" I ask, resting my elbows on my knees. I know it hasn't been more than a few minutes, but time seems to slow.

"I have a confession to make," Rhett says in response. His words are the last things I want to hear after asking him where the hell he's taking me.

My chest tightens, and once again, I search the side mirror with the Jeep. "I swear there better be a bar. Don't think I won't fight."

Rhett turns on his blinker and swerves right onto a gravel road. Dust sprays behind us with the sudden movement. I grip the door, a blip of fear sneaking up on me.

"I wouldn't expect anything less." Rhett punches the throttle, speeding down the road. "You know, I've been searching for you, and you have been one hard woman to find."

Fuck. "And why would you be looking for me? Did my aunt hire you? I told her that I needed my own life. I couldn't live with my mom's past straining our relationship."

"Your aunt, Delphia?" he questions.

"What did you call me?" I snap, fear sneaking up on me.

"That is your name, isn't it? Delphia Drakovich." A flash of light pops through the darkness, and I grip the door handle, wondering if I'd survive if I jumped out. Rhett shouldn't know my name. I've only ever told Galaxy. I haven't even heard it since I up and left my aunt and uncle in the middle of the night with only a note. There was a reason, and now my past seems to come back to haunt me.

"Stop the car," I say instead of responding to him.

"Not yet."

I squeeze my eyes shut. "I said stop the car!"

"We are stopped," Rhett says, his voice lowering. "Look around."

CAGED BY HER DRAGONS

Fluttering my eyes open, I stare at the empty parking lot outside the bar. Galaxy honks the horn on his Jeep, startling me.

"What the fuck?" I shout, flinging the door open.

"Delphia, wait." Rhett reaches for my hand. "Please."

I don't wait. I don't want to be alone with him for another second.

I flee.

Chapter 2

The Den

"NOVA!" STAR CALLS from behind me as I rush...who knows where. Shit. How am I going to explain any of this? Rhett acted surprised that I mentioned my aunt, which makes me even more afraid. If he didn't know Aunt McKayla, it means he knew my mom...and she wasn't exactly a model citizen. She was a thief and liar, and it all added up until the law caught up with her and she ended up

CAGED BY HER DRAGONS

behind bars where she lost her life. My dad too. I don't remember them, but Aunt McKayla told me what I needed to know in case...and it looks like I needed the information now. Because fuck.

"Where you going, kitten? The bar is that way." A tall, attractive man steps from what looks like a shed, startling me.

I nearly eat shit on the ground, but the guy catches me by the wrist.

"All that's out here is forest and wild animals. You wouldn't want to get mauled, now would you?" he adds, his lips pulling into a smile.

"I—"

The man spins me around without waiting for my response. I crash right into Orion, who stands a few feet from Rhett's car. He frowns and steadies me on my feet. Confusion washes over me. I know I was farther away than this. And the man? I swivel on my feet and peer around.

Orion releases a grunt, never being a man of many words. "Nova, are you okay?" I must really look crazy if he even asks.

I open my mouth to tell him that I need to get out of here, but Star claps and laughs, more amused than anyone over standing outside an unimpressive bar that looks empty. It gives Rhett a chance to exit the car. He looks at me from over the roof with a cocked brow. I don't know who the fuck Rhett is, but I don't want to find out.

"Sorry about the sudden turn. I've lived here several months now and still almost always miss the drive." Rhett continues to stare at me, though he raises his voice to speak to everyone. "Welcome to The Den. I know it's not much, but I hope to change that."

Rhett waves his hand at a stone building nestled against a dense forest. I swear I see sparks escape his fingers with his gesture. And shit. It can't all be in my head that this guy is creepy as hell. Something is going on here. Did he drug me? I can't remember if I ate or drank anything after my performance. I just—

"Need anything else before we go, Rhett?" The familiar voice draws my attention back to the man from the shed. I gawk in surprise, unable to keep my gaze to myself as two other really tall, really buff men stroll up next to him.

Rhett shakes his head. "I think I can manage the rest. I'll call you if I need you. See you around, Drekis."

The three of them stare between me and Rhett before just up and walking into the forest. Dragging my attention from them, I take a few steps away to put more space between me and Rhett. I need to think of a casual reason to get Galaxy and the others to leave. The fact that Rhett's been looking for me and knows my real name. Fuck.

I've always known that my parents' deaths remained unsolved, which is why my aunt and uncle were always hesitant to give me any freedom growing up. My mom's sister only did so out of pity with the gymnastics, but it didn't stop her from constantly reminding how awful things were. And now I can't help wondering if Rhett was involved with my mom or anything revolving around her convictions.

Taking another automatic step back, I bump into Orion again. I glance at the Jeep, considering how screwed I'd be if I tackled Galaxy and stole his keys to get out of here. Rhett follows my gaze like he can read my thoughts and struts next to Galaxy. I swear he looks like he's protecting him, slightly putting his body between me and Galaxy.

Orion nudges me to get my ass moving, pushing me to follow behind Star and Galaxy as they stride in the bar's direction upon Rhett's gesture to go ahead. Impatient with my slow movements, Orion dodges past me and abandons me in the gravel parking lot.

"Delphia," Rhett says, once again saying my real name. "You don't have to be afraid. I'm not here to hurt you. You've misunderstood my intentions."

I twist to look at him, my hair whipping behind me with the motion. It pisses me off that he calls me out, which helps turn my fear into anger. "Don't call me by that name. Don't even try to step closer either. I don't know who you are or why you are stalking me, but you need to leave me the hell alone. I'll call the police if you don't."

His light blue eyes blink with a spark of purple. The air

buzzes around us, sending invisible heat crawling over my skin. What the hell?

He snatches my hand. "Relax, Delphia. I'm not your enemy or here to cause you any trouble. I just—"

I rip my hand away from him, my skin still crawling from his touch. "Who are you?" I ask, cutting him off.

"An old friend of your parents, and I'm here only to talk. I've been instructed by them to find you." Rhett runs his hand over his hair, combing it back for a second before letting it fall in his eyes. He tightens his jaw with his words.

"Bullshit," I say, searching the area for the best way to escape. I wish I had my own car. If I run to the road, I'm sure Rhett will continue to follow me. "They've been dead since I was little."

He sighs and shifts on his feet, kicking gravel around with the toe of his designer shoes. "I know, and it's a shame. Your mother was quite the desired commodity back home. Wanted by many. Like you."

Ah, hell.

The purple electricity lights Rhett's eyes again as he captures my stare. "Your mother made it nearly impossible to find you. She—"

"Hey, Nova!" Star calls from the bar behind Rhett. She waves her hands over her head to grab my attention. "If you're planning to bone him, at least dance with me for a bit first. Galaxy and Orion are boring as hell."

CAGED BY HER DRAGONS

I grimace at her remark. "I'm not planning to fuck anyone tonight, but especially not him."

Star's face lights up in surprise, and she waves her arms again. "Then get your ass in here. It's time to celebrate, and I have a drink with your name on it." She turns her attention to Rhett and winks. "Maybe you'd like to hang out with me instead. I'm more sugar where Nova-babe is all spice."

"I can picture that." Rhett remains expressionless at her suggestion, acting as if he's not being a creepy fuck. The purple electricity fades from his eyes, and I wonder if I imagined it because of the glow of the bar sign.

"You won't have to picture my sweetness, honey," she responds with a laugh. Star is probably the boldest person I've ever met. For the first time, I've never been so glad for her kind of blunt interruption.

"Perhaps I'll take you up on it in a bit, sugar. I have some business to attend to now that I think about it." Rhett flicks his gaze to me. "You are welcome to join me. I have a private office if you'd prefer to hear me out there. Your parents—"

I shake my head. "No, I'm good. I'm not staying long, and if you even think about—"

"Nova, hurry your ass up! I love this song." Star whistles into her fingers.

Rhett glances at her, and I take advantage of his distraction. All I have to do is go inside the bar and find Galaxy. I can complain that I'm sick and want to wait in the Jeep. Then I can leave.

"Coming!" I shout. I half-expect Rhett to grab my hand to stop me from running away, but he wisely lets me go, so I don't have to punch him or some shit. A shiver shudders down my back in a cool wave at the sensation of his gaze following me.

I haven't thought about my parents, but especially about my mom, in a long time. I don't remember her or my dad, but from what my aunt has told me, my mom was wild and untamable. The type of person whose presence could captivate a room a second before blowing it up. But Aunt McKayla also told me how she hated that I was nearly the same. And maybe I am. I like living life as a free spirit, after all. And maybe that's what scares me most about Rhett. Bringing my past back to haunt me…I can't let the life I built get ruined by people who ruined enough themselves. It isn't fair. It was bad enough growing up with a woman who insisted on reminding me.

I jog the rest of the way to Star and fake a smile, sliding my arm around her shoulders. "Thank God you came for me. That guy is weird as hell. He asked me if I'd consider being a performer here."

Star tips her head back with a laugh. "We're aerial acrobats, not strippers!" Her voice rings through the air.

CAGED BY HER DRAGONS

I hold my hand over her mouth. "Shhh. He's stalking me now."

Star smells like she already helped herself to a tequila shot. "Stalking you? No way. I'd noticed. Even so, who cares? He's cute, rich, and he can't take his eyes off you. I can't believe you already rejected the puppy dog-eyed bastard. Fuck, Nova. If he makes us pay—"

I drag Star inside to shut her up, ensuring she doesn't try to turn and talk to him again—or worse, ask him to join us because she thinks she knows I secretly want him. Laughing again, she twirls toward the middle of the spacious bar, spinning me with her. Music hums through the air in beat with the colorful lights.

"Whoa." I gawk at the crowded place.

People dance around the entire room, not caring that there isn't a dance floor. A crowd hangs in front of the bar where several bartenders pour colorful drinks. Where the hell did these people come from? The parking lot was practically empty. I wonder if it's walking distance to a town or some shit.

"Amazing, right? You couldn't tell from the outside," Star says, twirling again. Her flowing dress sweeps the floor with the motion. "Come on. The guys got us a booth. V.I.P." She enunciates the P with a puff of breath.

"Hey, Delp...Nova." Rhett's velvety voice draws my attention to the door behind me. I was hoping he'd take the hint and leave me alone until I could make my escape.

I lock my fingers tighter around Star's hand without responding. If I don't engage, I won't open up any more lines of communication.

"Please hang out for a bit. I'll be at the bar when you're ready to talk. But I must warn you. If you choose to leave without doing so, I promise to show up to every one of your performances until you do." His words sound like a threat, despite the smirk lighting his features. "I'm a persistent man."

"And a creepy asshole," I mutter.

"Who are you talking about?" Star asks, peering around.

I motion my hand towards Rhett, but he's gone. Damn. What the hell? "Uh, that guy over there," I say instead, waving toward a man towering over two attractive women at the bar. "Look at him sneaking pictures of them."

Now that I notice one of the patrons, I can't help but take a more intent look at those here. I should've known not to expect anything less, considering this is Rhett's bar. They all look like they belong somewhere in a big city, dressed in designer, screaming money, and not in some tiny bar in the middle of nowhere. Things don't really add up, and it's freaking me out even more.

"Whoa. Look, there is another one..." Star's voice trails off. "Shit, the fucker is looking at us. He knows we caught

CAGED BY HER DRAGONS

him."

I reach out and grip her hand, my concern over Rhett disappearing with the fear of being leered at by a perv from across the bar. "We should just leave. Where did you say Galaxy was?"

"Ew, yeah." Star scrunches her nose, following my line of sight to the man. "Oh, God. Look at the other guy again. He's moving on to those girls. What a creep. We should tell Rhett."

I shake my head and tug her arm. "No. I bet Rhett told him to. I have a bad feeling about him and this place. It's like no one cares about that guy, either. There are at least three guys that can see him and are pretending he's doing nothing. Fucking sick-fuck." The second the words leave my mouth, the man jerks his attention in my direction.

Our eyes meet, and I step back, my body suddenly wanting more space between us. The man cocks an eyebrow and gives me a once-over, trailing his creepo gaze down my long legs and to my boots.

"Wait there," he mouths. "Your sweet ass is next." He has the nerve to smile and wink at me before turning to another group of women to sneak more pictures of them.

And then he touches a blonde on her shoulder.

The woman drops to the floor, convulsing and jerking her body. Star gasps from beside me, bringing her hand to her chest. Neither of us moves from our spots. Galaxy is the only one with a phone, but I notice a dozen people pulling theirs out.

A strange flash of light erupts from above the woman. It draws my attention from her and to the creepy man. He stands a few feet away with a leer on his face. One of the women's friends shouts and rushes to grab a purse from a nearby barstool. Before she can turn back around, the man slaps his hand over her mouth and drags her through a swinging door into a brightly lit kitchen.

Oh, fuck.

"Star, shit. Star. That man." I can barely get the words out of my mouth. "Did you see that? He took that woman. We have to help."

A tingling sensation prickles over my skin, the air filling with static. I shiver from the feeling as every hair on my body floats in the invisible electric currents. Squeezing Star's fingers, I swing her hand, trying to get her attention. Something's incredibly wrong. The air grows heavy, pressing in on me. The edges of my vision shadow. The chaotic noise of the bar fades until the only sound remaining is my heart beating.

"Star?" I repeat, my voice refusing to sound above a whisper.

"Star is no longer your concern." The hoarse, guttural voice shocks the fog from my mind, sending the world into overdrive. "She's mine."

CAGED BY HER DRAGONS

I gasp a breath, the weight of the room releasing me along with Star's hand. I cringe at the sudden blast of the music and cover my ears, composing myself. I spin to find Star, catching sight of the pervert man lacing his fingers around her elbow.

"No!" I scream. "Stop! Leave her alone!"

Rushing forward, I grab the front of Star's dress and try to drag her back. The man doesn't relent, yanking me along as he races toward the kitchen. My heart slams against my ribcage, panic engulfing me. Why isn't anyone helping? Who the fuck is this guy anyway?

"Stop, you asshole," I yell, scratching my nails at his arms.

His lips split in an unnerving smile—almost monstrous—and it startles me enough that I lose my hold on Star. Stumbling, I trip over someone's foot and land on my stomach. Star reaches out for me, her eyes capturing mine. Fuck. I'm going to lose her. That horrifying man is going to steal the woman who has been like a sister to me ever since I found Galaxy Gold's.

I push up on my hands, scrambling to my feet. Something about the bar feels off. No one even looks at me. I shove into a man blocking my way, and he doesn't react. No one does. Only the man and Star as she flails, giving the guy one helluva fight.

"Delphia, get down!" Rhett's loud holler cuts over the

sound of the music.

I do the stupidest thing possible. I hesitate. Fear freezes my insides, only my gaze darting in the direction of the bar. Rhett's handsome face clears from the blurring crowd, his light blue irises shining with impossible purple light.

And then a strange ball of electricity ignites in his palms with the unfamiliar words he calls.

The floor beneath me trembles.

Star screams.

Brilliant light steals my vision, and I fall to my knees.

The light consumes me.

CHAPTER 3

Beasts

"NOVA?" STAR'S SOFT voice whispers my name. "Please, wake up. Please."

My head throbs with what feels like the universe's worst hangover...except I didn't drink. Jerking upright, I expect to see our cluttered yet clean living area of the RV. Because that was one helluva crazy-ass dream.

"We have to get out of here." Star shakes my shoulder,

drawing my attention to her. "Can you walk?"

I drink in the sight of her face, her heavy eye makeup smeared down her cheeks with her tears. Red spots of color stain the torn bodice of her ivory dress. Star shakes me again, getting me to look into her watery eyes. I can't recall a time I've seen her cry, and she sniffles and tries to blink her tears away.

"Please, Nova. Say something. Are you hurt?" Star scoots closer to me, the urgency in her voice sending panic clenching my chest.

It's now that I realize we're squished together underneath one of the booth tables. A man lies face down on the ground a few feet away, blood staining his white dress shirt. Fuck. There's more blood. I don't think I've ever seen so much. And it's not only from the man.

"Holy shit," I whisper under my breath, gawking around the floor of the club.

Men and women all lie on the floor, battered and bleeding. My stomach twists in repulsion and fear. I can't believe this is happening. Maybe someone drugged me. It had to be Rhett. He threatened me. He said he was looking for me. He also knew my real name.

"Well hello, baby."

Star screeches and crashes into me, pushing me into the seat of the booth. A man with wild white hair locks his hands to her ankles and drags her out from under the table.

CAGED BY HER DRAGONS

I feel around the ground for anything I can use as a weapon, but nothing but a nasty napkin and a torn menu lie within reach.

The man squats down and bares his teeth at me in a cruel smile. His face contorts as his teeth elongate into jagged fangs. Static buzzes between us, and I grab onto the table leg. Like hell will I let this fucker get me so easily.

"Your turn, cinnamon," he says, reaching for me with a snide smile. "You smell fucking delicious." He looks ready to eat me too.

Fear explodes through me, kicking my body into action. Jerking my leg out, I strike him in the knee with the heel of my boot. He falls to his back, a gurgling laugh escaping his throat. I scramble from the small space and push to my feet. Blood from the floor coats my hands, and I fling the liquid into the guy's face with an annoying screech. I hate that I can freefall unexpectedly and remain composed but surprise blood freaks me out.

"Nova, watch out," Star calls, struggling in the arms of the creepy man from earlier.

He covers her mouth again, but I already heed to her warning and spin on the balls of my feet. A third man materializes out of nowhere. He startles me so much so that I swing my hand out and clock him in the side of the face. He hollers and clutches his cheek, a flash of red igniting from his skin. The glowing-red handprint fades with his unfamiliar words. I take advantage of his hesitation and snatch a fork from the table.

I do the only thing I can think of and jab it into his shoulder.

"Capture her!" the man shouts, his voice ringing in my ear. "I know ten clans who will want her."

A strong hand grabs me by the hair and drags me back. I fly off my feet and lock my fingers around the creepo's wrists, digging my nails into his flesh. Star stands frozen a few feet away. Her wide eyes remain unmoving like the rest of her. It sends my heart slipping into my stomach.

"Where have you been hiding, sexy little thing?" a hoarse voice says from my right as the man restraining me pinches my wrists harder as he adjusts his hold. "You're not from around here, are you? Your kind doesn't ever get to leave home, not with all those assholes keeping you caged."

My kind? Caged? What the hell?

"Now, be a good girl, and I won't hurt you." A cool blade touches my throat. "I only need a few drops."

I close my eyes, feeling the sting of the knife nicking my skin. The floor shakes around us, causing the man to let me go. I spin and high-kick him in the head, using my strength and flexibility to my advantage. Purple sparks rain down from the ceiling, and the bar quakes again, the tables and chairs falling over.

"Release her, brother. She's been claimed," Rhett says.

CAGED BY HER DRAGONS

The man squeezes me tighter. "And I plan to change that. You should've just looked the other way. Now look what you made me do. Lazlo will come for your head because of this. We had a deal."

"The deal didn't include her." Rhett pulls himself from the floor by the bar, using the counter to support himself. The sleeve on his suit jacket smokes and crackles with purple flames eating away at the fabric. "Delphia, run. Run and don't stop. I'll find you. Go!"

Rhett jerks his hands out, sending electric light toward the man with white hair. The man retaliates by throwing a dagger with perfect accuracy. It sinks deep into Rhett's chest. Rhett hollers and throws another ball of electricity, now chanting strange words in a language I don't know.

Something inside me warms, the sensation pushing away the cold dread threatening to drop me to the floor. Gasping, I stiffen with an intense muscle spasm. A wave of pain shoots through my very being, stealing my breath. I tremble in hot anticipation. My whole body clenches. Shadows crowd around me, shrouding my vision. The only light left in the bar radiates from Rhett. And he blasts it at me.

I expect to explode into dust. I expect to be electrocuted. What I don't expect is for the strange light to absorb into my skin and set my veins aglow.

"Delphia," he says, his voice turning soft with my

name. "Let her free. Now! Save yourself! They are counting on it."

They? The world disappears, my mind and body separating. I lose my senses, my consciousness floating in an absence of everything. Did I die? Is this it? The thoughts fade as quickly as they arrive, and the world blinks back on around me.

"Delphia." Rhett's voice snaps my attention in his direction. "It's going to be okay. You're okay. You'll free her completely soon enough. Just embrace her."

"Free who?" I ask, realizing part of my costume is shredded.

"Your true self. She will help you. She will keep you safe from the man who did this." Rhett coughs and groans.

"Who are you talking about?" I rub my temples.

My head pounds, my heart rapping in overdrive. A comforting warmth swells inside me, heating me enough to send sweat dripping down my back. The man with the white hair lies on the ground in front of Rhett, torn in half. His guts stretch from one piece of him to the other in the most disgustingly horrifying sight. My stomach tightens and heaves, and I cover my mouth, gagging while I turn away. Fuck. Fuck. Fuck.

"Lazlo Infinity." Once again, Rhett's words drag my focus to him. Blood drips from his mouth, eyes, and nostrils, and he clutches his chest. The purple light dims from his eyes with the warmth in my body. "This was his doing."

Rhett slumps forward, landing face-first in a pool of blood. Star's quiet whimper kicks my body into action, and I search over the bar, finding her kneeling next to one of the booths. Galaxy crawls out from under it, his face a series of hard lines. Our eyes meet, and he points a finger at me.

"Monster!" he screams. "This was your fault! You killed Orion!"

I tense at his words, his voice sounding strange, almost robotic. Pushing from the floor, he grabs Star by the wrist and pulls her along with him.

"You did this," Galaxy says, flinging his arm out at the massacre. "This is your fault."

"W-what?" I ask, my words quivering. "No, it's not."

"This is your fault. We both saw you," Star says, straightening her shoulders. "You're a monster. You killed them all."

I gawk in confusion, unable to move from my spot under their accusation. I mean, what the fuck? Star witnessed everything. She knows I had nothing to do with this. It was those men. The real monsters with the strange light power and scary teeth. They were trying to kill me.

Star and Galaxy stroll in my direction, pointing their fingers at me. I take a few steps back, only to trip over a body. I land hard on my ass, and cool blood soaks into my costume. I try to get up, but I slip. My body won't stop shaking, my fear pressing in on me.

"This is your fault," Galaxy says, continuing to step toward me with Star.

I scramble away, finally managing to get to my feet. "Stay back," I say, holding my hand out.

"You killed them," Star says, her eyes unblinking. "You're a killer."

Shit. I think they're possessed.

Galaxy picks up his speed, striding closer and closer. I hop and stumble over at least a dozen bodies, running toward the back of the bar. I don't know what the hell is going on, but the unnerving look in my friends' eyes pushes me to run. I need to get out of here. I need help. This night is far beyond the realm of reason, and maybe if I put some space between me and this place, I'll wake up with a massive hangover, and this will all be me tripping on some bad drugs Orion might've slipped me.

"This is your fau—" Galaxy drops to the floor, his words cutting off with the thunk of his body.

Star drops next, landing on her stomach. I freeze for a second, fear exploding through me. I can barely get my legs to move. My mind struggles to think. It takes everything in me not to run to them to see if they're okay. Something wild and feral claws at my insides, screaming at me that I need to leave. I need to run and never look back.

Slamming my hands against the back door, I thrust it

open and dash into the cool night. An eerie blue glow washes over the dirt drive, leading deeper into the forest. Fuck that. Searching my surroundings once more, I head toward the side of the building to follow it around to the front. Silence greets me, and I run to the Jeep behind Rhett's Porsche.

I reach the door and stick my arm through the open window to unlock it. Hopping into the driver's seat, I look at the ignition and smack the wheel. "Fuck!" No keys. They'd be in Galaxy's pocket.

Instead of risking trying to get them, I grab the tire iron from under the seat and make a run for it. My best option is the road. I can follow it back to the RV. I know Galaxy keeps a spare key for it hidden in our stage equipment. Then I can call the cops and figure this bullshit out.

Swiping my hands over my face, I try to dry the uncontrollable tears leaking from my eyes. The fact that blood stains my fingers only makes it worse. I probably look like the number one victim in a horror flick about to meet my end. Any Good Samaritans on the road tonight will probably avoid me altogether. I wouldn't blame them.

The headlights of a car illuminate the stretch of street at the end of the gravel drive. I push myself to run faster, hoping to reach the road before they pass by. Even if they don't stop, they might call the police.

Gasping, I stop right in the middle of the road and hop

up and down, waving my arms like crazy...except there isn't a car on the road. The light I see? Fuck. I don't know what it is. I spin on my feet and don't waste any time waiting to find out what lies within the eerie glow. I've seen enough alien movies to know that curiosity kills people. That weird light could transform into a beam to incinerate me. I've had enough of this bullshit for one night.

Too bad the universe seems to disagree.

I watch in shock as a huge winged creature drops a man from at least a hundred feet above. The animal soars away faster than my brain can process what I'm seeing. A gust of wind knocks me back, and I fall hard to the asphalt. My poor ass will be bruised for the next damn week. I drop the tire iron by accident, and it clatters a few feet away.

"Stay back!" I scream, crab-walking backwards until I get my footing. I snatch the iron from the street and hold it out in warning.

The freakishly tall, overly muscular man slows and cocks his head to the side. And damn. I recognize him. He was in the parking lot of the bar earlier.

His eyes light with a strange orange glow, almost like fire ignites within their depths. His long, dark hair blows around his sharp, handsome face. For the second—no, third—time in my life, I question the possibility that he is something other than human. Alien. He dropped from the fucking sky and not in the same way I do. Shit.

CAGED BY HER DRAGONS

Summoning my nerve, I once again shout, "I said, stay the fuck back, you asshole. Come any closer and you'll regret it." Did I really just say that? I'm like a twig in comparison to all his hulking muscles.

The man's lips curl into an amused smile. He obviously agrees my threat is as lame as it sounded coming from my mouth, my voice a squeaky, panicked pitch.

Ignoring my words, he steps forward again but keeps his hands at his sides. We lock gazes, and heat swells in my middle. Something about his presence awakens a weird sensation inside me, freezing my feet in place. He flares his nostrils and finally breaks his gaze to trail it down the rest of me. His cocky smile vanishes, and he narrows his eyes. I can't decipher his expression, but it darkens enough to make me think he might capture me to devour later.

I stiffen and grip the tire iron, glowering at him. "I mean it. Stay back."

"What about me, doe eyes?"

The smooth voice scares me half to death, and I drop the tire iron. A hand locks onto my shoulder and spins me around. I gawk at another hot as hell man with a mop of waves tousled around his head. He was around earlier too.

His hazel eyes meet mine, and he drinks in my features, studying every inch of my face. Now he looks like he wants to devour me right this second, but only in a way that'll leave me buzzing. "Where's Rhett? We got his call for help," the guy says, lifting his eyebrow.

I don't respond.

He frowns. "And you look like you need some too. Where is he? You were with him earlier. I wouldn't forget a face as beautiful as yours."

My throat closes, refusing to let me speak. Did he compliment me even though I'm covered in blood and am on the verge of sobbing again?

"Doe eyes? Hello?"

I realize my hands press to his chest, my fingers attempting and failing to dig into his bone-hard pecs. His heart pounds under my hand in rapid beats, the thrum a melody I can feel in my soul. My fingers refuse to move or do anything. I don't know if it is due to the absurdity of tonight, but I'm nearly certain my brain has disconnected from the rest of me.

"Is she broken, Rowan?" The question comes from behind me. It must be the third guy from the group earlier. Fuck. I should've known that someone so hot couldn't be human. I wish I could get my head to turn so I can look at the guy again.

Warmth radiates from Rowan, sending my body buzzing. It's like the firelight I saw in his eyes courses through the rest of him, emitting a wave of heat like rays of sunshine even on this dark night.

"I think she's frightened, Maddox. Feel her. She's

trembling so hard it's like she's vibrating." The man with hazel eyes, Rowan, touches my cheek. "You afraid, doe eyes? Is it me? I haven't even said…" His eyes ignite with fire, his handsome features morphing into something unrecognizable—like tough scales burst from his cheeks. "Boo."

Jerking my leg up, I knee the fucker as hard as I can in the balls. He roars, sending hot air into my face. My hair flies back, my body finally getting its shit together. I shove my palms against him and try to force him back. His muscular frame doesn't budge under my force, and it's like my hands slam into stone.

"Maddox. Rowan! Get your asses over here." A third man materializes from the trees, a long, shiny dagger gripped tightly in his hands. It's the same guy who came out of the shed when I first arrived at the bar. "Rhett's dead."

The two men release me and run toward the other guy without as much as a glance in my direction.

"Call it in to the High Council, Kash," Maddox says, combing his fingers through his long hair to scrub the back of his neck. He turns his attention to me. "And keep an eye on that one. She might be the only witness."

Oh, fuck.

I don't let my fear freeze me this time and bolt away. These assholes might be huge, buff…hot weird aliens, but I sure as shit do not want to hang around. I don't care if I could be the only witness. They are obviously not the police. I need the actual authority to help me. Or at least to hide. Because if they knew Rhett, maybe they know of my parents' crimes. When they find out, I'm doomed.

"Oh, no you don't, kitten. You're staying with me." A hand locks to my shoulder and pulls me back. Damn it, if these fuckers are fast.

My back slams into a hard chest, winding me. My body gives out, my legs buckling while I try to suck in air to scream. A strange noise rumbles from deep in the man's throat, and his arm slides across my stomach, gently but firmly, locking me in place.

Warm breath tickles my neck, and Kash says, "If you fight, you'll experience the best snuggle session of your damn life, so try it. I dare you. This is your only warning, feisty little human."

What the? I thrash in Kash's arms, kicking and flailing in an attempt to hurt him. He laughs and stays true to his word, throwing me into the air so high that I screech and expect to get eaten alive from that scary flying monster that dropped these assholes into my life.

But the world spins and my stomach rises into my throat. Without anything to grab onto, all of my training as an aerial dancer vanishes. I'm going to splatter on the ground. And not even after giving my best damn performance.

Hot arms wrap around me, breaking my fall, and I gasp

and meet Kash's eyes, the same color as Rowan's. Firelight flickers in his intense gaze, his eyes trailing over my face like he can't resist studying me.

And then his eyes widen, and he drops me. I slam my ass on the gravel ground and try not to scream out in sudden pain. All I care about is putting space between us as something hardens his features, his playfulness gone with the curl of his lips into a scowl.

This fucker.

"It was you," he snaps, releasing a growl. He stomps closer and points his finger. "You did this. Maddox! Her glamour cracked. She isn't human."

I don't get a chance to respond or argue or beg or anything.

A flash of light ignites the world around me. I lose access to all my senses, losing myself to the blinding light. My hearing returns first, then my touch. I smell the strong scent of cinnamon. Footsteps shuffle. Digging my fingers into the ground, I push myself to my feet and shield my eyes the best I can. Fear zings through me as a gigantic silhouette cuts through the light.

"Restrain her!" a woman shouts, but I can't see anything through the strange light. Her voice rings through the air as she calls command after command in a language I don't recognize. How I know she's commanding people? I'm not sure. Her voice, perhaps. The strange need to bow.

To give up.

Something scorching hot snaps on my wrists, making me scream. The flesh on my wrists burns under the electric restraints as I fight. I drop to the ground, the intense pain shooting up my arms to spill into the rest of my body. Several figures stand above me, looking down as I writhe on the gravel. Through bleary eyes, I catch sight of the giant winged monster soaring high above us. It's the only thing keeping my focus so that I don't pass out. If I don't struggle, the pain lessens.

"Does she have an I.D.?" another voice asks. "A mark? Brand? Tattoo? Anything?"

"A Mortal World driver's license. Nothing else that I could see without stripping her completely," Maddox responds, appearing in view. His dark hair blows in a suddenly hot breeze. The idea of him stripping me sends a strange sensation through my body. What the hell is wrong with me? I don't actually like the idea, do I? "She's playing mortal, but the magic shield she uses falters. We can assess her more when we transfer her."

Transfer me? Transfer me to where?

The thought remains locked in my mind, my mouth afraid to move or speak. My body fears more unbearable pain from these definitely not-human creatures.

The woman huffs, crouching down. Her red-glowing eyes lock onto mine. "Nova Noble, what is your Magaelorum name?"

"Huh?" My word comes out as a whisper. It hurts too much to properly answer her. "What's that?"

"We don't have time for this, High Priestess. The Mortal Authority will come at any time. Several reached out. The shield won't last long."

The woman flares her nostrils. "Very well. We'll extract the information from those with malleable minds." She stands tall and kicks my side with her boot. "As for you, Ms. Noble. Under Magaelorum Law, you are to stand forth in front of the High Council under the accusation of murder and will be considered guilty until proven innocent or convicted. Do you have anything you'd like to say?"

"What the fuck?" It's the only thing I can spit out through my clenched teeth.

The woman claps her hands, sending brilliant light through the air.

The world disappears.

Chapter 4

Falsely Accused

"YOU HAVE THIRTY seconds to tell me which warlock or witch made a deal with you. Was it the Lavarock Isle Coven? Seaview Hill? Fire Mountain Clan?" Maddox leans across the table and into my face. Fuck, why does he have to be so hot playing the bad cop? A part of me begs for this nightmarish trip to turn into a full-on fantasy, because none of this feels real. I expect Galaxy to pop through the door at any second to tell me this was all a stunt to get us onto some show. Maybe Rhett was a part of it.

But that's impossible. Rhett knew my birth name. I fear that's what the people here want, but what the hell is Magaelorum? I've traveled all across the United States with Galaxy and never once heard of anything like that.

I remain silent, continuing to plead with my mind to hurry up and strip his damn clothes off. There is no other way I want this weird situation to turn out. If he doesn't, that means I'm screwed and not in any way I enjoy.

Maddox slaps the table, startling me. Damn it. No fantasy and just one awfully bad trip or something. Because my mind can't fathom any of this being real. No man's eyes can glow like his. I swear if they penetrate me anymore, I might smolder under his glare, a glare I'm growing used to staring at.

Because for the first five minutes upon waking up in this dank cell, I was terrified. I might have sobbed for a moment and yelled for someone to let me out. I even requested a lawyer—no such luck, by the way. Wherever the hell I am, the people don't think I deserve help. I'm guilty until proven innocent. But how? No idea. It's complete shit.

When I realized as much, my fear turned into anger, and I've been surviving on the high of my fury for at least a few hours. Maddox only makes it worse with his accusations. My brain struggles even to process anything—from the sexy beast man to the creepy woman who eyes me without intervening in Maddox's interrogation. I can't stop from looking at the glowing restraints or around the room at the strange shimmering walls.

I think it helps that I'm not alone, even if it's with two people who somehow think I'll admit to something they think I'm guilty of when I'm not. They might be persistent in their accusations, but I refuse to give up on trying to prove my innocence. Because they're wrong. I'm not a murderer. There is no way I could kill a room full of people. It's ridiculous to even consider.

"Tell me, damn it!" Maddox's warm, cinnamon breath blows tendrils of my hair from my eyes, bringing my focus to him. I hope he screams in my face again. A few strands stick to my clumped eyelashes, annoying the hell out of me more than the strange-ass restraints that heat up if I so much as think of moving a muscle.

I blink a few times, twisting my lips. "For the thousandth time, I have no fucking clue what you're talking about. I think I've been drugged. Something is wrong with my vision. I'm hallucinating." I squeeze my eyes shut, willing for his glowing stare to return to normal.

He yells in frustration, finally clearing the hair from my face. "Stop playing games. You can't pull off this human façade here. The magic will break, and when it does, you're mine, cookie. You're going to wish that you complied." He says cookie like he only uses it as a threat to devour me.

"What fucking magic?" I ask and cringe, my restraints shocking the hell out of me as I absentmindedly try to throw my hands up.

"The kind blocking your true form." Maddox jabs his finger right between my cleavage. I expect pain to explode, my sternum to break under his force or something. What I don't expect is for a zing of electricity to spark against his hand, getting him to jerk it back.

I press my lips, my mouth wanting to laugh and taunt him for being a prick for hours now. "I don't even know what the hell you mean. I am in my true form, asshole."

Maddox composes himself, shifting his gaze from me and to the shadowy figure in the corner. "We will find out. Give it time. Your lack of cooperation will make things harder on you."

Turning my attention to the woman, I lock my gaze to hers. She hasn't said a single word this whole time since she arrested me and instead sits quietly in the corner as Maddox shouts, belittles, and accuses me over and over of things I can't process. Witches? Warlocks? Hell. Maybe that's what Rhett was with his purple eyes. Or the creepo white-haired man.

"I am cooperating. I've told you everything I know. I'm not a murderer or whatever the hell you think I am," I comment to the woman instead of Maddox. If Maddox is the bad cop, then she might be the one I can reason with. "It was the psychos I told you about. I'm not from wherever the hell Magaelorum is. I'm from Golden Trails Valley…at least, I was."

Grabbing my chin, Maddox forces me to look at him. Fire ignites in his golden brown eyes, and I swear a tendril of smoke trails from his flared nostrils. In the dim lighting, his face lines with shadows, enhancing a long, red scar that cuts across his cheek and over his jaw. "Bullshit! You have to be working with someone. Hiding. There are no records of Nova Noble with the High Council, and a shifter doesn't just end up in the Mortal World without access to one of the gates. Not to mention that you're alone. Where is your pack?"

"My pack?" I ask, the hardness in my voice dissipating. "My pack of what? I left my purse at the bar."

"Your pack of—" Maddox slams his hands on the table again and proceeds to lift it up and throw it at the wall. I'd react if this wasn't the third time he's thrown the damn table. The man has some major anger issues. "Damn it! Your clan, your pride, whatever the hell you identify your family as." He swings his attention to the woman again as if she might be the one in charge. Locking his fingers to the back of his head, he adds, "Give me permission to interrogate her my way, High Councilwoman Laveau."

Something shifts in the woman's features, and she

glances from Maddox to me and back to him. Nerves bunch in my stomach, fear finally breaking through my anger. I'm nearly certain whatever his way is might be the end of me.

High Councilwoman Laveau stands from her chair and straightens the few dozen strands of beaded necklaces draped around her throat. "We are out of time, CO Dreki. Judge Witherton has called upon us for the verdict. The court's decision has been made."

Huh? When the hell did this happen. The woman hasn't even moved or spoken on the phone. How the hell can she know that?

With one last nod to Maddox, she disappears, blinking out of sight.

Whoa, fuck.

I gawk at the empty space she left behind, missing the fact that Maddox closes the distance to tower over me. He puffs out his chest with his aggressive breathing. If I were to pant that hard, I'd probably pass out from hyperventilating. A part of me hopes he does. Another part of me thinks it would be my luck for him to pass out right on top of me to smother me to death.

I tip my head back to gaze at him, trying not to let him intimidate me. But damn it. I'm a bit scared now that we're alone. He could do whatever he wants and claim I attacked him or some shit. I'm not naïve. I watch crime TV shows.

"You will regret your decision to remain incompliant,"

Maddox says, his deep voice lowering even more. His full lips puff out with his breath, the cinnamon scent reminding me of the holidays with my aunt and uncle. I can almost taste it. If Maddox moves any closer, I might.

"I've been nothing but compliant. I—" I screech as Maddox drags me from my seat, cutting off my words.

He tosses me onto his shoulder and spins toward the door. My weight crushes my arms between our bodies. Blazing pain burns through me as the restraints explode with heat once again. I wonder if they hurt so badly to stop me from fighting during transportation, like having a bone-hard shoulder digging into my belly isn't enough.

I grind my teeth, wriggling in hopes to shift my arms out from between us. "Let me walk. You're hurting me."

"Toughen up, cookie," he growls. "Where you're going will make this feel like a dream. I'll ensure it."

I groan. "You're a fucking dick." I want so badly to threaten him with retaliation, but fear grips me tightly enough to steal my bravado.

Maddox shoves the door open and continues to stride with me down a dark stone corridor. Shit. Is this a dungeon? A real, godforsaken dungeon? A man's yells echo through the dank air. Fu-u-u-ck.

Strange green flames glow within sconces, turning the world eerier than I thought possible. Raising my chin, I try to look around, but there is nothing but the cold concrete and flashes of emerald firelight blinking on the walls with Maddox's fast pace. The jerk probably carries me because he knows I'd never be able to keep up with his long legs, but being carted around like this makes me feel less than human.

He jogs up a set of stairs at the end of the tunnel, bouncing me harder. I huff and grunt and swear, the pain of the restraints kicking my body into action. I spread my legs into the splits, contorting my body in a way not many people expect, and manage to jerk myself off his shoulder. Maddox is so focused on climbing the stairs that he doesn't notice until he reaches the top.

Dropping to the ground, I land on my feet as gracefully as if I'm performing in front of an audience. I should run. I should try to escape. But one look up at Maddox sends my mind screaming to drop to my knees and beg him for mercy.

"What the fuck?" he mutters to himself, jumping from the top of the staircase.

He lands so close to me that I fall back on my ass. I freeze, curling in on myself as small as possible. I expect him to rip me off the floor by my hair and to just toss me up the stairwell, but he hesitates.

His muscles ripple, his eyes burning into me. His sudden stillness unnerves me.

"Please," I whisper, tipping my head back. "You've

made a mistake. I don't know who or what you think I am, but you're wrong. I'm a Sky Dancer for Galaxy Gold. I'm part of a traveling aerobatic show. I hadn't even planned on going to that bar, but this guy offered my boss free drinks and he forced us all to go there." Now that I think of Galaxy, I can't help but think of Star and Orion. Pain clenches my chest. They acted so strangely before they dropped—fuck I hope they're not dead.

"Stop lying! There were witnesses." Maddox swings his arm and punches the wall, sending fragments of stones pelting over me. The rumble of his intense fury sends trembles through me, and I dig my nails into my palms to chill myself out the best I can.

"Witnesses? Everyone was dead..." I let my voice trail off as I cringe. The way the words come out of my mouth sound all wrong. They sound almost like I'm disappointed that anyone survived such a massacre. "The men I told you about—it was them. They were monsters. They tried to kidnap women and came after me. One second I was fighting and in the next, they were all dead."

Locking his hands under my arms, he lifts me back to my feet. He sets me upright and herds me like an animal with his massive frame until my back hits the wall. Maddox grabs my chin in one big hand, his thumb and middle finger grazing each of my ears. He leans in with his fire eyes, forcing me to share his cinnamon breath. I automatically inhale, ultra-aware that his leg rests between mine, my thighs squeezing him a bit as I remain steady. If he's aware of how close he is, he doesn't react. His steely face remains sharp with his fury.

"You mean Rhiordan. White hair, tall. One of the most powerful warlocks I've ever met?" Maddox's eyes search mine as he pins me. The warmth of his body heats me up everywhere we touch each other. And damn it. I like it. My hands do too, because I risk the electrocution of my restraints to ball the front of his uniform between my fingers.

"There were three of them," I say, nodding.

"None of them were monsters, cookie. You will soon see what real monsters look like. That, I promise you."

It's my turn to glower. "You can't see that because you're fucking like him. A monster too."

Maddox roars in my face, making me flinch. Releasing me, he takes a few steps back and heaves a breath.

My legs turn to jelly, and I prop my back on the wall until I steady myself enough not to fall over. Strange golden-green scales sprout across Maddox's cheek before disappearing with the fire from his eyes.

"Fucking Rhett," I mutter under my breath. I tilt my head toward the ceiling. "If you weren't already dead, I'd kill you for this."

Maddox must have some crazy hearing, because he jerks his attention to me and glowers. Swinging his arm out, he catches my wrist restraints and tugs me so hard that I fall forward. Without hesitating, he drags me with him, not giving me a chance to run behind him. My knees throb with each stone step he lugs me up until he kicks the door open and tosses me through. I screech and skid across the floor, bright light engulfing me. A golden chandelier sparkles overhead, sending starbursts of light over a blue, jewel-encrusted domed ceiling.

"Rhett was a good man and my damn best friend," Maddox snaps, looming over me. His massive frame blocks out the beautiful view of the ceiling, forcing me to stare into his smoldering glower. "I don't know what you got out of this, but I will find out. You will not only rot for the rest of your damn life, but you will suffer."

His words slap me like an unwanted promise. I open my mouth to argue again, to swear my innocence, to beg for someone, anyone to believe me, but Maddox reaches into his pocket and pulls out a rectangular piece of fabric. I scramble on the floor, slipping and sliding on the tile. He catches my foot and drags me to him faster than I can get away.

"Under the authority of the judge, you will not speak. Now it's time to get what you deserve," Maddox says, lurching forward.

"Wait! Wait! How can I prove my innocence if I can't speak? I want a lawyer. I want to talk to the judge," I beg.

CAGED BY HER DRAGONS

"You had your chance but chose to play dumb, cookie," he whispers, picking me up from the floor to pin me to him, facing me out.

"Please. This isn't fair. Don't do this. Don't—"

Maddox ignores me and presses the fabric to my mouth. It buzzes before practically melting to my skin. At least the shit isn't hot. Because I don't know how much more I can take. The longer I remain trapped here, the more I question my sanity. I hope and pray and beg that none of this is real. I'll wake up at any second to find I had one helluva night with Star, drinking way too much.

I shiver over the sensation of his breath against my ear. My. Stupid. Body. Tingles prickle across my skin despite my mind begging for my body to chill out. This man is a monster. He threatened me. He handled me like I'm the dirt in the tread of his boots. I should not find him even the teensiest bit attractive. But damn it. He and his cinnamon breath smell good.

"Don't tell me what the fuck is fair. The death of sixteen people isn't fair. This?—it's time to find out how pathetic you truly are now that you can't shift and no longer have the power given through the deal of magic. Your witch can't save you now." Stomping toward a grand set of double doors, Maddox kicks one open so hard that it bangs against the wall.

He pushes me into the brightly lit room only to turn

around and exit. I glare at the closing door, wishing with everything in me that this sticky fabric didn't prevent me from speaking. I'd call him every bad word I could think of. The fuckhead asshole. Screw him and this strange-ass place. Screw everything.

At least I won't ever have to see him again, I hope. The judge will see that I'm innocent. Whoever these beings are and wherever I am can't imprison me forever. I didn't do anything wrong. I don't belong here.

"Guards, please show Ms. Noble to her seat." A booming voice draws my attention from the door and to a man wearing all black, sitting on a high throne. He holds a scepter by his side, the top garnished with a shiny, multi-faceted onyx stone.

Two massive shadows cut across the floor in front of me as the guards close the distance to me from behind. I don't get a chance to turn to look before one of them grabs the back of my costume and tugs me to my feet.

A hint of cinnamon wafts from behind me. I stiffen, half-expecting Maddox to suddenly reappear to man-handle me all over again. But it's not him, though these two guards are just as bad.

Kash pushes me toward a long table with a single chair. His knuckles dig into my spine, his strength completely unnecessary. I'd move regardless. I want to sit in front of the judge and plead my case to the best of my ability. Then maybe I can take whatever light portal or whatever the hell brought me here the hell home.

Yanking the chair out for me, Rowan takes over for Kash and motions for me to sit. He locks my restraints in place on a ring welded to the center of the table. My arms ache from the strange position. The table restraint seems to have been made for a much larger person, and I have to sit on the edge of my seat as to not overstretch my body.

A loud knock startles me, and I whip my head to the man sitting on the ornate golden throne. When our eyes meet, he flashes two long fangs, like those of a snake, and points his scepter at me. I flinch and duck, expecting a ball of electricity or fire to spew from it.

"Nova Noble, trickster of the Mortal World, you have been accused of treachery, intent on seizing territory, and the murder of sixteen men and women, including one of our most powerful gatekeepers." The judge shifts in his seat and points to a group of the strangest people I've ever seen. They look humanoid, but like the judge, something is slightly off. From glowing eyes to fangs, weirdly textured skin to wings. Even a snarling wolf-like man-thing sits on the end of the bench. "Jury, what is your verdict?"

Wait, what? Their verdict? I haven't even gotten to plead my case. Bouncing in my seat, I struggle to speak, to beg the judge to hear me out, but I can't rip the sticky fabric off. I can't do anything but mumble and whine. The woman in the interrogation room wasn't kidding about this bullshit happening without me. And now I can't even prove my innocence. This can't be happening. It can't.

"With undeniable evidence brought forth by the two sole-surviving mortal witnesses of what I consider the vilest, most wicked massacre I have ever seen in my three-hundred and two years of existence, we, the jury, find Nova Noble permanently guilty under Magaelorum Law."

I scream, trying to make more noise. The fabric grows wider, creeping toward my nose. I panic and thrash against my restraints. I will not stand here and accept this bullshit. I won't go down without a fight. I don't belong here.

The edges of my vision shadow, my rage burning through me hotter than the magical restraints biting into my wrists. The air turns heavy around me, slowing the world. I gasp, struggling to breathe as the fabric blocks one of my nostrils.

I black out.

At least I think I do.

One second I'm thrashing in the seat, bound in place, and in the next Kash and Rowan restrain me. I catch sight of the chains on the floor, black and burning and no longer glowing with the strange magic. Voices yell through the air, and the judge stands in front of his throne.

"Seize her! Bind her ability before she shifts!" the judge yells, motioning to someone I can't see.

CAGED BY HER DRAGONS

I thrash and kick, using the two hulking guards as my support to swing my body up into the air. Landing on my feet, I hold my hands up. The woman from the cell—High Councilwoman Laveau—hesitates, a glowing metal brick in her hand.

A heavy body tackles me, skidding with me across the floor. I yell, my voice muffled under the fabric, but it's no use. Maddox grabs my wrists and pins me beneath him. He straddles my body, clenching my hips between his thighs.

I sink under him, giving up on my fight. It's pointless. I can't escape.

"Nova Noble, under Magaelorum Law, I hereby sentence you to life without retrial in the Maximum Magical Penitentiary," the judge bellows, whacking his scepter to the floor.

My eyes widen with his words. No. No! If only I could speak. If only—fuck. If only nothing. No one would believe me anyway.

The judge waves his staff. "High Councilwoman Laveau, please proceed."

I can't move or fight or do anything as Maddox flips me over to pin me on my stomach. Hot fingers lace around my wrists, bending my arms in a position that zings pain through my muscles.

High Councilwoman Laveau whispers a few words under her breath a second before scorching pain blazes over the backs of my hands. It lasts only a second, but I feel the agony all the way to my soul. A part of me dies inside, a wave of hopelessness consuming me.

"Inmate D64901 is ready for transfer," High Councilwoman Laveau says. "Please notify the victims' heirs that justice is now served."

Chapter 5

Convicted

"I KNOW YOU don't believe me, but this is a mistake. I don't belong here," I say, glancing at the tops of my hands for the billionth time. My identification number glows in what I can only describe as a magical brand, three digits on each hand. It only hurt for a second, but it's ugly as hell.

"Strip and face the wall," Rowan says, ignoring me. It's just my fucking luck that the guys who found me at Rhett's bar also happen to work in this prison. What's worse is that Rhett was their friend.

"Please, you have to let me explain," I beg. I wring my fingers through the front of my torn and dirty costume, half the sequins missing. It doesn't help that the last thing I want to do is to lose the last thing I have that connects me to the Mortal World. Ugh. I hate calling my home by another name.

He flares his nostrils and glowers. "I said strip!"

"You first!" I snap, refusing to let him intimidate me. I'm not a criminal and will not be treated like one despite what these assholes say.

My words catch him off guard, and Rowan widens his eyes for a split second, something indecipherable crossing his handsome features. Unlike Maddox, he's free of facial scars, but I spot a weird, swirly brand that weaves from his wrist to his elbow on the inside of his arm. It flashes orangey-red with his flexing muscles like fire burns through his veins.

He tightens his jaw and trails his gaze lower, mapping out my body in a slow, sizzling sweep. "Inmate D64901, if you do not comply, I will remove your clothes for you."

Shit. My body totally loves the idea.

He obviously does too.

I swallow, catching a flicker of desire in his hazel eyes. And damn. Why does this douche have to be so hot? Why do I suddenly want to test his threat to see if he'll actually do it? If I wasn't so nervous over being wrong about his look, I would. Instead, I straighten my shoulders and stretch my arms behind me to unfasten the clasp on the back of my neck, holding my sequined top securely in place.

The fabric loosens at the same time I tug the bow on my halter top to untie it. "You know, the last time someone demanded I take my clothes off was proceeded by a good time." I flick my gaze from the floor and to him to see his reaction.

He doesn't give one apart from clenching and unclenching his fingers.

"Do you know what a good time is?" I continue, his silence drawing out my nerves. "Probably not. Assholes like you turn women off with one word. Mood killers."

Again, he doesn't respond. He doesn't avert his eyes either. I'm not naïve toward his lustful curiosity. I bet this perv is just like the monsters in the bar. He thinks he can just intimidate someone into compliance. But he's in for it with me, because I'm pissed the hell off.

Summoning my anger is the only thing stopping me from breaking down. From believing that this is it and this is how my life is going to be. I won't let him break me, and I'll never give him that kind of power. If he wants to watch me strip out of my clothes, then he can be my fucking guest. He'll regret messing with me, because I know how to play games too. And I know his type. He wouldn't be here in this position if he didn't crave to hold power over people. It's not that he's serving justice. It's about stroking his damn ego.

"Enough, inmate. You're wasting time," Rowan finally says.

Raising my chin, I offer him a smug smirk before darting my eyes down his tight-fitting uniform and straight toward his groin. My stare makes him shift on his feet and adjust his belt. I bring my gaze back up and ease my top down, steeling myself for what might be the last performance of my life. Too bad I'm wasting it, but if I'm stuck here against my will, I won't be the only one suffering. I'll use what I have to make life torture.

Goosebumps prickle across my skin, my body reacting to the cool air and the intensity of Rowan's gaze. Shifting on his feet again, he blatantly drinks me in, the firelight back in his eyes. His chest rises and falls with his breathing, and he winds his gaze down my stomach, following the glittering fabric of my costume as I take it off.

"Everything must go," he says, his deep voice humming through the air.

Fuck. Me. "Would you like me to bend over while I'm at it?" I quip. "I don't know how the hell this prison works, but I've seen enough TV."

He opens his mouth to respond, but the door to the

concrete chamber flings open. I automatically cover my bare breasts and turn to face the wall. Maddox storms into the room and thrusts a one-piece, black jumpsuit at me with my ID number sewn over the breast.

"Get dressed, inmate!" Maddox yells. "Next time I catch you trying to manipulate a CO, I'll throw you into the damn pit."

The pit? What the hell is that?

I don't get the chance to ask. Maddox shoves Rowan toward the door and follows him out, leaving me alone. The metal door slams and the lights flick off. Utter darkness consumes me. Only a sliver of light seeps in through where the window cover slides open a few centimeters from the force of Maddox's anger.

"What the hell are you thinking, brother?" Maddox's sharp voice hums through the closed door. I don't think he intends for me to hear him, but I'm thankful that I can. "I told you to tell her to change and then leave her. Not fucking stay and give her an ounce of power over you. That's probably how she got so close to Rhett. Whoever sent her knows Rhett had a damn soft spot for the unclaimed. Her acting is solid, and I will not allow her to make you a fool."

The unclaimed? What does that even mean?

"Lighten up, Maddox. I knew what she was doing. If she wants to play these games, I'm going to enjoy every last one of them," Rowan says, his voice light, almost amused.

"You can't deny she's hot. Feisty when pushed. You wouldn't call her cookie if you didn't love the idea of her crumbling beneath you to enjoy her every sexy morsel. Those perky tits of hers—"

Maddox growls and something slams against the door, startling me. "Just fucking stay away from her. We need to follow the damn plan. For Rhett."

Rowan sighs. "For Rhett."

The metal door flings open once more, and I stumble back, searching the ground for the discarded jumpsuit. Maddox glowers at me. If he could blow me up with his gaze, he would. He's obviously not the one I can test. Not like Rowan. I can't stop from stretching up to try to look behind him to see if he lingers, but he's gone. Damn.

"You have five seconds. Get dressed or this is how I'm taking you to the pit," Maddox says, straightening his back to fill more of the room. "I'm sure the inmates would love a little show of your sweet meat."

Ew. This guy.

I rush to get into the jumpsuit, no longer willing to test my luck. It was one thing to tease a guard in private. It's a whole other hell to give a show while being paraded to whatever the pit is. Sliding on the sleeves, I adjust the bodysuit in place and cross my arms. Maddox turns his gaze from the ceiling to me and waves his arm.

"You will fulfill your sentence in Cellblock S. Until we

CAGED BY HER DRAGONS

can assess what work you're capable of doing that doesn't include taking off your clothes, you will report to the corrections officer on duty at the Work Center in your block." Maddox knocks his knuckles between my shoulder blades, herding me along a corridor that ends in a barred door.

It automatically opens for us. I tense at the noisy, grand concrete room. I can't stop my jaw from slackening in shock. I don't know what I was expecting, but it wasn't this. I mean, come on. People aren't supposed to have wings. A mixture of men and women, all with wings sticking from their backless jumpsuits, eat something strange from bowls at metal tables. Maddox shoves me to get me to move my legs, and I sweep my gaze across the room.

At least a hundred pairs of eyes all turn in my direction. If Maddox wasn't herding me, I'd probably cower behind his massive muscular body, which is more solid than a block wall. Even with his snarling and yells and shitty asshole attitude, he doesn't exactly scare me. It's hard to fear someone your vagina appreciates and wants nothing more than to take for a ride.

A man jumps from his seat and bares his sharp teeth at me. He gnashes his jaws, his face distorting into a series of hard lines that make him even more terrifying. Maddox yanks what looks like an iron baton from his belt and whacks the man on his shoulder. His skin smokes, and he scrambles back but continues to look on the verge of trying to devour me. I expect him to take flight as Maddox swings the baton again. He tries, bending his legs, but all he does is hop back. It's now that I notice a series of rings clipping his wings together, preventing him from flying.

Maddox ushers me through the room, the sudden silence digging into me. It feels as if the whole cellblock might be plotting for my demise. At least I can thank the universe that I won't sprout magical wings that would ensure my stay in this section.

"Look too long and you'll lose your eyes," a child-like girl says with a hiss. She stands on the bench of one of the tables and expands her arms. Jumping from the table, she lands on her feet a few feet away. "Hear what you shouldn't and lose an ear. Touch what doesn't belong to you and lose your hand. Heed my warning, beast. It's the only one you'll ever get."

Maddox waves his baton again, sending the winged girl back. He doesn't say anything and ushers me the rest of the way through the room. The next barred door opens for us and immediately closes to lock in place. A few of the inmates slap their hands to the bars, trying to get me to look back. I don't. I decide it's best to stare at the floor and not to give the world around me even an ounce of attention.

"Fucking fae," Maddox mutters under his breath, sliding his baton back into his belt.

A guard steps from a doorway and greets Maddox with

a stern nod. My damn eyes disobey my request to remain locked to the floor, and I glance up and catch sight of the prettiest man I've ever seen. Despite his glare, his delicate features make him anything but a hard ass. And he also has wings—brilliant metallic wings that look to have been brushed in gold. Unlike the inmates, his aren't clipped together.

"Get your fucking block under control, CO," Maddox snaps at the man. He whacks him on the back. "You're too damn lenient."

The man untucks his gloved hand from his pocket and grabs his iron baton from his belt. Without a word, he disappears into the fae people's cellblock. Fae. I repeat the word over and over again in my mind. I used to pretend fairies were real as a kid—but these winged-creatures are far from the beautiful, tiny flying princesses I imagined. Some of them were taller than me. And buff. Sexy.

Maddox forces me to lead the way, even though I have no clue where I'm going. I drag my bare feet, wishing I'd gotten some shoes. Each step down the concrete corridor feels colder than the last. I descend down a set of stairs to the next barred gate. It opens with Maddox's presence, and I shuffle into the next cellblock.

Holy. Shit.

No one has to tell me what type of creatures remains imprisoned in this section. A dozen silver-flashing eyes zone in on me as I follow the painted, glowing pathway through the dimly lit, windowless room. And damn. I break the looking-rule the fae girl warned me about and devour the closest hot-as-hell guys with my eyes. Even in their inmate jumpsuits, I can see the definition of their bulky, delicious muscles. One of the guys—a dark-haired man with piercing black eyes—raises a bag of dark liquid and winks at me.

He smiles, revealing his fangs and...what the hell? They've been capped. A vampire with capped fangs? I can't stop the surprise laugh from escaping my lips. I know I shouldn't, especially with how quickly his smile vanishes, but damn it. This place gets to me. And now I'm pretty sure the guy will try to get to me for laughing at him.

I puff out my bottom lip and mouth, "Sorry. You're still hot."

Maddox must notice the small exchange that softens the vampire's features, because he shoves me in the back hard enough to make me stumble.

"Damn it, Maddox. Chill out!" Ohmyhellno. I did not just scream at him, using a name I wasn't given permission to use.

A few of the vampires inhale sharp breaths, and another guy laughs. I tense and squeeze my eyes shut, willing myself to disappear. Where is the brilliant portal light when I need it? Because if the sudden heat warming my skin wasn't bad enough, the nearly overwhelming cinnamon breath of

CAGED BY HER DRAGONS

Maddox sends my heart sinking into my stomach.

I prepare for a monster's wrath, for unbearable pain, for my end to come. What I don't prepare for is the whack of a baton to my ass. I startle at the sting that weakens my knees for a second but manage not to fall over.

"Gotta do it harder than that, CO. I think she liked it," an inmate says.

I glance in the guy's direction, blush crawling up my face.

The world falls out from under my feet, and Maddox dangles me on the crook of his elbow like a doll. He stomps his way through the room and then to another and another, not allowing me to look around. We reach a barred door leading into a dark hallway, but Maddox turns and pushes a door open with his shoulder. He kicks it closed and swings me up to slam my back into the wall of what looks like some sort of office.

He huffs a few warm breaths in my face. "Never, and I mean *never*, use that name again. I'm CO to you, Nova."

His eyes burn with the orange glow, his glower smoldering over me. My name sounds so sexy coming from him that I can't stop myself from sucking my lip between my teeth. It'll either drive him crazy or piss him off. Either way, I hope I get to him. Fucker.

"You mean Inmate D64901." I know I should keep my mouth shut, but a part of me wants to test him and show him that I've dealt with a damn hot-headed man of a boss for a while. I put my life at risk every night since joining Galaxy Gold's. There is no safety in a traveling stunt show like that. "*CO.*"

Punching the wall near my shoulder, he sends flecks of stone to the floor with his strength. "Shut your fucking mouth and listen to me. You were damn lucky that wasn't my cellblock, or your life sentence would've turned into the death sentence half the High Council thought you deserved."

I crack under his words, unable to stop my mouth from frowning. "You mean you, not the whatever council. You wanted me dead."

"What I want is answers," he mutters, pulling away.

The empty space he leaves in front of me grows cold, making me shiver. Something strange flickers in his hard gaze. Sorrow? Grief? I'm not sure. But it prods at me, drawing me from my place against the wall. Why in the world do I feel the need to comfort the asshole who spent all day screaming in my face? The douche who wouldn't believe a word I said? The one responsible for me being here? Because for a split second, I understand. He lost someone close to him. Whatever evidence they found points to me. Would I believe me if our positions were changed? I don't know.

If only my movement didn't destroy that soft flicker in his eyes that made him look like a lost man rather than the asshole who acts tough to fulfill whatever expectations he thinks he must meet. The absence of emotions and his sudden roughness, the way he grabs my arm and yanks me toward the door, screams at me that trying to get him to listen to me or believe anything I say is a lost cause. The only thing I can expect from this intimidating, hard-ass man is a whole lot of torment.

Guiding me to the next door with the letter S engraved on a placard on the wall, Maddox nudges me through without following. "Go to the CO in the supervision office and get your assigned cell and provisions."

And like that, he slams the gate closed and disappears.

I touch my hand to the barred door, nearly begging him to come back, but a shock crackles through me. I jump away and clutch my hands, the brand marks stinging worse than a baton smacking my ass.

A soft whistle echoes through the air from behind me, and I stiffen at the sound of footsteps. It doesn't take me more than a second to realize this place is nothing like home or any prison I've seen on TV. For one, it's full of creatures I still can't believe are real. And two, it's co-ed. I'm not sure which one is worse. Considering I'm not a real criminal, and I'm attractive enough, number two might be far worse in this moment.

A hand touches my shoulder, and I panic, my heart crashing against my ribcage. A thousand horrible thoughts flit through my mind. I prepare to fight.

"Well, look at you, sweet thing. Fresh meat—"

Spinning around, I perform a high kick, clocking an old man in the side of his head. He stumbles toward me, falling right into my bent knee. He howls in pain, landing on his side while clutching his junk.

I've never been so thankful for the self-defense classes my aunt signed me up for at the local fight gym. My aunt said it was the least she could do to protect me from my mother's mistakes. Mistakes I don't want to think about. The instructor even gave me extra lessons because of my aunt. He used to always tease me about how my graceful alterations to the moves would leave any attacker in complete shock to take them down. I think he might've been right.

"Mmm, I like them feisty," someone comments, tightening a knot in my stomach.

I tense and get my feet into their proper place to keep my balance. "And I like forcing assholes to their knees."

A few guys laugh and someone claps. I nearly take a bow before catching myself. This isn't a damn performance. What is wrong with me? Apparently I still thrive on applause, no matter how low it comes.

Silence draws through the cellblock, and I jerk my attention to the rest of the room for the first time. I brace myself to see a ton of hideous monsters, but everyone looks normal—at least as normal as one can look within the magical walls of this penitentiary. By the overgrowth of facial hair and some seriously other hairy extremities, I doubt they get razors here, and all these people are a bit beastly, not like the fae or vampires.

Mostly men sit at the metal tables, consuming disgusting raw meat. All the women I can see sit together at one table in the back, eating with their hands, but none of them look up in my direction. Whether that's good or bad—ah hell. They have their own prison clique, and I'm not sure if I'm prison bitch material, not that I'd want to be.

"Hey, kitten. Retract those claws or you'll spend your first day in your cage." The husky voice comes from across the room. A few inmates grumble at the threat, but I would gladly hide in a cell. "Be a good kitty-cat and slink your ass over here."

I inhale a few short breaths, trying to get my nerves under control. I regret the gesture as the air permeates with a foul smell. Just the sight of the inmates' bloody meal grosses me out. If that's the only option, I won't last here.

"Now." Kash stands on the top step leading into an enclosed office with window walls to get a view of the main room of the cellblock.

Someone meows and hisses from a nearby table, but I refuse to give the fuckhead any attention. Straightening the front of my jumpsuit like it matters, I cross the room to where Kash trains his gaze on me. Our eyes meet, and something about him captures my attention so much so that I can't get myself to look away. Neither does he. And now this staring match tests the both of us to see who breaks first.

"Let's make things simple, shall we?" Kash says, pressing his lips together. "Because from what I gather, you've managed to avoid Magaelorum Law until now."

"I haven't avoided anything. This crazy-ass fucking world is not common knowledge on Earth. Where exactly is this place anyway? Another planet? I know you came for me from the damn sky." My curiosity gets the best of me as I snap. The fact that no one cares to listen to me—or to explain anything to me for that matter—has me on the verge of a breakdown.

Kash tips his head back with a roar of a laugh. "That's cute of you to even suggest we're even on the same plane, kitty-cat."

"Wait, what?" I raise my eyebrows. He's serious. Really-fucking-serious. I don't even know how to respond.

"Enough questions, inmate." Kash closes the space completely and holds out a stack of items he picks up from a wall compartment. "You refused to cooperate with CO Dreki, so any and all questions you have can screw off with all the fucks I don't give for you."

Except maybe the good fuck he wants to give *to* me. I

see him checking me out. I'm not naïve to the lustful looks from men. I perform in tiny costumes, stretching my body into difficult positions. I know plenty of men fantasize about me. I've been told as much. Galaxy is always first to boast how Star and I bring sexy to the stage, being his little moneymakers.

A buzzer sounds through the air, making me cringe. All of the inmates suddenly get up from the tables and line up to dump their bloody plates into a bin. Two inmates remain nearby with janitorial equipment to clean up after whatever the hell meal this is. I haven't seen a single clock and can't figure out what time it is.

"All right, kitten. Time to see your new home," Kash says, pushing past me. "You're in the cell that gives me the perfect view. Say goodbye to your privacy."

Great. "Does watching women go to the bathroom turn you on, CO? Is that why?" I cross my arms over my chest. If he thinks the lack of privacy will bother me, he's wrong. I lived in an RV with three men and Star.

He doesn't respond to my quip or motion for me to follow him, but he doesn't have to because someone growls from nearby. I can't stop my legs from dragging me behind him to stay within his shadow like it'll somehow hide me. I have to jog to keep up with his long strides and consider grabbing onto the back of his uniform to let him drag me instead. We skip the staircase that takes us to the second level, and he leads the way to the last barred door nearest what looks like another office.

My gaze darts to the open door, and I catch sight of Rowan sitting at a desk with his legs up. He looks like one of the lazy cops from movies, just kicking back and watching something that's clearly not the video feeds from security. Naked breasts, followed by a crotch shot, lights up the screen. My heart jumps in my chest, spotting him catching me looking. He cocks his eyebrow and winks at me. I can't help thinking about the whole strip down. He obviously can't help himself either, because I swear I catch a damn smirk crossing his gorgeous face a second before his eyes glow with firelight.

Rowan distracts me so much with the naughty gesture he does with two fingers that I don't realize Kash stops in his tracks. I crash into his back, knocking the breath from my chest as I collide into the wall of muscle he creates. A hot hand locks around my wrist, yanking me forward to stop me from falling on my ass. I stumble right into Kash's body. Locking my free arm around him, I hug him to steady myself, practically clinging on for dear life. My hand squishes between us, and I flatten my palm against the even thrum of his heartbeat picking up.

And my damn body refuses to pull away. A strange buzzing sensation washes through me, and I lose myself in his hazel eyes, the same beautiful color as Rowan's.

CAGED BY HER DRAGONS

"Kitten, step away or you'll find your ass on the ground. One nice gesture toward a damn murderer is all you'll ever get." Kash flares his nostrils, his chest puffing against my hand, pressing harder to me.

"I'm not a murderer," I say, risking my limb by smacking my palm to his taut pec before hiding it behind my back. I feel the burn of Rowan's gaze penetrating the side of my face as he listens, and I turn to give him a second look. "I swear. I don't know what the hell kind of proof you have, but it wasn't me. I didn't even know witches or warlocks or whatever existed. Whatever the hell you are either. Or anyone here for that matter. I'm human. I don't belong here."

"You're not," Kash snaps.

"Then what the hell am I?" I ask, throwing my arms out. "You keep calling me a cat. Is that it? Because I'm damn sure I'd know." Shifting on my bare feet, I look at Rowan. "Or am I deer? You called me doe eyes. So which of those things am I?"

Kash greets me with silence. He swivels to glance at Rowan. He wears the same indecipherable expression.

"Tell me," I say, anger rising in me. "Tell me what kind of creature you think I am."

Again, neither of them responds.

"It's because they don't know, you enchanting woman. They only call you prey names because it's what they hope for. Someone they can boss around with them being at the top of the predatory chain." The voice comes from within the cell we stand near. I hadn't realized someone was inside, lying on the bottom bed of the bunk. The young guy twitches his fingers at me. He's scrawny compared to Kash and Rowan, but something about his smile makes him cute. "Now why don't you leave the COs alone and come in here and get settled. I'll gladly try to answer your questions if you promise not to punch me for making any sudden movements. And you don't have to worry. I can't bite."

He says he can't bite, not that he doesn't. Usually, I'd laugh something like that off, because people joke like that, but he's not human if he's here, and he probably means the words he says. I shift on my feet to look to Kash to see what to do. He stares at the guy in the cell for so long that I have to clear my throat to draw his attention to me.

"I'm staying with a man?" I finally ask. I can't believe this. It was one thing knowing the guards would watch me, but this guy is a stranger. He might be friendly, but I don't know what got him behind bars. For all I know, he could be like the warlocks from Rhett's bar. "This is so messed up. You can't do this."

"Red, those lionesses will tear you up and spit you out if you are assigned to share a cell with them. Their pride allows no outsiders, and you don't even seem like you're from this realm." The guy sits up on his bed.

I glower at the side of Kash's face since he still doesn't

look at me. "That's what I've been trying to tell everyone. This is a mistake."

The guy graces me with a smile, turning him from cute to sexy. "Well, you can tell me all you want. I'll listen. I feel rather lucky to get a doll like you as a cellmate. This could be a lot of fun."

Kash suddenly reacts and grabs my arm, yanking me away from the cell. He pushes me against the wall, sandwiching me to it with his whole body. Every muscle of his ripples against me, sending my heart racing. Boots clomp nearby, and I listen to the guy's cell door open. A deep growl reverberates through my bones. The guttural sound that escapes from Rowan's throat as he drags the guy out of the cell freaks me out just a bit.

"Inmate D64876, you are being relocated to cell twenty," Rowan informs the guy.

"Of course I am." The guy chuckles. "Careful, CO. I might start to believe you like that gorgeous woman. What would the warden think?"

"CO Dreki, take him to the pits," Kash says, putting an inch of space between our bodies.

The man grumbles under his breath but doesn't fight. I manage to shift a few inches to get a clear view of Rowan grabbing him by the collar. The guy tightens his jaw and jerks his neck to look back at me.

"I'll find you when I can, Sky Dancer. Don't let these

asses push you into submission. You are not theirs," the guy says.

My eyes widen at his reference to my job. "How did you know?"

"I knew your m—"

Rowan slaps his hand over the guy's mouth and drags him away. I try to dodge around Kash's huge form, but he blocks me with his arm and herds me toward the open cell. I stumble inside and twist on my feet to look at him. He stands tall, watching me watch him as the door slides shut.

Anger washes over me, and I rush forward and link my fingers around the bars. "You're an ass!"

Kash scowls at me, closing the distance. He laces his big fingers around mine to prevent me from moving away. A zap of electricity sparks between us, sending my hair floating with static. Kash's eyes devour me. He puckers his brows, flaring his nostrils.

And then he leans in super close.

My body gets trapped in his gravitational pull, and I mirror his movements, standing on my tiptoes to erase the distance between us. I lick my lips at the same time he swallows, sending his Adam's apple bobbing in his throat. I prepare for him to kiss me, to grab the back of my head to keep me in place to do so. I suddenly yearn for it, crave it, feel as if I'll explode if I don't experience the sensation of our lips caressing together.

CAGED BY HER DRAGONS

"Let's get one thing straight, Nova," he whispers, his soft voice like a feather-light kiss to my mouth. "I have one job, and one job only. To ensure you don't ever see the outside world again. You will pay for your crimes."

I exhale a breath, my heart racing in overdrive. His words weren't what I expected or wanted to hear. I fucking should've known better. Clearly, this strange attraction is all in my head, my mind still begging for this nightmare to turn into the best fantasy of my life.

"I'm innocent," I manage to say.

He releases my hands and steps back. "As far as I'm concerned, you're not. And now your life is mine. Understand? You're mine."

I don't get the chance to respond. Kash spins on his heels and disappears, leaving me alone and breathless in this dank cell.

Fuck this prison life.

Chapter 6

Prison Life

I'M GOING CRAZY.

I have no idea how much time has passed, but it has been long enough for the buzzer to blare. I stand at my cell door, waiting for the bars to open, but to my dismay, it remains closed. The muffled voices of the other inmates trickle from the main room of the cellblock. I can't get a good view from the hall apart from a round mirror that allows the guards to see behind them as they walk.

CAGED BY HER DRAGONS

After doing a few body lifts, using the bars as support and treating them like one of the set pieces on Galaxy's stage, I practice my floor routine as best as I can in the small space. I don't know what else to do. I can't just forget my life outside of this cell so quickly. I have hope that this is all some crazy hallucination, and I'll wake up and have to prepare for the next show.

If Kash didn't come stomping down the hallway, I could pretend a little while longer. With one glare, he shatters my hope to pieces. It crashes onto the floor with the plate of bloody meat he drops through a slot without waiting for me to try to catch it. Juice splashes over my bare feet, and I jump back.

"Ew, what the fuck," I say, kicking my foot to get the cool drops off.

"Eat up, kitten. You're going to need your strength for your duties today." Kash's lips twitch with his words.

"My duties?" I remember Maddox mentioning that I'd be put to work. Who knew I'd actually want to? Why the hell am I excited?

"I'm to assess your capabilities." He remains expressionless with his arms crossed over his broad chest. I trail my gaze from his pristine boots and up his muscular body. I stop at his collar, noticing the edge of a tattoo peeking out on his neck.

He remains expressionless and silent under my scrutiny. Nerves bunch in my stomach as he returns the favor and draws his gaze down my body, stopping at my breasts, my nipples tight and pressing against the fabric of my jumpsuit, clearly enjoying his attention. My. Damn. Boobs. This would be a lot easier if I could just kill the attraction rising in me.

Clearing my throat, I meet his startling hazel eyes. Something warm washes through me as he locks me in a gaze I can't break. Whoa. What is wrong with me? He obviously looks just as surprised, his eyes widening for a split second.

He flicks his eyes from mine first, finally releasing me. "You have five minutes. Eat up or starve."

"Can't you at least tell me what my options are for duties? I'll tell you if I can perform them or not." I expect him to glower at me, yell at me, something.

He freaks me out a bit by smiling. Not only because something dark lines in his eyes but also because he looks hot as hell doing so. He grabs the bars of my door and squeezes them in his fingers. "No. You will do whatever I tell you to do." He says the words like he's absolutely certain that I'll comply with whatever he demands. Bastard.

"That's what you think," I mutter under my breath.

"I know," he practically purrs under his voice. He smacks the bars, startling me. "Now eat up." He doesn't turn away or anything like he plans to watch me suffer trying to eat something completely inedible.

I drop my gaze to the strange, raw meat on the floor. I can't tell what the hell kind of animal it is, but I'd rather starve than even consider getting it near my mouth. So instead, I straighten my shoulders, turn my back on him, and stroll to the bunk to flop down.

Uh-oh.

The cell door buzzes and slides open. I remain frozen on the cot as Kash storms into my cell and picks up the meat. Before I can react, he drops it onto my chest, pelting my face with meat liquid. I screech and fling it off, smacking him in the stomach with it. It splats to the floor, splashing juice on his pants and boots.

Ah, hell. He looks ready to force-feed the gross meat to me.

"If you even think about it, you better just throw me in whatever the fuck the pit is now," I say, clenching my fingers into fists. "I'm not eating that shit."

His eyes light in an orange glow. "Fine. Then starve."

Kash grabs me by the wrist and drags me out of my cell with him. I can barely keep my feet moving to stay with his long, fast strides. My bare feet squeak on the cold tiles, and I consider just giving up.

"Keep up, inmate," he mutters.

This. Guy.

I know better than to open my mouth and argue. If only the huge, annoyed part of me could resist fighting him. Because I'm not the criminal this damn world makes me out to be. I shouldn't be here. The last place I belong is in a world full of creatures from my nightmares.

I summon my nerve and go flaccid in his arms. He drags me ten feet before realizing that I slide across the floor. Releasing my wrist, he drops me with a growl. I huff, my back hitting the tiles. I don't try to get up or move or anything. I freeze under his fiery stare, his eyes feeling as if he burns my jumpsuit off me to peek at me naked.

"Get up now, inmate," he says, towering over me.

"No." I tense as the sharp word explodes from my mouth. What is wrong with me? Something about Kash prods at me and makes me want to rebel and push boundaries. If this was a prison back home, I doubt I'd resist like I am now, even if I was innocent. It's just—this place. Fuck. This guy even. I have so many questions, and with how he and the other guards act, I swear that the only way I'll ever get answers is if I somehow either beat it out of them—which, yeah-fucking-right—or seduce them and screw it out of them. Is that even possible?

Maybe.

I know I'm not imagining the weird-ass attraction buzzing through me, even now as I lie on the floor right in front of him. He swallows, his jaw shifting with the gesture. For a split second, he looks like he has no idea what the hell to do. His confusion goads me on even more.

I prop up on one elbow and fling my hair out of my face. "If you want me to keep up, you're either going to have to drag or carry me."

His eyes flash with something indecipherable. Annoyance? A teensy bit. It's something else too, something that quirks up the sides of his lips in a half smile. "All right, kitten. If this is the game you want to play."

Bending over, Kash locks his fingers around my ankles and lifts me upside down by my feet. I shriek at the sudden spinning of the world around me as he tosses me into the air. He catches me in his arms and glares at me only to drop me halfway. Locking his hands around my knees, the bastard hangs me upside down right in front of his damn groin. My nose brushes his pants, and I stiffen.

He releases a strange, deep noise in his throat and shifts me a bit, but it's not before his body reacts to my closeness. His pants grow in my direction, and his surprise boner brushes my cheek. And holy hell is this guy hung. And so incredibly hard. Now I can't stop thinking about his hot body or how his clothes smell a bit like a fireplace and cinnamon and a few unfamiliar scents that I can only describe as warmth and sunshine. Nothing like his cold eyes.

"Do you mind?" I ask, risking stretching my neck to look up at him. All my gesture does is make me rub my head harder to his crotch.

He releases a low, deep groan in his throat.

One second I'm swinging upside down with his quick pace, and in the next, I fall a few feet. I brace to hit the floor, but a soft cushion breaks my fall. I shoot up and look around a quaint living room. Kash strides a few feet away and kicks the door closed.

My heart beats wildly, his eyes drinking me in from his spot across the room. I feel naked even in my clothes and wonder what the hell I'm doing. I don't know what the prison rules are, but I'm nearly certain Kash is breaking them to get me alone.

"What are you doing? I'm not going to bang or blow you, if that's what you think," I say, clenching my fingers into fists. "That kind of fun must be earned, CO." Who the hell said that? It sounded like me, but it doesn't feel like me.

Kash scrubs his hand over his face. "You're right about that. Now, don't even think about getting up. If you move an inch, you will end up back in your cell for incompliance."

"Not the pit?" I ask, remaining on my back.

"I can't watch you in the pit." Turning his back on me, he unfastens his belt. "You're my inmate. You will learn who's in charge the way I want."

"Maddox—" I cringe as I say a name I shouldn't. "I mean, the other CO threatened me with that."

Stripping out of his uniform shirt, Kash twists on his

CAGED BY HER DRAGONS

feet. "I doubt it was a threat. CO Dreki doesn't make those. He only makes promises." Dreki? That's what he called Rowan too. Not only are these guards coworkers and friends, I'm nearly certain they might be brothers or cousins or something. How could I miss this?

My eyes roam down Kash's neck and to his taut, broad chest. The bastard is totally doing this on purpose because of my banging comment. And his games are working. Because, damn. Tattoos paint his golden skin, from his chest and up his neck and down both arms. I devour each of his bone-hard muscles, how his abs clench and flex like he can feel my gaze actually touching him.

"But not you?" I ask.

His jaw tightens and he continues to strip from his clothes, not even caring that I watch him kick his pants off. And holy shit. His boner is even more impressive without the fabric of his uniform pants keeping his body contained. His black boxer-briefs do the opposite, giving me the best damn view.

Without answering my question, he says, "I'm going to shower. Like I said, stay here. If you move, you'll regret it. Once I get out, you'll start your tasks."

"Will it include drying you off?" I ask, my mouth smirking. I think he underestimates that nothing his sexy self can do will make me uncomfortable. "That seems like an awfully big task since you keep growing. If I didn't know any better, I'd think you liked me."

It takes everything in me not to laugh at his reaction. His steely face cracks under my words and he covers his mouth to stifle the lusty growl that comes from his throat. He surprises the hell out of me by dropping his underwear and kicking them into his pile of clothes. I shamelessly stare at him, my eyes glued to his delicious body. He doesn't react under my scrutiny, but I swear he shifts to give me a better view.

I remain utterly still, wondering what the hell is going on. I don't even flinch under his bravado, and I wonder if this is all some sort of test. Why the hell would he drag me from my cell and bring me to what I'm nearly certain is his personal living quarters? If my brain would stop obsessing over the sight of his rippling muscles as he enters the bathroom, I might be able to process this. But maybe not.

He leaves the door to the bathroom open, and I risk sitting up on the couch. Peering around the room, I take in the green carpet, small coffee table, and open kitchen. The bed sits on a raised platform in a loft area. Disheveled blankets hang over the edge, spilling onto a desk beneath it. Other than an open closet of nicely hung uniforms and a pile of dirty laundry on the floor, there isn't much else to look at—not pictures, a TV, or anything. No wonder these COs are like this. They're basically in their own prisons here.

CAGED BY HER DRAGONS

I listen to the sound of the running water and push up, tiptoeing across the room. I sneak toward the small kitchen, my stomach rumbling at the sight of the fridge. Getting thrown back in my cell will be worth disobeying his orders. I realize how hungry I am as I spot the bowl of fruit on the counter.

Snatching up a banana, I peel it and shove half of it into my mouth. I moan at the sweet flavor, my belly still screaming.

"Inmate!" Kash yells, startling the hell out of me. He stands in the doorway to the living room butt-ass naked, his chiseled body glistening with water and suds of soap.

I shoot my gaze to him, my mouth still full with the hunk of banana. He shakes his head, sending water pelting the wall. Rushing in my direction, he leaves a trail of footprints across the carpet.

I do the only thing I can think of.

I chew as fast as I can and shove the rest of the banana in my mouth, throwing the peel right at Kash. It splats against his chest and falls to the ground. He stops a foot away, his chest heaving, his body tense with his anger. I cringe and swivel, cowering just a bit under his intimidating presence.

Grabbing my shoulder, he pulls me to him, closing the space. He leans in and glowers, his eyes lighting with fire. Heat zings from his fingers and to the rest of me, warming my core from inside out. My breath catches in my throat, and I finally swallow the banana, half-expecting him to stick his finger down my throat to see if he can remove it from my body.

"I-I'm sorry," I whisper, trying to keep my voice even. "I couldn't help myself. I'm so hungry."

"And I brought you dinner," he snaps, digging his fingers more into my shoulder.

"Something I can't eat. If I can even stomach that bullshit enough to get it down, I doubt it'll stay down. I don't know what you think I am, but it's not some beast. I'm human. I eat fruit and vegetables. Carbs. Cooked meat on a good day. Not something that looks like you found it on the side of the road and skinned only to torment me with." My chest heaves with my breath, my breasts grazing his bare chest. And then I remember he's naked.

So does he.

Raising his hand, he points to the couch. "Go sit and wait for me, damn it. I mean it."

I release a haggard breath and bob my head, my whole body quivering under the freezing air the lack of his presence leaves behind. With one last look over his shoulder he disappears into the bathroom.

He obviously doesn't trust me to leave me alone for more than two minutes because he returns to the living area rinsed of soap with a towel slung low around his hips. I rub my lips together, taking a peek at him again, imagining his towel dropping to the floor.

Stomping to the kitchen, he grabs a box of something from the cupboard. My stomach rumbles at the picture of what I think might be crackers on the front. Something shifts in Kash's hazel eyes the closer he gets to me. His jaw twitches, his stone-hard expression softening for a split second.

And then the fucker dumps the box of crackers on the floor in front of me.

"Clean this shit up," Kash says with a scowl. "After that, take care of the rest of the damn place." Crossing his arms, he trains his eyes on me. "Now."

I glare at him, wanting to tell him to clean his own damn place and that I'm not a maid, but he grabs my shoulder and tugs me from the couch to knock me on my ass on the floor. Without even getting dressed, he slumps onto the sofa and plops back, his smooth, muscular hip and leg showing off from his tied towel. Because I don't move right away, his knee brushes between my shoulders. My skin tingles under the simple touch of his body to mine.

He intakes a deep breath and holds it, stiffening behind me. "Nova..."

The softness of his voice grabs my attention, and I swivel and look at him. My heart picks up speed at just the caress of my name on his lips. I want to hear him say it again to assure myself I didn't imagine it. Something strange comes over me the longer I look into his eyes. A dozen thoughts light with fire, turning his beautiful gaze orange.

"What am I doing here?" I finally manage to ask.

"I'm assessing your capabilities." He remains serious, despite his muscles rippling. "To assign you work."

My gaze breaks from his to travel down his pecs and to his chiseled abs. I've never seen muscles like his. Where Galaxy, Mars, and Orion's muscles were lean and sinewy, Kash is like a concrete wall carved into a man and sexy as hell. No art piece I've ever seen quite has a body like his, especially his once-again hardening dick, set off under my scrutiny.

"Have you never seen a man's erection before?" he asks, snapping my attention from his impressive cock—hard, long, and thick enough that I imagine being able to show him quite the performance with my acrobatic pole skills.

I lick my lips. "A boner? Yes. A beast of one like yours? No. I told you already that I don't belong here. You're obviously not human, and I'm not whatever the hell you think I am."

He howls a laugh and suddenly sits up. "You want to see it again, kitten?"

I gawk at him in surprise. I mean, what the hell? Is he for real? "Yes." Whoa. Shit, did I just say that?

CAGED BY HER DRAGONS

I'm not the only one surprised by my word. His face darkens with something indistinguishable, his handsome smile fading. Silence draws between us, and I shift more to face him. His eyes trail away from mine and to my mouth, studying my lips so intently that they tingle in anticipation. A crazy-intense need overcomes me, and I risk Kash yelling at me for getting to my feet.

Sitting up straighter, Kash leans forward, his large hand encircling mine. He pulls me closer, catching me between his knees. His warm thighs sandwich me between his legs, and fire blazes in his eyes like he plans to devour me.

"Kash..."

The second his name escapes my lips, I inhale a sharp breath. My legs tremble in panic, the memory of Maddox threatening me because I said his name before freaking me out about Kash's reaction. But Kash doesn't react the way I expect. He reaches his other hand up and glides his fingertips over my hip and to my side.

Our gazes meet once again with me staring down at him. His nostrils flare, his jaw tightening.

A bang sounds on the door, startling me. I stumble away, crunching my feet into the crackers littering the carpet. Kash hops up and catches me before I eat shit on the floor. Another thud hits the door, and Kash releases me.

He points to the mess. "Clean this up, inmate. Don't say a word. Got it?"

I can only manage to bob my head, my emotions churning wildly inside me.

Kash crosses the room, leaving me in my spot. I kneel on the floor and swipe a few crackers up, stuffing them down the front of my jumpsuit. Gross? Most definitely. But my stomach growls in desperation, Kash's distance now reminding me of more important things than checking out the hot body of one of the cruel guards who might try to break me.

"CO Dreki, what the fuck?" Maddox appears in the doorway to Kash's living space. "You disobeyed my order."

Ah, hell.

I snatch up as many crackers as I can and shove the ones I can't fit between my boobs into my mouth. A shadow casts over me, and I chew as fast as I can. Hands lock to the back of my jumpsuit and haul me from the floor. Maddox dangles me in front of him, huffing deep breaths. His cinnamon scent engulfs me, filling my airspace.

"She's going to the pit," Maddox says, glowering past me.

"What for?" Kash steps closer, his presence warming my back. "It's my shift, so I can do with her as I please."

"Do not undermine my authority." Maddox shifts me onto his shoulder.

"Fuck off. She's mine." Kash locks his fingers to my hips and tries to jerk me away.

CAGED BY HER DRAGONS

"Yours?" Maddox's voice rumbles from his throat. "*Yours?*"

I screech as the world falls out from under me, and my knees hit the carper. Heat blazes around me, the air turning hotter by the second. Panic ignites inside my core. I don't have a chance to move or do anything as Kash shoves his hands against Maddox's chest. Maddox stumbles under the force and hits the wall with a crack.

His skin ripples, his gold eyes sparking orange. It's like lava flows through his veins as deep, metallic scales shimmer across his arms with his strange transformation. But he doesn't turn into the beast I can't get from my mind—the flying creature unlike anything I've ever seen—but he doesn't need to. He releases a deep, throaty growl from his throat before fire explodes from him, singeing across the carpet to surround me.

Shadows edge my vision, the intense heat threatening to devour me.

The world turns dark except for the orange and yellow flames.

They swallow me whole.

Chapter 7

Criminal Games

SOMETHING WET PELTS me in the side of the face, drawing my attention to the world above. Two unfamiliar inmates hover over the grate that separates me from the prison yard. The scent of smoke wafts through the air, jerking my attention to my body. My jumpsuit smolders across my stomach, between my breasts, and on the tops of my legs. It's now that I remember the fire that burst from Maddox. How I'm not a pile of ash or how the sizzling fabric doesn't burn me, I have no idea.

Another splatter of liquid hits me, this time on my leg. Smacking my palms to my jumpsuit, I pat the smoking fabric until it stops.

"Aw, so soon, sexy?" one of the men says from above me. "I was imagining all the ways you'd enjoy my spit all over you to squelch out your fiery desire."

His words sink into me, and I gag and scramble to shove myself as close to the dirt wall as possible. I don't know what I was expecting, but it wasn't an actual pit. I thought it would be something like solitary confinement. At least it's not a damn fire pit, though with how my jumpsuit looks, maybe it was at some point, and I just happened to survive.

A deep growl rumbles through the air, getting the two guys to move on without another word. I curl my knees to my chest, hoping that whoever scared the guys away isn't even worse than they were. I don't think I've ever been spit on in my life, even during my worst performance, and gag. Those assholes.

"Chow time, cookie." Damn it. I can't catch a break. Maddox's voice erupts the memory of him spewing fire in anger to the front of my mind. "You want out or not?"

Something sounds different in his voice, but I can't put my finger on it. Slowly scooting back into view, I tip my head up to meet Maddox's golden gaze. The scar on his cheek glows red before fading, and I wonder if I'm imagining things.

"If it's that nasty raw meat, then I would prefer to stay here. This pit is better than suffering through that torture." I brace myself for his anger, but Maddox remains expressionless.

He links his fingers to the metal grate and heaves it off the mouth of my pit one-handed and drops it beside him. "As much as I'd prefer that, I can't have you trying to escape me just yet." I can't help but wonder if he's implying what I think he's implying. "You're no use to me dead."

Hell. I was right.

"I'm no use to you at all, so why don't you just leave me alone and let the other COs handle me?" I tighten my mouth. "Then you never have to see me again."

I don't get a chance to prepare myself before Maddox slides into the pit, holding the edge with one hand. He secures the grate and locks us in together. Jumping into the pit, he lands in a crouch beside me.

Metallic scales erupt on his arms, breaking through his rippling muscles. I don't know what comes over me, but my hand takes on a mind of its own, and I bend down and caress my fingers over the strangely magical sight.

Sparks shock me, and I retract my hand, cradling it close to my body. I expect Maddox to shove me into the dirt wall and yell in my face, but he stills without looking at me. Several breaths draw out the silence. Tipping my head back, I look up to see if I could launch myself high enough to brace my feet on each side of the narrow tunnel leading up to the grate. If I could get a teensy boost, I could do it. I know I could.

Inhaling a small breath, I try to talk myself out of the dangerous stunt I'm about to pull. But I need space between my body and Maddox. My heart won't stop racing, my skin still buzzing from the shock of my fingers touching his...scaly skin.

I suppress my good senses and jump on Maddox, using his muscular back to launch myself into the air. He grunts under the unexpected force of my move but doesn't topple over. I extend my legs out into near splits, catching myself on the section of the pit I can climb out of.

"Nova, what the hell are you doing?" Maddox asks, my name sounding deep and husky on his lips. I expected him to roar in rage, to call for the other guards, something, but he remains beneath me without even attempting to stretch up to snag my leg.

"I don't know," I say, using the strength of my legs to push me up a foot closer to the grate. "I just—I need to get away from you."

I summon my strength again and jump another foot, catching myself on the dirt walls again. The ground below crunches with Maddox's movements but he still doesn't attempt to grab me. Instead, he plops down on his ass and watches me try to get out of the pit.

Sweat prickles on my forehead, the exertion of having to use my strength in such a way reminding me of some of my tougher performances. Except the freefall toward concrete is not nearly as scary as a drop toward that infuriatingly sexy man-beast who seems to enjoy the show.

"Cookie, you're going nowhere," Maddox says from below me. "You'll never get away from me."

"Wanna bet?" I ask, finally reaching the top.

Linking my fingers to the grate, I test its weight by shoving my hand against it. And shit. It weighs a lot more than I expect it to. And then the fucking metal sparks with electricity, zapping my hand. I lose my balance and drop toward the dirt, preparing to break or twist my ankle from the fall. I press my lips together to stop any noise from escaping, the sensation of flying toward the dirt something I'm used to.

Except I don't hit dirt.

Maddox catches me by my waist, and I automatically wrap my legs around him and dig my fingers into his broad shoulders. Energy hums between us, his cinnamon breath overpowering the scent of dirt. Our eyes meet, and a burst of tingles warm between my legs, my damn vagina begging me to do something, anything, to get a moment with this gorgeous man naked.

Maddox's body arouses at my closeness, and I shiver in anticipation, his hardening cock testing the barrier of his uniform and my jumpsuit. Sliding my fingers from his shoulders, I move them around his neck and close the space enough to where he could kiss me if he just would lean forward. The fire in his eyes screams he wants to. So does the friction of our bodies rubbing together as he pulls me against him, digging his fingers into my ass.

His lips puff with a soft breath. "I told you that you couldn't escape me," he murmurs, staring deep into my eyes. "You're mine."

Why the hell do I love the sound of that? It doesn't sound threatening but just a fact. The truth of my existence. But fuck that. I belong to no one, especially not this hot-headed asshole who refuses to believe me.

"Are you sure about that?" My voice comes out all breathy. "Kash—CO Dreki claimed me already."

His eyebrows peak on his forehead at my words. "He thinks you belong to him, but I'd know it if he staked his claim. And he won't. Not with you. Never with you."

This conversation has taken a weird turn, and I don't even know how to respond to that. So instead, I ease myself back, trying to put another few inches of space between us.

"I don't want that either," I say, tightening my mouth.

"Because you want me." Is he for real? How audacious

of him to even say the words out loud.

Anger rushes through me but not because of his implication. I'm angry because he might be right. How can I be so damn attracted to a guy who yelled at me for hours? Who refuses to hear me out? The man who runs hot and cold and wants to be cruel for the sake of making my life miserable? Who whacked my ass with a baton...okay, so maybe I liked that a little. But it doesn't matter. Whatever I'm imagining in my head is wrong. I need to focus on more important things and not how good his damn arms feel around me, or how I want him to prove his strength by ripping my clothes off to sink his raging boner inside me. Or how I want him to kiss me—

My lips brush against his, my body turning my fantasy into reality. Heat sparks from our kiss, and Maddox tightens his arms around me, spinning me toward the dirt wall to kiss me harder, deeper, like our mouths are suddenly at war with each other. His tongue plunges into my mouth with hot desperation, his passion igniting every cell on my body, sending the warmth from his kiss to shoot down the rest of me, turning me on. I crave more of his touch and desire. Slick warmth builds between my legs with my sudden raw, almost feral need.

I imagine yanking his belt open and sticking my hand into his pants to pull his cock free. My whole body buzzes in anticipation, needing to really test this uncontrollable attraction. He'll be rough on me for sure, but I wouldn't mind. I don't even care that dirt will coat my back if he chooses to use the wall to brace me against.

I act first on my desire, dragging my nails down his back until I manage to bunch the fabric of his shirt enough to pull it from his belt. A deep rumbly moan vibrates against my mouth. He's imagining the same fantasy as me. It burns hot in our kiss, our tongues exploring each other's, his hard-on threatening to break through our clothes to experience more of me.

"No, cookie," Maddox says, snatching my hand to pin between us. He squeezes my fingers in his large hand, breathing against my mouth. Caressing his lips to mine again, he says, "Me first."

Maddox sets me on my feet, breaking our kiss. I lick the cinnamon flavor his scorching tongue leaves behind, my body buzzing and begging for me to ignore him and to proceed however I want.

Reaching up, he brushes his thumb to my lip, stretching it out with the movement. And then he kisses me once more before spinning me around toward the dirt wall. He presses into me, combing his fingers through my hair to pull the strands from my neck. He sucks the skin on my throat hard enough to leave a mark and make me moan.

"Don't make a sound," Maddox commands, sliding his big hand around my stomach to where he can pop open a button on my jumpsuit. "If you disobey me, I will stop. You won't get what you crave."

Get what I crave? I'm nearly certain he has that twisted. Instead of saying as much, I go along with his need to hold power over me and slowly nod my head. A dozen thoughts swirl through my mind and the more reasonable part of me screams that I better not lose focus or start to like Maddox no matter how hot he is. This is nothing but a hopefully good time and a chance to play his game until he loses. When he loses, he'll see he's made a big fucking mistake. Because I don't belong here. I will break free.

"Not a single sound. Not here," he says again, slowly unfastening the buttons of my jumpsuit.

I inhale a small breath at the warmth of his hand sliding into my clothes to explore the sensitive skin of my breasts. His hard cock pokes into my lower back, his desire as prominent as my own. It feels massive, intimidating, but something I'd experience given the chance. I don't know if it's this fucking place, my whirlwind emotions, or just a carnal need because I haven't had sex in months, but whatever it is. Fuck. Me. Fuck it.

Biting my lip, I stop a moan from trying to escape my mouth as Maddox traces his fingers lower, mapping the smooth planes of my stomach. A line of heat trails after his touch like he brands my skin but not in a way that hurts me—it excites me and teases me. It's a shadow of a remind-

CAGED BY HER DRAGONS

er of how his touch feels as he does whatever the hell he wants with me. I can't wait to find out. My body screams in good anticipation the closer he gets to where I want him to go.

"You're so soft," he whispers, slipping his fingers into my panties. He hums under his breath. "So smooth."

I brace my hands to the wall, my knees shaking in anticipation as he grazes his fingers over my sensitive skin. My breathing quickens, my heart thrashing like crazy.

Maddox glides his tongue down my neck and kisses my shoulder. "You're so warm and wet. For me." Lifting me up slightly, he adjusts his raging boner between my legs from behind. "Feel what you do to me, Nova? Do you like that?"

"Mmmhmm," I whisper so quietly under my breath that I'm not sure he heard me.

"Do you like this?" With his question, he slips his finger across my clit to rub circles over my body.

I dig my nails into the dirt wall, bracing against it, a dozen sexy thoughts racing through my mind. It's so hard to stay silent as he works me over with his fingers, adding speed and pressure like he's determined to make me orgasm faster than I ever have before.

Maddox whispers my name, sinking his finger inside me to find out exactly what he does to me. I can't believe this is happening. I never in my wildest dreams ever thought I'd be convicted a murderer, locked away in a magical penitentiary, while also experiencing the best foreplay of my damn life—with a hot, broody, beast of a man who might explode at any second without warning. I have always been a thrill-seeker, living on the edge. But this is far more dangerous than any aerial performance.

My body builds until I almost reach my peak, and an uncontrollable moan escapes my mouth. Maddox stiffens behind me, his muscles rippling against my back. Tugging his hand away from my body, he spins me around and glowers, his eyes flashing with fire.

"I said no noise," he snaps, his nostrils flaring.

I open my mouth to apologize but then my good senses return with the foot of space he puts between us. Annoyance and frustration rush over me, because fuck. My body still buzzes even as my damn almost-orgasm skips away from me, taunting me about how stupid I was to fall for this game. I bet a man like Maddox never follows through to ensure a woman orgasms.

Stepping forward, I shove my palms to his chest and push him back. "I don't give a damn about what you said. If you want me to be silent then don't touch me like that again. Better yet, don't touch me at all. I don't know what the hell twisted thing you're thinking, but I'm not yours. I will never be yours. You're why I'm in this godforsaken place."

He bares his teeth at me, releasing a low growl. "Get

dressed, inmate. It's time to return to your cell."

It infuriates me that he doesn't even respond to my comment and instead acts like we weren't just making out or getting off.

Without giving me the chance to comply, he closes the space and snaps the front of my jumpsuit up. He tilts his head and glowers at me, trying to intimidate me or some shit, but all I do is meet his glare with my own.

"With the way you teased and failed to bring me to completion only shows what kind of man you are. The noise bullshit was only a damn excuse. I bet you couldn't actually do anything." I purse my lips, trying to think of another few things I could say to mess with his ego. "And you know what else?"

Maddox doesn't respond but instead looks up toward the grate.

I poke him in his chest. "I'm damn near positive Kash would be better than you. He's not afraid to show off his sexy as hell body. I bet he'd—"

Maddox releases a growl and snatches my hand from his chest. Pulling me closer, he pins me against him, sliding his hand around my lower back. A wicked smile curls his lips, and he leans in and surprises me with a kiss. "Nice try, Nova. You can't use my brother—either of my brothers for that matter—against me."

That's what he thinks. Because now I'm more determined than ever to figure out which one of these guards I can get close enough to. In doing so, hopefully I can somehow prove my innocence.

"Now, be quiet, cookie. Tell no one I'm here. I'll get you to myself again soon. We're not finished." Maddox releases me and nudges me toward the center of the pit by smacking my ass.

I startle at the warmth left blooming on my butt cheek, even through my clothes. Swiveling, I peer at him from over my shoulder, but he hides within the shadow, a foot of space shielding him from anyone who looks into the pit.

A whistle sounds through the air, and I catch sight of a silhouette blocking the sun above. I glance at Maddox again, who holds his finger to his lips to tell me to be quiet. He licks his finger with a wicked smirk, firelight glowing in his eyes. And now I'm confused as hell. I mean, what the actual fuck? This guy is so hot and cold. I hate how my body loves the idea of him finding me again. This is so twisted, but so is this place and all the magical creatures within this impenetrable fortress.

Something bangs on the grate a second before it slides off the opening to the pit. A rope ladder falls down to me, and I stare at it, wondering if I should just tell whoever is above that I'd rather just stay in this damn hole. Because hell. I'm a little afraid of what will happen. Those guys who spat on me earlier might seek me out again. Or someone else.

"Don't make me come down there, Inmate D64901," Rowan says, smacking what I think is his baton to the side of the grate. "Grab the ladder. It's my shift, and I've decided I'd prefer you in your cell."

I link my fingers around one of the rungs on the rope ladder. "So you can watch me like the creep you are?"

"Exactly. Now hold on tight."

My heart flies into my stomach as he yanks the ladder out of the pit instead of allowing me to climb. Wind whips through my red hair, and I can almost envision being on stage with Galaxy. I forgot how freeing it felt to propel through the air, upward with a precise leap and not the annoying unexpected freefalls.

I land on my feet beside him, and he steadies me by the arm. Tingles explode over my skin where he touches, the sensation stealing my attention before I even look around the prison yard. Rowan captures me with his hazel eyes. His sudden intensity burns over me, sending warmth between my legs, my lust still running rampant from Maddox.

"What? No shriek? Not even a little squeal?" Rowan asks, cocking an eyebrow.

"Before you assholes dragged me to this hellhole I was a performer in a traveling aerial acrobatics show." I don't know what comes over me, but I have the urge to try to prove myself truthful. Getting into position for one of my floor routines, I dash a few feet from Rowan and perform a flip. "So no, no screeching."

"Hey, CO, I know how to make the lass scream." The gurgly voice sounds from behind me.

"Inmate, no!" Rowan shouts.

A hand slaps over my mouth while another tangles in my hair. "Mmm, pretty girl. You looking for a master? I'll take good care of—"

"Release her!" Rowan hollers. "She's mine!"

The strange man drags me back, locking his hand across my neck. I close my eyes, preparing for him to choke me to death, to do something crazy. This is the bullshit I get for trying to prove my innocence by showing off my talent. Too many gross assholes around here are fully ready to give me their unwanted attention.

"How badly do you want her, CO?" the guy asks, tightening his fingers around my throat. "Enough to—"

Rowan roars, his skin rippling.

Power hums through the air, and I stare in shock as Rowan rips through his clothes and transforms into a giant reptilian beast straight from TV. His dark green scales glitter with metallic gold. He unfolds his wings, his massive form bigger than any animal I've ever seen.

Then the beast blows fire, setting the dry grass ablaze by my feet.

The inmate releases me and shoves me forward.

CAGED BY HER DRAGONS

I can't believe what I'm seeing. Rowan is a dragon. A real fucking dragon.

Flapping his wings, he bends his legs and launches at me. All I can do is brace myself to be devoured.

But instead, the beast rams his head into my stomach, not giving me a choice but to grab onto his big snout. My skin buzzes, my heart beating wildly. Even though the dragon's body feels cool under my touch, I can still feel warmth radiating between us.

And then we're flying.

Chapter 8

Dragon Men

FUCK. FUCK. FUCK.

The ground speeds toward me as the dragon—I mean, Rowan—descends toward the far corner of the main structure of the prison. I grind my teeth, keeping my mouth shut no matter how much I want to scream. This is faster than free falling.

Squeezing my eyes shut, I brace for impact. My body

jostles for a moment before the world stills. I'm afraid to move or even open my eyes. I cling onto the dragon until a weird sensation crawls over my skin, sending an intense wave of emotions through me. It's like everything good I've ever felt in my life sneaks back to me to push the twisted direction my future heads away. As quickly as the feelings come, they disappear.

I fall back and hit my ass on the ground. Snapping my eyes open, I gawk at Rowan. He stands a few feet away from me and completely naked. My eyes betray me and dart from his handsome face and straight to his cock and back up...and back down again. I continue to stare at the well-hung appendage that swings with his movements as he closes the distance and offers his hand out to me.

I screech and crabwalk backward and not because of the close proximity of his impressive manhood—because damn—but because he just turned into a dragon. A *dragon*. And I rode on his fucking head. In. The. Air.

Rowan lifts an eyebrow. "There are those doe eyes again. You afraid of a naked man?"

I open and close my mouth, trying to suck air into my lungs. "It's not your cock."

"Good, because it won't hurt you. You'd enjoy it." His lips curl into a smile with a flash of fire in his eyes. "Promise."

I crinkle my nose and narrow my eyes. "Not happening, asshole."

"Yet. A life sentence is a helluva long time." Rowan closes the space again, this time not offering me his hand and instead sliding his fingers under my arms to haul me from the ground and onto his shoulder. My eyes stare down at his firm, smooth ass, and if I could reach it from my position, I'd smack him so fucking hard. "Now, try to be quiet. We've already drawn enough attention as it is."

"We? *We?*" my voice rises with my words. "You turned—you turned into a fucking dragon. You blew fire all over the prison yard. And now you're standing here butt-ass naked. Don't include me in this attention drawing bullshit."

Rocking forward, I surprise him by managing to pinch the top of his ass cheek. Rowan shifts me on his shoulder, dangling me farther down. I scramble to clutch his sides, afraid he'll flip me off of him completely. But he doesn't let me go.

"For every damn pinch, slap, bite, whatever the hell else you want to do to me will only make me return the favor, Nova. Think carefully if that's something you want to happen. This is your one warning from now on." His voice grows husky and deep, longing even. He dares me to test my luck, and I suddenly want to.

"It'll be worth it," I snap, swinging my hand out. I smack him hard enough to make my hand sting.

He doesn't give me a reaction. Not a startled jump.

CAGED BY HER DRAGONS

Not dropping me. Nothing. Instead, he ignores me. It pisses me off, and I swat him again harder. This time, he chuckles.

"All right, Nova. Your turn."

The world jostles as Rowan stomps his way toward a guard-access only door. I regret testing my luck the second he hauls me inside, marches down a long hallway, and enters what looks to be his private quarters. My heartbeat picks up speed, listening to the door click closed.

"What are you doing?" I ask, bracing myself on his hips to arch my back to glance around the messy room. Rowan's room looks like he just drops clothes where he takes them off, sets dishes wherever he wants, and probably never dusts. His small studio is chaotic, where Kash's was tidy and bare.

"I warned you that I'd return the favor." Rowan flips me off his shoulder and sets me on my feet in front of him.

I place my hands on my hips. "You're fucking joking."

He twirls his finger, motioning me to turn around. "One pinch and two spankings."

I widen my eyes, heat blooming up my cheeks. "Fuck that."

"I could make you strip too. You are filthy from the pit," he says.

Shit. This guy. What a cocky bastard with a control complex. Just like when I first arrived here, Rowan undresses me with his eyes, probably fantasizing about me being as naked as he is. I know he wants to play games. I heard him arguing with Maddox about it...and now? It makes me want to fuck with him too.

"You can thank Maddox for that." I know I shouldn't mention Maddox. It could turn this hellhole even worse, but I can't help it. "He thinks I'm his."

He flares his nostrils.

"So does Kash," I add.

Rowan growls under his breath, his eyes flashing with firelight. Without him having to say a word, I know I might've gotten under his skin. A smile curls my lips, and I comb my fingers through my messy hair, pulling it out of my face and off my neck. I twist on the balls of my feet and glance around his room.

"So maybe you should just take me to my cell." I feel his burning gaze darting over me, and I purposely keep my eyes elsewhere. "After a shower. Because you're right. I am filthy, and I bet your shower is better than what awaits for me out there."

Turning away from him, I head toward the bathroom door, his room having the same layout as Kash's. I pop open the buttons on my jumpsuit and ease it down, slowly showing off my shoulders and back, letting it hang on my hips a bit until I enter the bathroom. Soft footsteps follow behind me, and I smirk to myself, wondering what the hell Rowan would do if I shut the door on him. I'd kind of love to watch him break it down.

CAGED BY HER DRAGONS

I don't get the chance. A warm chest bumps my back, pushing me into the small room. I automatically turn around to glare at him. Rowan fills the doorway, his muscles bulging as he grips the sides of the frame. His smoldering eyes trail down my body to check out my breasts and then continue lower, burning across the planes of my stomach.

I lick my lips, trying not to react to the blatant desire crossing his face. I won't let another Dreki CO turn my mind to mush like I had with Maddox. I've learned my lesson, and there is no way I'm leaving this bathroom in sexual frustration. Rowan can suffer blue balls.

"Do you plan on watching me the whole time?" I ask, even though I know the answer. "That's kind of creepy."

Rowan enters the bathroom and closes the door. "No. I'm joining you."

Ah hell. "You are so not."

My body loves the idea as my vagina clenches, and I squeeze my thighs together. This damn situation can only go in two directions, and I'm not even sure which way I should take it. I know which way I want it to go, but I have to guard myself from Rowan. I know he's playing games, flexing his power, and will want me on my knees. I know this. He only thinks of me as a prisoner he can do as he pleases with. He has already admitted as much as he plans to lay claim on me, especially knowing that Maddox and

Kash have tried to do so too.

    The smart thing to do would be to not test my luck. I shouldn't feed into this crazy-ass situation. I'm nothing to these COs except the supposed murderer of their friend. This could be some sort of plot to torture me as they try to get under my skin and tease my desires. My good senses scream that all they will ever be is the men on the other side of the cage I'm in, only letting me out to play with to their heart's content before shoving me back in. I'm basically an animal to them. Their prey. They'll tease me until they've had enough and then devour me.

    Rowan turns the water on, dragging my attention from my thoughts. He enters the shower first, releasing a soft groan when the steamy water cascades over his muscular body. And this bastard. He reversed the roles on me.

    He shakes his head, flinging water in my direction. "If you want to shower, you can join me then. Your choice, doe eyes."

    I inhale a few deep breaths and stare at him as he turns his attention back to the shower stream sending rivulets of water down his body that now awakens seemingly for me. Maybe because I can't stop gawking at the rod of flesh turning as hard as the rest of him or because I'm also doing so while standing half-naked. Either way, I appreciate what I see. I think he might even be bigger and thicker and a bit more intimidating than what I felt of Maddox, though I

CAGED BY HER DRAGONS

can't be sure comparing him to Kash.

"Letting the warm air out. You better decide in the next ten seconds, because this is your only chance. Once I'm through, I'm taking you back to your cell before the night inspection." Rowan shifts and looks at me. "Five seconds."

Shower with hot guy or—what kind of question is this?

Tugging the rest of my jumpsuit down, I kick out of it and enter the shower. Rowan pulls the glass closed behind me, and I squeeze past and step in front of him. I stick my face into the hot water, using the sensation to try to distract me from the fact that there is barely enough room for the two of us, and I can feel the tip of Rowan's raging hard-on against my lower back.

After an intense silent minute between us, I ease my face from the water, bumping my head into his taut pec. "Can you watch that thing? It's uncomfortable jabbing me in the back."

"Where would you like for me to put it?" he asks, his voice lowering. "You're in my shower. By your choice."

I spin around and smack his chest, my movements in the small space causing his dick to slide up my pelvis because it has no other place to go. And fuck me. I nearly say as much the second my gaze meets Rowan's. My skin buzzes, his closeness setting off my lust and desire and something strange yet inviting, begging me to make a move already. Because he wants me too. I know he does. It's part of his game. He wants me to prod him just enough to give him a reason to take control and have his way. He enjoys his position of power, but under that cocky-bastard grin, those fiery eyes, and his tough-ass presence hides a man who won't force me into anything I don't want. I don't know how I know this, but it's an overwhelming and undeniable feeling that lights hope inside me that maybe he'll eventually see the truth. That I don't belong here.

Rowan draws his big hand up my arm, tracing my skin from my elbow to my shoulder. Pushing my wet tresses away, he slowly turns his gaze from mine and to my body. "Nova," he says, his words coming out softly. "Tell me to get out."

Get out? That's suddenly the last thing I want.

My heart ricochets around my ribcage, pounding so hard that it's like each beat nudges me closer to Rowan until my body molds flush against his. Slowly gliding my fingers across his muscular shoulder, I link my hand to the back of his neck, using his solid form to brace against as I rise on my tiptoes. His cock slides against my pelvis again until it slips down and between my legs where I have to straddle his boner because his cock has no place else to go in this position. How he resists picking me up by my ass to slip inside me? I wish I knew.

I realize in this moment that Rowan's far better at these

games than I am. I'm not some sneaky, hard-ass criminal. I'm a free-spirited Sky Dancer who likes to challenge myself and smile in the face of danger so I can brag that I survived. It's turning into the adrenaline rush I crave and less of everything else.

I'm doomed. Really fucking doomed. The only thing I have going for me is that I manage to keep my lips from his, despite how close the rest of our bodies are.

"I don't want you to get out," I finally whisper, closing the space to his mouth yet leaving an inch. I don't care how torturous this feels. He's going to make the first move. He needs to make the first move. He has enough power over me already. "Unless that's what you want."

Rowan hooks his hand around my waist and lifts me off my feet by my ass. My back hits the cool tile wall as I wrap my legs around his hips, anticipating him to enter me. But instead, he crashes his mouth to mine, kissing me so passionately, it's almost violent like he wants to break me but yet it feels so good. His lips taste amazing, similar to his brother's yet sweeter like sugar sprinkles through the cinnamon flavor. His hands twist in my hair as he holds me close and slides his tongue between my parted lips. The heat of his skin warms me up hotter than the shower, and I gasp and comb my fingers through his hair, craving more of everything he has to offer. With my mouth battling his for control, our tongues practically wrestling for a better taste and feel, the rest of the world fades from my mind. It's just Rowan and me and the steam of the shower, the desire sparking between us, and the hot intensity of our passion that could destroy the universe and neither of us would notice.

I've never experienced such fervency in my life—like his kiss is my punishment for trying to beat him at his game. Our breaths mingle, our lips and tongues and teeth exploring each other, sucking and nipping and tasting like one of us will die if we don't give in to the raging desire exploding between us. I scratch my hands down his shoulder, rolling my hips to grind my body to his. Rowan returns the favor by digging his fingers harder into my ass cheeks, holding me tightly to ensure I can slip and slide against him to my body's content. And damn does it feel good.

"This isn't enough," I murmur, stretching his lip between my teeth. "Get a condom."

"No. I want you to tell me you're mine," Rowan mutters through a kiss, breaking away from my mouth. He glides his tongue down my throat to the sensitive crook where my neck meets my shoulder. He sucks in my skin between his teeth, giving me a hickey. "I want to hear it first."

I hum under my breath, stretching my neck more to the side. "Not happening. I belong to no one." My breath gasps with the words.

CAGED BY HER DRAGONS

Rowan growls, the sensation vibrating against my skin. Pulling me up higher, he sucks my nipple into his mouth hard enough to make me moan. I arch back, giving him better access to my breasts, lacing my hands to the back of his neck. I comb my fingers through his hair, grinding my body against his chiseled abs, each hard muscle creating friction between my legs.

"You belong to me, Nova," he says, slipping his hand from my ass cheek to in between my legs. He teases me with his finger, not getting carried away. He wants me to break first, but I refuse to. "Now tell me."

I shake my head, sending my wet hair splaying over my shoulders. "Make me. The only way I'll ever say it is if you make me."

Rowan slides me down his body until my feet touch the tiles. He doesn't stop though, getting on his knees only to stretch my leg over his shoulder. I moan so fucking loud as he pulls my body to his face and kisses my clit with another rumble from his throat. I cling onto his head, pulling the wet strands of his hair between my fingers. He flicks his tongue with expertise, sending tingles exploding from my groin and to the rest of me. My leg trembles, my body turning to jelly under his attention. If the wall wasn't propping me up, I might fall.

"Rowan," I murmur, the sound of his name escaping my lips a second before I realize what I've said.

He slides his hand between my legs from behind, sinking a finger between my heated flesh to send my body into a state of ecstasy unlike anything I ever expected to feel with this beast of a man. Where he breathes fire, he also ignites a different kind of flame within me, setting me ablaze to my very soul, awakening a rawer, darker, more feral part of me.

"You're mine," Rowan says as he works over my body. He curls his tongue around my clit and sucks it with enough pressure to make me weak in the knees. "Tell me."

"I—" I snap my mouth shut, my brain refusing to give in to his demand. If he thinks by turning me on and stroking my desires that I'll bow before him, he obviously knows nothing. It makes me want to resist more. Get him to do more. "I will consider it after you make me orgasm." I moan again, loving how his frustration turns into determination. I will enjoy every last moment of this while I can. I thought I was losing these power games, but he's the one on his knees for me. He will be the one to beg.

He growls again, the vibration nearly buckling my knees. The only reason I remain upright is because Rowan's hulking frame prevents me from doing anything else. He continues on his mission to make me declare his claim on me, rolling his tongue while sucking my clit just right until my body explodes with my intense orgasm, my muscles tightening and pulsing in a wave of indescribable feelings that make me moan so incredibly loud the whole prison might hear our passion. I scratch my nails into his shoulders hard enough to leave eight red lines on his skin. He eases away from me and kisses his way back up my stomach like he can't get enough of my taste, like he wants to experience every inch of me.

"Nova..." He eases away from me to look into my eyes. "You're beautiful."

I suck my bottom lip between my teeth and inhale a few slow breaths, trying to get my brain to function despite my body wanting to just enjoy the lingering pleasure rolling through me.

"I'm more than that," I finally manage to say. Because complimenting my appearance doesn't change anything. "I want you to get that straight right now."

A smile curves his lips, turning him even more handsome, his sharp expression softening. "You're stubborn. I like that. Feisty. Strong-willed. Determined."

I raise an eyebrow. "Why? Because I won't let you win these games you're playing with me? I know what's going on here. I know exactly your type, Rowan. Tough-guy, always gets his way, power-hungry—"

Rowan shuts me up with another kiss, groaning as our lips meet. My skin tingles in anticipation, his kiss shocking me like he broke through an invisible cloud of static. He snakes his hand around my ass and pulls my pelvis to his, his hard cock sliding against me.

"You know nothing about me," he says, pulling away. His hazel eyes search mine for a moment. "But I'd like to change that. This was all…" He swallows, letting his voice trail off.

What the hell? He looks like he has a dozen thoughts on his mind and also like he doesn't want to share a single one of them. I don't know what changed, but he feels different, softer toward me, almost relieved. It's the weirdest thing.

"All what?" I ask, deciding to pry when he's not quick to give me a clue as to what is going on.

"Unexpected." Rowan puts space between us but doesn't let go of me, keeping his hand locked to the small of my back. "Unbelievable."

I furrow my brows, his words making no sense to me. "I don't understand you, you know. What are we even doing? Why are you even doing this? Is this part of getting into my head in an attempt to break me? Torture me? What? You're obviously willing to risk your job, so whatever this is can't be good. I'm not dumb."

He blinks a few times, his mouth tightening as he continues to stare at me. "It's not like that, Nova. I'm not playing any game with you."

"Bullshit!" The shower and his closeness suddenly feel like they're suffocating me. I swivel on my feet and reach out, trying to push open the glass door to let cool air in. But

Rowan doesn't let me go. He holds me close, my heart pounding against him, my emotions turning wild. "You think I killed your friend. You want revenge."

"I don't," he says quietly, reaching up to touch my cheek.

"Yeah-fucking-right," I snap, pressing my hand into his chest to push him back. "If that were the case, you'd believe me when I say I don't belong here. I'm innocent."

"I know." The words come out so softly that I'm not sure if I imagined them. Rowan touches my chin, tipping my head up to look at him. "The last place you belong is here."

Confusion washes over me, and I search his eyes, trying to determine whether or not he's lying to me. This could all be a part of his twisted game, giving me an ounce of hope only to steal it away.

"If you were guilty, I'd have felt it," he adds softly. "And after feeling you in my dragon form..."

What the hell? I can't believe what I'm hearing. "What is that supposed to mean? Why didn't you say something to the judge if you knew I wasn't a murderer? Why drag me through this bullshit if you knew I was innocent? What the fuck, Rowan? Fuck. Fuck!"

I squeeze my eyes shut with my anger and bat my hands against his chest. I can't believe the words I'm hearing. He made me believe that he thought I was guilty all along, and now he's admitting he knew I was innocent. What a bastard.

"Nova, please. You have to understand. I didn't know for certain until now." Rowan traces his thumb across my cheek, pushing my wet hair behind my ear. The warmth he had brought to me now dissipates despite the hot water still steaming around us.

"You're not making any sense," I say, trying not to savor his touch. "I don't understand any of this."

I try to reach around him to turn the water off, but he grabs my hand and links his fingers through mine. Without saying a word, he studies me for a moment, his hazel eyes flickering with indecipherable emotions. His chest bumps against mine with every breath he inhales, the intensity of this moment threatening to send me into a hurricane of confusion.

"You really don't know about Magaelorum." It's more of a statement rather than a question. If I didn't know any better, I'd think he might feel a bit sad. His smolder diminishes the longer we stay together, just opening up for the first time. "Or what you are. You don't know anything."

I shake my head. "I'm human. I'm from Earth. I was just an aerial performer. Rhett approached my boss after one of our shows and freaked me out. He said he had been looking for me, but I don't know why. He was stalking me and promised to follow me around until I let him speak his mind, but he never got the chance."

Silence falls between us as Rowan thinks over my words. I shift on my feet, still holding his hand. It takes me squeezing his fingers to get him to pull himself from his thoughts. I find myself tracing my finger over his pec with my free hand like my body can't understand that I shouldn't be so close.

"Because he knew," Rowan finally says. He grumbles with the words as he lets them sink in. "He had to have."

"Knew what?" I blink my eyes to clear the drops of water from the shower off my lashes.

Without answering, Rowan swivels on his feet and shuts off the water. He drags me from the shower and grabs a towel from the rack, draping it over my shoulders. I stand in surprise as he starts to dry me off, swiping the towel across my body like he's afraid the fluffy fabric might accidentally hurt me. Or maybe he's afraid he might.

"Get dressed," he says, pointing to my dirty jumpsuit.

I frown, hating the idea of putting it back on.

"I promise I'll bring you clean clothes. You'll get another shower. I just—I have to get you back to your cell and talk to my brothers." Rowan slings the towel around his hips and disappears from the bathroom. He returns with a way-too-big T-shirt and what I'm nearly certain are a pair of his boxers and holds them out to me. "This will help. Now please, get dressed."

The fact that he says please doesn't go unnoticed by me. If it was yesterday, he would've demanded it. But now? Something has changed. I don't know what, but I think it's something important. It's more than the fact that we kissed and fooled around in his shower.

Rowan disappears, leaving me alone in the bathroom. I consider arguing a bit more, but the clothing he brought for me feels so soft and inviting compared to the roughness of the jumpsuit. After slipping the T-shirt over my head and then the boxers up my legs, I take a minute to comb my fingers through my messy hair the best I can. I spot a hickey at the base of my neck, peeking from the drooping collar of the T-shirt. I graze my fingers over it, the memory sending lust shooting between my legs again.

"I couldn't help myself," Rowan says from the doorway. "I saw one of my brothers already left a mark on the back of your neck."

Heat burns up my chest and into my cheeks. It was Maddox, and not even that long ago. With the thought, I can't help grimacing at myself. Did I really mess around with two guys in the same day? That's a first for me. Star would laugh her ass off and tell me to get it. She was even more free-spirited and confident than me. And now I miss her.

My lack or response and frown makes Rowan clear his throat. "You don't have to say anything," he adds. "I'm not bothered if you're worried."

I bob my head and release a breath like he was right about my thought, even though he wasn't. But I'll accept it because I wasn't planning on getting into anything with him right now.

Rowan scoops up my jumpsuit and shakes it out, sending dirt pelting to the floor. He holds it in front of him and bends slightly, silently asking me to get dressed. I use his shoulders and step into the jumpsuit, not even getting the chance to button it up before Rowan snaps it in place. His jaw twitches as he meets my gaze again.

"Can I kiss you once more?" he asks, touching my cheek. "I know I don't deserve your affection, especially now, but...please?"

My head nods before my mind can process, and Rowan bends down and brushes his lips to mine, softly and sweetly, and nothing like our first kiss. I still crave for him to do it again when he eases himself away. I enjoy the closeness of his body far more than I realized, especially after seeing this side of him.

"Tell me you're mine," he whispers, his Adam's apple bobbing in his throat. "I know you feel it."

I frown. He just had to go and ruin it. "I don't know what you're talking about. Why do you keep insisting such a thing? I can't be yours. You can't own me."

The corner of his lips quirk up. "You will understand

soon. Now, come on. I have to get you back to your cell."

His words send a blip of fear through me. Rowan locks his fingers tighter through mine, not letting me pull away. But fuck that. He just told me he knows I'm innocent. My cell is the last place he should take me.

"No," I say, finally breaking from his hold. "You're going to take me to the judge. You're going to tell him—"

Rowan lifts me off my feet, cutting off my demand. "I'm sorry I have to do this, Nova, but no. I have to take you back to your cell."

"You don't."

"But I do."

CHAPTER 9

The Dreki Brothers

"CO DREKI!" I yell for the tenth time. "I need to speak with you!"

I stare at the mirror that gives a view of the empty hallway, waiting for Rowan, or even Kash or Maddox for that matter, to show up. It feels like I've been trapped in here forever. It's been so long that I think I slept for a bit. Smacking my hand to the bars once more, I turn around and slump onto my cot. I yank the collar of Rowan's shirt from my jumpsuit and bring it to my nose. It still smells like him—cinnamon, sugar, and something fresher like the wind blowing during a storm.

The buzzer to my cell goes off, startling me. I hop back to my feet and push the T-shirt back into my jumpsuit. Loud footsteps thud against the concrete hallway, but I remain in my spot as the bars to my cell slide open. Anticipation courses through me the closer the person comes. I never thought I'd be excited for the return of one of the Drekis.

A strange scent wafts into my cell a second before an unfamiliar guard appears in front of the doorway. I take an automatic step back, darting my gaze to the floor. I've never seen this man, and something inside me panics, stealing the badass I've managed to summon to face the Drekis.

"Hands up, inmate," the guard says, pulling a chain from his belt. "You have a visitor."

A visitor? What? Who? Shit.

"If you're good for me, I'll give you some free time in the prison yard," he adds.

"That sounds like punishment," I mutter under my breath instead of berating him with all my questions.

If the CO heard me, he ignores me. I don't test my luck and raise my hands for him to secure the restraints on. They glow green with electricity, reminding me of the restraints Maddox put on me when I arrived in this stupid world. I grind my teeth and brace for the pain that comes with any sudden movement, but luckily, nothing happens. Something's different.

I want so badly to ask the new CO what's up, but he shoves his hand between my shoulder blades and pushes me from the cell to walk in front of him. Keeping my gaze on the floor, I stroll down the long hallway and try my best to ignore a few grunts and catcalls from the asshole inmates still in their cells.

The guard palms my back again, getting me to pick up speed when I slow down. We enter the main area of the cellblock with the tables, but none of them are occupied at this time. A few more inmates shout for the CO's attention, but he ignores them while he guides me toward an unfamiliar door that leads...outside.

I shiver at the gust of air that blows my hair off my neck. Sunshine stings my eyes, and I squint, really missing my favorite pair of sunglasses I left on the table in Galaxy's RV. Not like such a luxury is allowed here but still. Who knew I would miss something so small and simple.

"The visitation room isn't in the main building?" I say, finally getting the nerve to ask.

"No."

I was hoping for a better, more detailed answer but no such luck. I doubt he'd give me one anyway. He's steeled toward me, neither acting like an ass nor nice. He's just neutral, I guess. Whether that's good or bad, I have no idea.

"I didn't think I would get any visitors, considering I've never been to Magaelorum before this bullshit." I know I shouldn't continue to make conversation, but it's the only thing stopping my heart from trying to burst from my chest as we walk farther and farther away from the main building and to the outskirts of the prison yard.

"Don't know. Don't care. The warden approved Mr. Infinity's visitation. I expect you to be a good little girl and mind your manners. He's up for a High Council position within the next century." The guard comes up beside me as we near a building. "He could easily persuade the right people to end your life sentence." The way he says it doesn't sound like an early release but a change from life in prison to a death sentence.

I shiver at the thought and peer around. Electricity zings across the top of high walls, threatening to shock anyone who attempts to escape. I slow down until the CO whacks my back with his arm. He pushes me toward a single level building surrounded by a chain-link fence. If another CO in the same uniform didn't stand at a gate, I might panic more than I already am. Something about this supposed visitation center doesn't feel right. Why the hell does the name Mr. Infinity sound familiar?

Ice slides through me, cooling my blood. Everything has been so hectic and insane that I forgot Rhett's warning a minute before he died. He mentioned the name Lazlo Infinity. He blamed him for the massacre at the bar.

And now the fucker is here to see me.

I halt in my tracks and back up a few feet. The guard behind the gate hesitates without opening it. He stares at me, studying me from my wide eyes to my fingers wringing together. With a nod of his head, he gets the CO who brought me here to turn towards me.

I extend my arms in front of me protectively. If only the damn restraints didn't trigger at my movement and send pain blasting through me. My legs give out, and I drop to my knees with a screech. The edges of my vision shadow from the burst of pain lingering in every cell on my body.

"What's the matter, Inmate D64901?" the guard at the gate asks.

I groan and turn over on my side without getting up. "I changed my mind. I don't want to see any visitors. It had to have been a mistake."

"The warden doesn't allow for mistakes," he responds, opening the gate. "Get her ass up CO Lowe."

CO Lowe finally acts on the gatekeeper's command and drags me to my feet. He grips my shoulder so hard that I wince in pain. His strength is crazy, his fingers feeling as if they could easily break my bones. If that happens, I won't be able to perform for who knows how long. I could lose my position...fuck. I've already lost that. I've lost everything. This whole time I've been blaming Rhett—a dead man—but now I have someone alive and within my reach to blame. This could be exactly what I need to prove my innocence, except I'm freaking out. I can't help it. Whoever Lazlo Infinity is, he's a psycho. He has monsters working for him that hurt people. He should be the one in here. Not me.

I wish I had Star or even Galaxy here to give me a pep-talk. If I can face three damn intimidating dragon beast men, I sure as hell can face anyone. The thought is enough to get me to get my act together.

Straightening my shoulders, I raise my chin up, meeting the gatekeeper's gaze. He arches a brow, probably thinking I'm on the brink of losing my mind with my split second shift in my attitude and demeanor. It's a talent, I guess, my ability to take on a role and give my damn best performance. There have been many close calls with Galaxy and reacting negatively could ruin a whole performance. He trained me that I better damn-well smile and be confident even if I was about to splatter on the ground. For that, I'm thankful. Damn it, I miss him. I miss Star, Mars, and Orion. I miss being a sky dancer and traveling everywhere and anywhere. I miss the people and the RV that I called home.

"Arms up, inmate," CO Lowe says, not giving me much of a chance to dwell on everything this fucker waiting for me ruined.

CAGED BY HER DRAGONS

I raise my arms for him and wait until he unlocks my restraints that flicker out the second they drop free. Rubbing my wrists, I stare at the small, dimly lit room before me. CO Lowe guides me past the guard at the gate and inside, where the door closes behind us.

CO Lowe nudges me toward a blank wall. "Hands against the wall and spread your legs."

I frown but do as he says, closing my eyes as he pats my jumpsuit down like he suspects I'm hiding a ton of weapons. At least he doesn't ask me to strip.

"All right. You're good. Go on in. I'll knock when you have five minutes left of visitation." CO Lowe motions at the only other door in the room apart from the exit leading to the prison yard.

Fear prickles in my heart, and my chest clenches. "You're not coming with me?"

He remains expressionless. "The warden approved Mr. Infinity's request for privacy. I'll monitor you from out here, so don't try anything regrettable."

It's laughable that he thinks I'm the one who might do something insane when it's the asshole in the visitation room who is definitely here for something surely evil if he was involved with the monster men trying to kidnap women from the bar.

Instead of saying as much, I suppress my nerves with a deep breath. I can only pray that if this Infinity douche tries something, CO Lowe will intervene. Fuck, I hope that's the case. As I push the door open, I silently beg the universe for one of the Drekis to come and take this CO's place. At least they don't want me dead. Maddox thinks he'll get answers from me. Kash—I don't even know about him. And Rowan? Hell.

A man claps his hands together, cutting into my train of thought. The door slams closed behind me, and I whip my attention around at what appears to be the only entrance and exit into the room. A long mirror sits inlaid into the wall, and I imagine CO Lowe taking his place behind it to watch us.

"Delphia, you look just like your mother down to that fiery hair, green eyes, and even the damn jumpsuit. How's the bitch now? Grieving over your absence, I bet." A short man with long white hair smiles at me from a few feet away. Clapping his hands again, Lazlo Infinity sends a burst of sizzling blue light through the air, dimming the overhead light.

"I think there's been a mistake." I try not to react to the use of my birth name. "I don't know who Delphia is. My name is Nova Noble, and so you know, both my parents are dead."

Blue electricity blinks in his light gray irises. "I know a Drakovich descendant when I see one."

"A what? Who are you anyway?" I hug my arms over

my chest, deciding to go with scared and naïve instead of ballsy and infuriated. Maybe if he doesn't know that I know who he is, it might give me an advantage. If I can get him to say something to prove my innocence, I could get out of here.

Vanishing from his spot across the room, Lazlo materializes in front of me and proffers his hand. "Lazlo Infinity. I should be offended that you haven't heard of me, Delphia."

"Why? I'm not from wherever the hell we are now." I clear my throat and pout my bottom lip, trying to calm the annoyance from my voice.

Lazlo tilts his head slightly. "Let me guess. You're going to now tell me you didn't tear my brother in half. Is that right?"

I grimace at his words. "How the hell would I do that?"

One second I'm standing in front of Lazlo, and in the next, I hang a few feet off the floor, engulfed in a cage of blue light. I can't move or scream or do anything, and the door to the room remains shut. I knew I couldn't trust CO Lowe to intervene in this bullshit. He's probably laughing his ass off.

Lazlo stomps toward me, baring his teeth. They extend into long fangs. His eyes spark with blue light, and he mouths something I can't understand. Fire erupts on the tops of my hands, the pain so intense it feels like he's burning them off. Tears blur my eyes, but I can't defend myself.

He's casting some sort of spell over me.

And then he stops.

I fall to the ground with a gasp, jerking my hands up to see the damage his unexpected burst of magic caused. My inmate ID brandings glow red and orange like lava swirls through the numbers, but that's the worst of it. I blow a soft breath over them even though the pain dissipates. My body wants nothing more than to see the fire snuff out.

Lazlo locks his fingers through my long hair, yanking me off the ground. His face morphs into something even more monstrous, and I can't stop looking at his fangs. It's creepy as fuck. If I didn't think he'd devour me, I would look away.

Instead, I jerk my leg up and knee him in the balls.

He hollers, my attack surprising him. I shove my hands into his chest and force him away. Lazlo snarls, swinging his arm out in an attempt to grab me, but I'm too fast. I launch over him, pretending I'm jumping to a platform high in the air. My instincts kick on, helping me put enough distance between me and Lazlo that I reach the metal door before he can make it halfway across the room. I think my knee to his balls might've interrupted his ability to perform that glowy magic bullshit.

Pounding my fists on the door, I yell for the guard to let me out. If only I was strong enough to break the damn thing down.

CAGED BY HER DRAGONS

"He won't help you if he can't hear you, Delphia," Lazlo says, his voice echoing through the room.

Blue light casts over the door, and I slap my hands harder to the metal. Panic ignites inside me. I brace for pain, for death, for something, only footsteps tap across the floor.

"You have some debts to pay me." Lazlo moves closer. His magic illuminates more, blinding me to the room. "You'll be a dead woman otherwise. Either way, your beast is mine."

"I didn't kill your brother," I snap, trying to keep my shit together. There is no way in hell I'm going to cry. "I'm not who you think I am. I don't belong here."

"It doesn't matter." Lazlo digs his fingers into my shoulder and yanks me from the door. "The High Council needs someone to blame for not only the murders of so many poor, innocent souls. They need someone to blame for a break in the gateway. They'll soon discover what else you've done. What you will do now that you've escaped."

I glower at his implication. Whatever the hell he's up to, he's going to try to pin on me. "Fuck off."

"Close your eyes, Delphia. Be an obedient beast," Lazlo says.

I grind my teeth as he whispers something I don't understand, sending pain shooting over my hands again. It's now that I realize what he's trying to do. He's trying to remove my brandings. I know they're what help the High Council keep track of me or something. They contain whatever they think I am. If Lazlo removes them, he can take me. I wanted to be free of this prison, but I didn't want to trade it for what I know will be something far worse.

Unable to keep my mouth closed, I scream in pain, my body buckling under Lazlo's magic. He follows me to the floor, continuing to chant. I try my best to fight, kicking my legs and bucking my body. If I can hurt him again, he will stop.

A loud roar breaks through the hum and static of Lazlo's magic. He snaps his mouth shut and shoves me away from him. Blinking from existence, Lazlo disappears. The door flings open to the small room. Fire bursts from the figure, silhouetted in light from behind. My eyes water as the pain coursing through me vanishes. My brain screams to get up, to do something. I can't just lie here and do nothing. I can't. Lazlo could return any second. He'll kill me or steal me. Who knew that prison would be the lesser of two evils?

"What is she doing in here?" Kash's rumbly voice explodes through the room. "It's not visiting hours."

Another figure materializes beside him. "I—I don't know. She must've climbed the gate. CO Waters wasn't at his post. Probably pissing."

I groan, trying to push from the floor. "What?"

CAGED BY HER DRAGONS

Kash enters the room, a glower hardening his handsome face. Without giving me a chance to explain, he bends down and slaps a piece of fabric across my mouth. My eyes widen as fear rushes through me. He's not even going to give me a chance to speak. There's no way I can tell him that CO Lowe is lying.

Kash grabs my wrists and pulls me to my feet. While pulling out the magical chains, he looks over his shoulder. "This is on you. Go home until this gets sorted out. She shouldn't have even been brought out of her cell. She hasn't been granted permission to join gen. pop."

CO Lowe flares his nostrils. "I know that. It wasn't me."

I swing my head, trying to speak. My voice muffles through the fabric, and I point at CO Lowe.

Kash turns his attention to me. "Not now, Inmate D64901. Now hold your arms out. You must be restrained."

Narrowing my eyes, I glower at him, wishing I could smack him upside the head for not giving me a chance to speak. Kash remains expressionless as he binds my wrists with magical chains. Curling his fingers around mine, he pulls my hand closer to study my brand marks. They still faintly glow red, Lazlo's residual magic lingering.

But Kash doesn't say anything. Instead, he releases my fingers and presses his big hand to my lower back. He guides me to the exit and pushes CO Lowe out of the way. The two of them have a silent staring contest until Kash releases a low, threatening growl.

"I said go home, CO," Kash says, shoving his hand into my back to keep me moving. "Don't make me call the warden to discuss your indiscretions."

CO Lowe spins on his feet with a grunt and stomps away from us, exiting the building first. Kash glares behind him without a word but doesn't follow. He allows a minute to pass before he finally looks at me.

"I'm sorry I have to do this, kitten," he says, leaning in to whisper. "You okay?"

I shift on my feet and tilt my head up to meet his eyes. He searches my face and combs his finger across my forehead to pull stray strands of hair from my eyes. I remain utterly still under his touch, the soft sensation of his hand sending warmth over my skin that sinks into my bones. A mixture of emotions swirls through me, and I break my steely expression. I can't help it.

I shake my head, trying to fling the tear from the corner of my eye. Kash watches me with a grimace, his lips pouting, looking ever so kissable, I can almost imagine them caressing against mine.

"Let me help you," he whispers, running the pad of his thumb under my eye. "I need you to get your shit together to walk through the prison yard, okay? Seeing weakness is a treat for a lot of these fuckers."

"Then take this damn thing off my mouth," I mumble, my words only coming out as a series of hums.

"I can't just yet, kitten. You weren't granted permission to be out of your cell, but as soon as I get you across the yard, I'll take this bullshit off." Kash rubs his hand along the length of my back like he can't help trying to smooth away my annoyance. "And then we'll talk."

I can't believe he understood what I said. "Why are you being nice?"

His eyes flash with firelight. "Come on. Let's go," he says instead of responding. Maybe he didn't understand me and just assumed.

I have no choice but to let him lead me outside. The gate where the other CO stood guard is still empty. It's weird as hell, especially now that I see at least a hundred inmates from different cellblocks hanging out in the prison yard. And I swear they all turn to look at me as Kash nudges me forward.

Gripping the back of my jumpsuit, Kash pulls me closer to him and protects my back. I try my best not to look around as we make our way across the yard and toward the entrance leading into the S cellblock. A few guys catcall, but none of them risk getting close as Kash parades me around like a criminal.

"Hey, CO! Where's your backup?" a familiar voice

shouts.

Kash stiffens. "Stay back, inmate."

"You look alone out here," another inmate calls.

Kash lets go of my jumpsuit and swings his attention to a group of guys crowding together. I make the mistake of looking at them.

"Why don't you leave that sexy little thing with us? You do that and you'll have time to call for backup." A massive inmate punches his palm, shoving past a few of the guys. He smirks at me. "What do you say, girly? I'm sure you'd prefer someone who'll treat you like a queen. You give me what I want, and you'll be set here."

Fuck.

"Inmates, stay back!" Kash roars, sending a wave of fire across the dry grass in front of the guys. They all step back as his skin ripples and metallic scales eat away at his human self.

"Last chance, CO." The massive man has the nerve to step over the smoldering barricade. His eyes spark with orange not unlike the way the Dreki brothers' eyes do. And then I realize it's because the man is a dragon too. "Give her to me to claim or you won't make it out of this yard alive. By the time backup comes, they'll have to just clean up your remains."

"Nova, run," Kash says. "Now."

He doesn't have to tell me twice. There is no way in

hell I'm going to stand for another fucking attempt to possess me. Especially by an asshole that can't do anything to get me out of here.

Kash snarls with his transformation, and I break into a sprint, heading toward the open door leading back inside the building. Commotion echoes through the air behind me, sending my heart crashing around my ribcage. I gasp through the pain shocking my wrists, the chains binding me glowing brighter than ever. It's enough to slow me down. I can barely stand it.

"Hey, Inmate D64901, this way," a familiar voice says. It's the same one from the group of guys hell-bent on fighting with Kash. "Come on. I have somewhere safe to go."

I turn my attention toward the voice and spot the guy who was living in my cell before the Drekis kicked him out. His cute face lights with a mischievous smile, and he motions for me to hurry with a wave of his hand.

"You have my word that I won't hurt you. I just wanted to talk. I have answers for your questions, and I know I might not get another chance for a while. It seems the asshole guards want to keep you to themselves." The inmate strolls closer to me, showing me his palms. "Just five minutes."

I tighten my mouth and glance behind me, my heart stalling at Kash in dragon form, launching into the air.

"I'll take the gag off," the inmate says, drawing my attention back to him.

Kash flaps his huge wings, launching higher into the sky. Fear rises in me, his distance freaking me out. He left me alone and bound in this damn prison yard. He told me to run, but I have nowhere to go.

The inmate takes my hand and pulls me a foot. "Come on. It's now or never."

I swallow my fear and rush behind him. What else am I supposed to do?

Chapter 10

Answers

D64876. I MEMORIZE the inmate's stitched on identification on the front of his jumpsuit. If our IDs are assigned numerically, it means this guy hasn't been here for long. Even so, he looks to know the prison yard well enough to be able to sneak us to a utility shed around the side of the main building.

"Hurry up. The place is going into lockdown now. We

only have ten seconds to get inside." A girl with iridescent rainbow wings holds open the chain-link gate to the shed. She flicks the latch down when we're through and pulls out a key from...I don't even know where. I'm not sure I want to.

Inmate D64876 musses the girl's pink hair with his fingers. "I owe you big time, Rose. Now help me with the gag on her."

Rose, who I can only assume is from the Fae Block, rubs her hands together faster than humanly possible. She quickly pinches the corner of the magical fabric, and it peels away, allowing me to gasp in a breath.

"You bet your sorry ass you do." Rose motions us inside, giving me a quick once-over. "Though your girlfriend might have better luck getting me what I want. Removing a spelled gag hurts like hell."

"I'm not his girlfriend," I say, finally getting my lips working so I can speak up. "I don't even know the fucker's name."

Inmate D64876 tugs me into the shed. "It's Quillon."

"Of course it is," I mutter, rolling his name over my tongue. *Kill-on.* "Your parents sure set you up for this life."

Rose laughs, her musical voice echoing around us. "Damn. I like you. What's your name, anyway? I'm assuming it isn't Red, Ginger, or 'woman of Quillon's dreams' as he called you." She air quotes the last phrase.

CAGED BY HER DRAGONS

I don't know how to respond, so I just smirk at her and turn my attention back to Quillon. "Dreaming about me already? You saw me for a second."

I half-expect him to glower at me, but he returns my smirk with a full-blown smile. I bite my lip between my teeth, my nerves vanishing now that I'm nearly certain he didn't lure me out here to murder me.

"What can I say? It's easy to get caught up in dreaming about you when the whole place wants to get in your pants, but especially the guards. Can you blame me if I would love nothing more than for you to help me get under their fucking skin?" Quillon nudges my shoulder with his arm. "I can promise a good time. Better than sitting in a damn cell all day."

Rose groans. "Ugh, knock it off, Quillon. Show some respect to the female population. We're more badass than all of you supposed tough-assholes combined." She points to herself, jabbing her finger into her chest. "Killer here." She pokes me next. "Raging murderer there."

Quillon snatches her hand before she can jab him next.

"Unauthorized transportation of people from the Mortal World. You're in for what, like a month?" She grins at him.

"Two years." Quillon rolls his shoulders. "And who says I'm not a cold-blooded killer? Perhaps I was just better at not getting caught."

"At least you weren't falsely accused. I didn't murder anyone. I was set up by…" I let my words trail off. I just met Quillon and Rose. It's in my best interest not to treat them like long-time friends who I can trust. They could use anything I say against me. I'm sure I'll get punished for being here as it is.

"You were set up? No shit?" Rose says, flicking her gaze over me.

"I'm not even from this place. I'm human," I add.

That gets a chuckle from Quillon. "That she knows of. The poor thing has no idea of even what she is. Neither do the guards, but I'm sure they'll figure it out soon. It's only a matter of time. And when that happens—" Quillon snaps his mouth shut without finishing his thought.

"Don't be a dick. Tell me," I say.

He brings his gaze to mine. "They will murder you."

What. The. Hell. "Yeah-fucking-right." I regret the words immediately. By saying them, it could mean that Quillon and Rose discover my naughty little secret about my infatuation with the Dreki brothers and their weird need to possess me or whatever. If they call me out, I'll deny it. There is no way I'm letting anyone—no matter how nice they seem—get in the middle of my plan to win them over to get them to help me. I can already tell they'd have a lot to say about the twisted situation, especially because I've been fantasizing and nearly sleeping with the inmates' enemies.

CAGED BY HER DRAGONS

Quillon locks his fingers to my shoulder, his sudden strength startling me. "I'm serious...Red."

"Nova," I say, knowing I never did tell either of them my name.

His brows furrow. "Nova?"

"It's great, right?" I smile with my words. "I named myself."

"Mortals do that?" Rose asks, finally speaking up. "That's so strange. What do they call you before you decide?"

Quillon releases a soft guttural noise from his throat. "Not now, Rose. We're running out of time." He turns to me. "I want to meet you again. Tomorrow. If the guards don't let you out, I'll think of something again, okay? We really need to talk more."

"Why?" It's the only thing I can think about. "Why do you want to talk to me so badly? What do you get out of all of this?"

Moving in closer, he brings his lips to my ear. "I know who you really are, Delphia. I knew your parents."

I suck in a sharp breath, fear rising inside me. I swing my bound arms out and whack them into his muscular bicep. "Don't call me that."

"But it's who you are. You will have shamed your clan if they knew you took on a mortal persona." Quillon's eyes flash green for a split second. "You're the last of the Drakovich females."

"I'm not. My aunt is still alive. My mom's sister—"

He shakes his head. "Your mother only had brothers."

My eyes widen. "What?"

"Not many females are born in the sky clans, and when they are, they're promised to the strongest allied clans to continue powerful bloodlines." Quillon flicks his gaze to the shed door. "They're also killed to stop such a thing from occurring, which is why the Drekis will murder you. You're the last Drakovich female dragon, a clan at war with the Drekis. It's their duty to stop your bloodline."

"Fuck, we have to go," Rose says. "Someone's coming."

My mind whirls with Quillon's words, confusion and intrigue crashing through me. He can't possibly be right about me. I'd know it if I were able to transform into a dragon, right? And the Drekis? I don't know what to think. This is all so crazy.

A hand squeezes my shoulder. "Did you hear me, Delphia?"

I flare my nostrils. "Don't call me that, especially now."

He tightens his jaw. "I need you to distract CO Dreki. It'll give us time to get out of here. And tomorrow, I'll find you. Promise."

I don't even get the chance to agree as Rose leads the way to a small window at the back of the shed. Quillon stays on her heels and helps her fold her wings to squeeze through. I hear the clank of the chain-link gate smack closed and rush toward the door.

Sinking my weight into it, I try my best to block Kash's entrance. I know it's him without even having to peek. It's the strangest thing. He pushes against the door without forcing it open. If he does, I'll probably fly across the shed and hit the other side.

He taps his fingers on the door. "Nova, you don't have to be scared. It's me."

Sucking in a small breath, I hesitate without saying anything. I want to give Quillon and Rose as much time as possible.

Kash pushes against the door again, forcing it open a few inches. "You need to be stronger if you plan to keep anyone out. Remind me to take you to the gym. We'll start tonight."

"Uh, what?" I finally remove myself from my spot in front of the door to let him in.

"You need to be able to defend yourself." He enters the shed, dressed in a clean uniform, unripped by his transformation into a dragon. I don't know why it bothers me, but it does. He went and got dressed, leaving me to my fate. I shouldn't have expected more from him. "I can't babysit you every second, kitten, and something is going on around here. I was missing three COs, who were supposed to be on duty in the yard. My brother made a huge fucking mistake, trying to publicly claim you like he did. You will be tested, taunted, and possibly hurt because of that."

I groan. "Fucking great. That's your excuse for abandoning me?"

He surprises me with a chuckle. "You were far from abandoned, but yes. I will not make the same mistake as Rowan and make things worse. I'll make sure nothing happens to you the only way I can. I hope you like wrestling. I won't risk giving you a weapon."

I turn my gaze to him, annoyance rushing through me. How he can go from dickhead to suddenly concerned about me pisses me off. I have a clear enough head in this moment to recognize how twisted it is to be so attracted to the Drekis that they can easily make me forget how they treated me when I first arrived.

"I don't need your help, Kash. I'm not your responsibility." I steel myself toward his cocky-ass expression, because technically, I am his responsibility as an inmate. But now, I'm a bit nervous about it. If what Quillon said is true, I'm screwed. "Maybe the best way to help me is either getting me out of here or leaving me the hell alone."

"So...you want to walk yourself back inside?" he asks, smirking.

Fucker. I can play his game too. "Yes."

"Some inmates are still in the yard."

Ugh. I shake my restraints, wishing he'd take them off

already. His gaze breaks from mine, and he glances down and grabs my arm. Without a word, he unlocks them and lets them drop to the floor. My wrists throb, my skin tender and red from the magic and metal rubbing against me. Kash links his fingers through mine and pulls my arm up to inspect it. His fingers graze over my skin in a feather-soft motion, and I shiver, imagining him touching the rest of me like this.

"You're in need of care. The restraints trigger if you move too quickly..." His attention jerks from my hands and to my mouth, and I realize I'm no longer wearing the gag he put in place. "How did you get the muter off?"

I press my lips together, trying to remain expressionless. I have no good explanation for it, and I don't want to tell him about Rose. I need her and Quillon if things get even worse here. I need people who understand what it's like to be an inmate and not the ones in charge. "It just fell off."

"You're lying, Nova." His eyes flash with firelight. Swiveling on his boots, he peers around the small shed. His muscles bulge in his arms, his veins rising with his tensing. "Who was here? Who let you in? You must tell me."

I narrow my eyes and flick his shoulder. "I don't have to tell you shit. You left me to defend myself in the yard with a bunch of men who want me as their queen bitch while you were off flexing your power in beast mode. I'm lucky that someone was nice enough to help me."

"At what price? Nothing comes for free." He clenches his fingers into fists, his handsome face scowling as he looks at the window like he can envision Rose and Quillon sneaking through.

He's right. Rose did mention that only I was capable of getting something that she wanted. Sighing, I run my fingers through my messy hair, wishing I could put more space between our bodies. Kash keeps stepping closer, passing the invisible barrier of my personal space like it no longer belongs to me.

"It doesn't matter anyway." I chew my lip, trying to think of what I could possibly do for someone, and my mind flickers to what I expect a male inmate would want from me since I don't have basically anything but my body to offer. I just hate thinking it, and my face burns at the thought of saying it out loud. "I'll do what I have to do until I get out. Agreeing to giving a guy a blow job later isn't any worse than the meals you keep trying to force me to eat. I'd prefer to suck dick over that."

Uh-oh. Maybe I went too far.

"I don't believe you," he says, huffing a deep breath.

"Seriously? That nasty meat is—"

"Not about the meat. About the price of helping you. I know the assholes here, and if they wanted that, they'd have demanded it on the spot." He flares his nostrils, glowering at the thought. "And I'd kill whoever it was for even suggesting it. They know that. So tell me the truth. An inmate smart enough to help you knows they can get more than that. Because you're mine."

"But I'm not," I argue. "I don't belong to Maddox and Rowan either."

"Nova," he says, touching my hand. My skin buzzes, my body reacting to his gentle touch. It draws me closer until I rest my hand on his chest, feeling the thrums of his heart beating. "I need you to tell me. I don't like the idea that you owe someone because I failed you. I want to handle it."

I blink a few times with my confusion. Who is this man standing before me? This isn't the asshole who dropped crackers on the floor and demanded I clean them up. Is it possible that something possesses him, and he'll change the second I pull away? I have to know. I don't like being played with.

"What has gotten into you?" I purse my lips, drawing my gaze to peer into his hazel eyes. "You're being weird. What happened to the jerk who threw crackers on the floor or demanded I clean his apartment while you lounged around butt-ass naked? I feel like this is some kind of trick or test, and I refuse to be fooled by your charm."

He narrows his eyes and tightens his jaw. "Is that how you want me to be? Do you like that?"

I throw my hands out, swatting them to his chest so

that he takes a step back. "No, but I don't get any of this. What changed? Is this because of Rowan? Maddox?"

He grunts at the mention of his brothers. "Yes."

"Seriously? They have a thing for me, so now you do too?" I scrub my hands over my face. "What did they tell you?"

"It's not like that, Nova. We have a lot to talk about because however you ended up in the Mortal World hindered you of things you should've known." He licks his lips and takes my hand. "And I want to tell you as much as I can, but not here."

"Yes, here," I snap. "So tell me."

"Not here," he repeats.

"Damn it, Kash. I'm not leaving here until you tell me." I pull away, wishing he would just tell me what the fuck is going on.

Rowan flipped his attitude after our hot as fuck shower session because he said he knew I was innocent. But he never told me how. I hate the sudden hope rising inside me. What if Rowan told Kash, and Kash believes him? What if they can get me out? What if—

"Oh yes you are, kitten." Kash flips me onto his shoulder, surprising the hell out of me. "You need care, a change of clothes, and probably something to eat. I'll only talk to you when you can think clearly. It's a lot to take in, and I need it to sink it. You're not from around here."

CAGED BY HER DRAGONS

I smack my hand against his back, getting him to shift me off his shoulder and into his arms. I cling to him like a damn koala because he doesn't set me back down. I dig my fingers into his shoulders, leaning in closer to glare at him. "Oh, so now you believe me that I'm not from this shithole."

"Shithole? Maybe only Max. Now it's even more obvious that you've never seen Magaelorum." He chuckles, his cinnamon breath dancing around my senses. "And so you know, I knew the second I saw your face when I was amid transforming. The Dreki Clan rules the skies in this area. You acted like seeing me in my true form was...indescribable."

"It was all right. At least I didn't ride on your face like Rowan." Heat bursts in my cheeks at the way the words come out. What makes it worse is that the innuendo is quite true for that matter. And now my vagina wants to remind me.

Kash swallows, his throat pulsing with the gesture. "Next time," he says, his voice turning breathy. "You can ride me any way you please."

Fuck me. "Is that so?" Did I really just say that?

By the feeling of his hardening cock growing enough to feel his shaft grazing my thigh, I know I did.

"After I fix you up and feed you." He spins me with him as he turns toward the door. "If you want. I know I always chill out after a good time."

The audacity he has makes it impossible to think of anything else. What he suggests sounds like my kind of date, despite being in this hellhole prison.

"It depends. Do you take inmates to your living quarters often? Will your brother come barging in again to throw me in the pit? Will you—"

Kash moans under his breath, leaning in so close to me that all I can think about is how close his lips hover near mine. "No more questions. I need you to be quiet until I get you to my room."

"Then help me," I tease, searching his eyes. I can't help myself. He prods at something inside of me that wants to test his boundaries and will. "Make me."

"Nova," he whispers. "I shouldn't."

"I guess all the Drekis can't be rule breakers." My smile widens, loving his astonished expression like my remark totally offends him.

He reacts by closing the space between us, brushing his lips to mine while sliding his hand to my ass to hold me tighter against him. The world shifts with his sudden movements, and he continues to kiss me, tasting my lips, as he carries me from the shed.

His tongue slides into my mouth, caressing mine in deep, soft strokes, far less aggressive than either of his brothers. And now that I think of Maddox and Rowan, I can't

CAGED BY HER DRAGONS

help thinking about exactly what I'm doing now. I've kissed all three of them, and I'm nearly certain if Kash doesn't stop soon, I'll end up going even farther.

Something inside me is addicted to the rush of crossing the invisible lines, testing the restraints of these dragon guards. I know deep inside, none of this could end well. They don't seem like the type of brothers to let someone get between them, especially not an inmate despite whether or not they believe I'm innocent. And when they prove as much, then what? I'm not sticking around here. I'm going to find my way back to Galaxy and the family I made as one of his sky dancers.

My back hits a soft cushion, yanking me from my thoughts. I was so lost in Kash's kiss, how delicious his mouth tastes, how attracted I am to him...and his brothers, I didn't realize he somehow managed to take me back inside and to his living quarters uninterrupted by anyone. It's enough to distract me from Kash's kiss that he eases away and combs his fingers through my hair to push it behind my ear.

"You're safe here. We have a few hours for things to be sorted out," he murmurs, staring intently into my eyes. "You won't get in trouble."

"What about you?" I ask. "This can't be part of your protocol."

"Warden's out."

My mouth forms an O. "So you're just going to let the prisoners do whatever they want? You're not worried they'll kill each other?"

"They'll be fine." He runs his hand to the back of my neck. "You don't need to be concerned. The only ones they ever want to murder are us."

I highly doubt it, but I decide to drop it, especially after my two terrible experiences in the prison yard. Some of these inmates act like they want to cage me even though I'm already imprisoned. Since they don't have the power they have outside these magic walls, they want to flex whatever they can here. Being one of the few female...shifters—fuck, that's still impossible for me to believe—puts me at a disadvantage.

I bob my head, finally responding to him. "I guess you're right."

"I've been working here for years, kitten. This isn't the first time we've been understaffed. Hell, half the time, at least two COs are sleeping on the job. I've done it. Shit gets boring when you're required to stay on the property unless granted permission otherwise." Kash grabs my hand and pulls me from the couch. "But we can talk about that more in a sec. I want to take care of your wrists. I can't pin you how I want unless they're better."

Damn it, do I love the sound of his wants. My body is fully prepared to let him have his way with me, pinning me beneath him and all. But a part of me doesn't want him to know that. An even bigger part of me wants to keep my attraction to him completely hidden. He'd love it way too much if he knew I was already thinking about him ripping my clothes off to sink inside me, stretching me in ways that my body loves and wants and suddenly really fucking needs.

He releases a deep purr from his throat like he heard my thoughts. "You like the thought," he murmurs.

I raise an eyebrow. "Do you really think I'm going to let you do that?" I ask, silently begging myself to stop thinking about how warm his hand feels around mine and how I can nearly imagine the heat trail it'll leave over my body if I allow him.

"I do, actually," he says, smirking. "All I would have to do is kiss you again."

"I'm not that easy." At least, not usually. This place gets to me, and I don't care. I don't care about any standards the Mortal World put into my head. Because I'm not there.

"I didn't say that." Kash tugs me toward his bathroom and motions me inside. I can't stop the damn memory of Rowan pleasuring me in a shower identical to Kash's, and it turns me on enough that I shiver and inhale a small breath. "It's not your fault that I'm irresistible."

Tipping my head back, I release the loudest laugh. Kash grins at me, the intensity between us lightening a bit.

With the lightness smoothing his features, he turns from handsome to fucking hot, sexy, and fine-as-hell, that I can't help myself from sliding my hand around the back of his neck to kiss him again.

And my simple kiss sets him off.

Scooping me up, he plops me on the counter, spreading my legs open by my knees to stand between them. I squeeze his hips between my thighs as heat rushes through me, blazing from my lips to the rest of my body. His body feels so good close to mine that I rush to unbuckle his belt to unhook the clasp on his uniform pants. A rumbly noise escapes his lips, his teasing fading only to be replaced with scorching desire that sends every molecule on my body buzzing. Unzipping his pants, I reach into his boxer-briefs and pull his raging hard-on free. I stroke my fingers over his thick shaft, making him moan.

"That feels so good," he mumbles, kissing me harder. He squeezes my thigh. "I want to touch you too."

I nod my permission, allowing him to pop the buttons open on my jumpsuit. He pauses, glancing down at the T-shirt of Rowan's I'm wearing underneath. His jaw twitches, a look of first confusion and then annoyance crossing his features.

But I don't apologize. I won't.

He surprises the hell out of me by hooking his fingers to the collar, stretching the fabric so fast with his powerful strength that he rips the shirt right down the front, exposing my breasts to him. I gasp at the coolness of the room before Kash snakes his hands to my back and pulls the rest of my jumpsuit down. My heart and lungs compete to see which one can work faster as Kash bends down and sucks my nipple into his mouth. I moan under the good pressure of his mouth, stealing thoughts of Rowan right from my mind. All I can think about is the warmth of his body, the sensation of his mouth, how hard and ready his dick is...

He kisses a fiery trail up my neck and back to my mouth, expertly lifting me off the counter an inch with one hand while using his other to tug down the rest of my jumpsuit. He growls again at the sight of Rowan's boxers on me and rips them off as well, exposing the rest of my body to him.

He glides his hands up my stomach and around my back, tugging me even closer. Our tongues meet, his body ready and waiting to experience exactly what he does to me and to show me how good he feels inside me.

I hook my fingers to his shirt, and Kash arches down to let me pull it over his head. He rushes to kick from his boots and pants while holding my legs, the tip of his cock a mere inch from me.

"You're beautiful," Kash says, leaning in to kiss me again. "Sexy."

I ease away to look into his eyes. "What, you're not going to try to declare that I'm yours again?"

His eyes flicker with firelight. "Is that what you want?"

I smirk and align his body to mine. "How would you feel if I said you were mine? All mine. To do with as I please."

Something shifts in his expression, his eyes locking onto mine with all his heated intensity. I wonder if I took it too far, but if I did, he manages to brush it off with a cocked brow.

Sinking his fingers into my hips, he bows in. "I'd like it," he murmurs. "I'm yours."

Well, okay. If this is how he wants to play it. "That's right. Mine. You will give me whatever I want."

His breath picks up as he tests my body with the tip of his cock, sending tingles bursting through me at the pressure. "Tell me what you want," he murmurs.

Sucking my bottom lip between my teeth, I say, "You."

With my word, Kash slides inside me, making me gasp. I moan so embarrassingly loud, the pleasure his cock brings me turning my mind into mush. I cling onto his shoulders as he thrusts at the same time he pulls my body toward his by my ass. Leaning down, he brushes his lips to mine, kissing me with so much passion that all I can think about is how I never want him to stop. This unexpected turn of my day couldn't have been better than this.

Kash moans with his movements, breaking our kiss to

trail his lips down my throat. I explore his broad back with my fingers, mapping out every tight muscle and what feels like the grooves of scars, though I can't see them.

Bringing his lips to my shoulder, he sucks hard enough to leave a mark. I bend forward and return the favor, nipping his skin before drawing it into my mouth to give him a hickey. He moans under the sensation of my mouth and trails his hand between us to rub his warm finger over my clit. I gasp at the pleasure bursting through me.

"Fuck," I whisper. "Don't stop."

"Not until you scream for me, kitten," he murmurs, rubbing me with his even thrusts.

I rest my head on his shoulder, our breathing fast and in sync, the heat of his body against mine making my skin glisten with sweat. My moans come in quick bursts as he continues to work me over until my legs shake, my body tensing for my oncoming orgasm.

Sinking back, I smack my head against the mirror with my scream of pleasure. Kash pulls me back, swinging my body to his faster and faster. I dig my nails into his shoulder blades through the wave of ecstasy until he pulls out and cums across my stomach. He releases a guttural noise from his throat, his hazel eyes sparking with flecks of orange. For a second, his muscles ripple and his dragon peeks through.

A strange wave of emotions crashes through me, leaving me breathless. Kash freezes, still standing between my legs.

His eyes turn from my body and to me, and he opens and closes his mouth like he has something to say.

I reach up and pat my hand to his chest. "What's up? Do you regret letting me stake my claim on you now?"

He shakes his head, gracing me with a smile. "Careful what you say, Nova. I don't think you understand what you've just gotten yourself into."

"Uh-oh. I should've warned you that it's actually me who is irresistible," I tease, letting him pick me up to carry me to his shower.

"Addictive. I want you again and again," he murmurs kissing me.

"That's too bad. You'd have to break me out of this prison."

Kash frowns at my words with a groan. He doesn't respond to my comment, choosing just to kiss me again while he turns on the hot water. Steam fills the small bathroom, and I practically melt against Kash under the amazing stream from the showerhead. I can tell he wants to bang again, slipping and sliding me up and down the length of his shaft, but I wag my finger at him.

"None of that until I get to wash my hair," I say, nipping his lip.

He lets me wiggle out of his arms and to my feet. Grabbing the bottle of shampoo first, he nudges me to turn around and massages a palm full into my long tresses. Shifting my hair over my shoulder, he traces his finger in a circle before doing the same to my other one.

"Who marked you?" he asks, keeping his voice even. "It's not mine. Was it one of my brothers?"

"That's none of your business." I try not to react with annoyance in case he doesn't blow things out of proportion like I expect.

"I don't like it if it wasn't."

So he's cool if it was? "You don't have to like it."

"But you're mine, Nova. Can't you feel it?" Kash suddenly spins me around, cradling my cheek with his big palm. "When we touch, kiss. Fuck, did you not feel anything as I made love to you?"

Made love? I don't make love to people I barely know. "Uh, I had a good time?" My voice rises like I now question it.

"I realize you being here wasn't bad luck on your part. It was supposed to be this way. We'd have never found you otherwise." Kash's voice lowers. "You wouldn't have claimed me either."

Ah shit. What the hell? "I was joking. Playing a game. Teasing you. I don't actually think you're mine, Kash."

A strange look darkens his face, his chest bumping against mine with each of his deep breaths. "I know it's confusing, but I can explain. What you are—you're like me. You're a dragon. I can sense it. Feel the heat and fire inside you. Rhett must've known. I bet he was trying to bring you home for us."

Us? This is so strange.

"What do you mean by *us*? You claim I'm yours but you also keep mentioning your brothers. It's weird. My home is in the Mortal World," I say softly. "I have an aunt and uncle there. My friends. I've never turned into a dragon in my life. This is a mistake."

He sighs, his cinnamon breath wafting over me. "It's not a mistake. I'll help you figure it out. When my brothers get here, we'll all talk. It has to be us together. You're our inten—"

Something crashes from the living area. Kash tenses, his muscles rippling. Pulling me closer, he shifts to stand in front of me protectively. A growl resonates through the air, followed by a second, much deeper growl.

Rowan flings open the door with Maddox looming behind him. "Brother, Nova's gone—" Rowan snaps his mouth shut, his eyes darting past Kash to me. He devours me with his gaze, the fire in his eyes burning over me in a good way.

Maddox shoves past Rowan and crowds the tiny bathroom with his huge presence. He sniffs the air, his nostrils flaring. Without looking at me, he gets in Kash's face. "Damn it, Kash. What are you thinking? We discussed this. You should've stuck to the plan. It was unfair of you to allow this when Nova knows nothing."

"I needed proof," Kash says, crossing his arms. "She wanted me. It was fate."

I frown and slide past him, realizing a little too late that I'm naked and sandwiched between two sexy-as-hell men. "What are you guys talking about?"

Maddox ignores me and turns to Rowan again. "Get her some clothes and take her back to her cell."

My heart stalls at his command. "What? No. You can't do this. I want to know what the hell is going on. What proof? Why are you all here?"

"I said take her back to her cell, Rowan. Now!" Maddox grabs my shoulder and spins me toward Rowan.

"Don't touch her!" Kash yells. "She claimed me! We made love. I know she's my mate."

All three men freeze, turning their attention to me.

I shrink under their scrutiny, my heart ramming so hard against my ribs that it feels like it'll crash through at any second. Pursing my lips, I say, "Uh, what?"

"Not only yours," Rowan says, reaching over Maddox's shoulder to touch my cheek. "She's mine too. You know that."

"You are both idiots." Maddox combs his fingers through his long hair. "She can't be our mate. Everything she did—"

"Our mate? Our? As in plural? You're right, Maddox. I

can't be all of your mates. That's crazy. This is all insane." My mind whirls at his words. What the hell?

"She's innocent," Kash says, his voice softening.

Maddox surprises me by resting his hand on his brother's shoulder. "You can't know that for sure, brother."

Rowan nudges me forward as he steps inside the bathroom, leaving no room for me to move at all. "I feel it too, Maddox."

"I don't know," Maddox responds, turning his attention to me. He drinks me in like he can somehow see the same thing his brothers do with me in this vulnerable state. If he does, he doesn't let on to it. He hardens even more.

"I swear it wasn't me. I didn't do any of this. It was Lazlo Infinity." Pain shoots through my head at the mention of his name. Dizziness washes over me, and I squeeze my eyes shut. What the hell? I feel ill just thinking about the warlock.

"What?" Maddox leans in and grabs my chin. I can't move under his scrutiny. "What did you say?"

"Lazlo—" Agony bursts through my head once more, stealing all my senses away.

It feels as if my head will explode at any second. With the way all three Drekis look at me, shock and fear widening eyes, I think I might.

I scream.

Chapter 11

Claimed

"THIS IS THE kind of shit we'd call Rhett for." Rowan's voice tugs me from the numbing darkness of unconsciousness. "It was a spell. It had to be."

"I still think we should take her to the infirmary," Kash says. A warm hand touches my forehead and runs down my cheek and back up. "I've never heard anyone scream like that. I bet the asshole had something to do with my missing

COs. Lowe doesn't remember taking her to visitation, but he was there."

Maddox growls. "No. She's better here. It will give me a chance to sort things out. It's bad enough I had to log her into the pit. If the warden realizes she's not there—" Another hand touches my foot. "Hey, cookie. It's rude to eavesdrop. Sit up. I want to check you out."

I snap my eyes open with a grimace. Kicking my foot, I get Maddox to let me go. I peer up into Kash's eyes as he cradles my head on his lap. We're both on the couch—me covered in only a blanket and him in boxers—with his brothers sitting on the floor.

Rowan takes my hand and laces our fingers together. "You okay, Nova?"

I shrug. "I don't know, to be honest."

"You gave us a bit of a scare. I think you were cursed or spelled or something, but luckily, your brands work both ways. They suppress magic and block it. It's not foolproof, but it works enough." Rowan leans in and brushes his lips to mine like it's the most normal, natural thing to do. Like we've been doing it forever. "Thank the fucking High Council."

Everything comes rushing back to me in a wave of confusion. The visitation of Lazlo Infinity, Quillon's revelation of me being a dragon with a bloodline supposedly hated by the Dreki Clan, how I had mind-blowing sex with Kash,

CAGED BY HER DRAGONS

and...fuck. Apparently I'm his mate—and his brothers'—whatever that means. All these things add up to weigh heavily on me.

"I bet you're hungry, kitten." Kash draws my attention from Rowan, and I tilt my head back to peer up at him. "I did promise to feed you."

The second my brain processes his comment, my stomach rumbles loud enough that Maddox drops his gaze to it, furrowing his brows. He has the nerve to reach out and poke my belly. Swinging my hand out, I smack his shoulder. Then the fucker does it again.

"If you'd eat what was served, you wouldn't be hungry," Maddox says, the corner of his lips curling.

I whack him again, making him laugh and catch my hand. His smile falters, his eyes flashing with golden fire. The heat of his gaze burns over me as his eyes flick to my lips, reminding me of our kiss in the pit. His hot and cold attitude confuses the hell out of me. So does my attraction to him.

With a tug of his hand, he pulls me up so quickly that I fall forward and right into him. Maddox plants his lips to mine, surprising me with a kiss in front of his brothers. Neither of them says anything as I allow Maddox to kiss me deeper and tangle his hand into my hair. His other hand slides down the length of my bare back as he pulls me completely from the couch and onto his lap.

His body awakens against me, poking some sense into me, and I pull away. I slap him across the face, my breath panting with my desire. I lick my lips and scramble to pull the blanket tighter around me but my body refuses to move off him.

"What the fuck, Maddox," I say, pressing my hand to his chest. "You can't just kiss me whenever the hell you want, especially in front of your brothers."

"But you're ours." Did he really just say that again? This. Guy.

"I am not." My voice doesn't come out as strong as I want it to. "Even if that bullshit is true, don't think I have forgotten about the pit and what you pulled. Or how you treated me like shit and wouldn't believe me about my innocence."

He flares his nostrils. "I'm still uncertain. I saw some of the bodies. That wasn't caused by warlock magic."

I slam my hands into his chest and push away from him only to hit my ass against Rowan. Rowan hugs his arms around me, stopping Maddox from trying to pull me back. Kash growls softly, the heat of his hip radiating against my shoulder. My body totally goes out of whack, excitement building between my legs. I love and hate their attention.

"Another reason you can't just kiss me," I finally manage to say through a gasp of a breath.

"But you liked it."

CAGED BY HER DRAGONS

Ah hell. "So what."

"I'm only doing things you like." Is he for real? He sounds so serious, like it's no big deal.

I wiggle in Rowan's arms until he loosens his hold enough to break free. I scramble to my feet, gripping the blanket around me, and extend my arm out to point, keeping them in place. Being near them overwhelms my senses. I can't breathe properly because even a simple touch from one of them makes me gasp.

"I'm not your little toy to be played with nor will I allow you to use my attraction to you against me. Until you believe me that none of this was my fault and that I don't belong here, stay at least five feet away, got it?" I swallow, walking backward, afraid that if I turn away, one of the Drekis will close the space to test my resolve. "That goes for all of you. You can't just declare I'm your fucking mate. I've been here for like five seconds. That's not how things work. You can't exactly take me on dates, so this is all going to end nowhere. I'm leaving as soon as I can."

Kash cocks his eyebrow like I've said the most ridiculous thing. "Come on, kitten. Sit back down. I'll get Maddox to shut up. He is more...wild than us. He's our alpha and direct as hell so things don't get misconstrued."

I shake my head. "Yeah, right. And my answer is still no. I need space. I can't think with you all so close." I squeeze my eyes shut, gripping my fingers to the blanket.

Shit, I feel like a hot mess.

"Just make her something to eat already, Kash. That's probably why she's so reactive and grumpy. I wouldn't want to be your fucking mate either if I had to wait so damn long to be served." Rowan punches Kash in the leg to get him up.

"She wanted sex first," Kash argues, flicking the back of Rowan's head. "You assholes are why I haven't fed her yet."

"I'm fine. I'll make my own damn food," I call, already entering the open kitchen. Because damn. I can't listen to them argue about my needs and what should happen first. "You probably couldn't cook anything I'd like anyway."

Maddox gets to his feet next and crosses his arms. "We could if you weren't so damn picky."

I flip him off and turn my back on the three of them. They chuckle, sounding so cute that I can't help myself from peeking over my shoulder. Kash jogs the short distance and hooks his arm around my waist, spinning me toward Rowan and out of the kitchen.

"As much as I hate saying it, let my brothers help you dress. I still want Maddox to give you a quick exam. Your wrists still look tender," Kash says, opening the fridge.

I don't get a chance to see what he selects because Rowan scoops me up so quickly that I automatically wrap my legs around him. My heated flesh presses against him, and he grins like a cocky-bastard. Leaning in, he puckers his lips to see if I'll kiss him. And how could I not? He looks like he might pout or some shit if I deny him. Plus, our hot kiss from earlier flits through my mind.

Slowly, I caress my lips to his, sliding my hands around his neck. It should feel so strange kissing him after kissing Maddox and having sex with Kash, but no one says anything, so neither do I. While it would've been useful to pit them against each other if they continued to be complete assholes, I'm a bit relieved they're not fighting. I can't imagine being between three dangerous dragons could end well on my part.

"You're going to make me jealous, kitten," Kash calls, drawing my attention from the softness of Rowan's mouth. "If I didn't think my brothers would fuck up your dinner, I'd expect to be in Rowan's place right now. It is my apartment."

"Make me something better than edible and maybe I'll show my thanks any way you want," I tease.

Maddox enters the bathroom first and blocks the way, stopping to peer around. "Not happening now. You'll be going back to your cell when you're through eating."

"Seriously?" I gawk at Maddox. "What the hell? If this is how you're going to treat me as your supposed mate, then fuck off."

He narrows his eyes. "I should be the one scolding you, cookie. Do you know how inconvenient and agonizing it is that the one damn woman who was destined for me turns out to be a damn criminal? One who doesn't even know shit. You think you have bad luck—"

Rowan jabs his fist out and punches Maddox in the solar plexus, winding him. Maddox slams his fist into the wall instead of retaliating and turns his back on us to grab a few things from a cabinet in the bathroom.

I want so badly to say something, to retort and tell him that he's crazy to think I'm fated to be his, but it feels like Maddox might start spitting fire. Rowan's tense muscles also feel like I might be the only thing stopping him from acting as well.

"Fuck, brothers. Chill the hell out or you both can leave. You're making Nova uncomfortable." Kash waves a spatula. "And Maddox, before you open your damn mouth to insult her again, you better think carefully. I won't try to convince her to ever give your sorry ass a chance. You know what will happen if she denies you."

Maddox stiffens at Kash's words, but only grunts his response. I crinkle my nose and look at Rowan, hoping he'll tell me what Kash is talking about. Instead, he kisses me again, his warm, soft tongue slipping between my lips to ensure I don't try to say another word.

"All right, Rowan. Let me get a look at her. I will not do this shit while you kiss," Maddox mutters.

Rowan eases away just far enough to whisper, "Don't

worry. I'll gut him if he says anything else stupid, okay?"

I blow a breath through my nose. "You better."

Maddox motions for Rowan to set me down. "You would obviously do it yourself, cookie."

I only respond with a glare and plop down on the couch where Maddox points. He opens up a medical kit and sets a few jars of unmarked liquid on the floor by my feet. Pulling out a folded black cloth, he stretches the strange fabric across his knee and squeezes a sparkling gel from a silver tube along the middle.

"Next time, don't fight against the restraints. No one has ever been able to break out of them," Maddox says, grabbing my forearm to hold it out. I had no idea he could be so gentle, but he carefully drapes the black ribbon of cloth over my wrists and wraps them so softly that I barely feel them.

"I didn't fight against the restraints. I was running from a damn prison yard fight." I shift my gaze from my wrists to look into his golden eyes.

"What?" he asks with a frown.

Kash saunters across the room with a plate mixed with some familiar and unfamiliar foods. He squeezes on the couch next to me and rests his hand on my bare knee, the sheet bunched between my legs. "I told you the COs on duty didn't show up for their shift."

Fire lights Maddox's eyes. "You failed to mention Nova

was in the middle of a fight. She shouldn't have been in the yard in the first place."

"CO Lowe said he found her in visitation," he responds, trailing his finger in a circle over my skin.

"Why were you there?" Maddox asks, turning to me.

I realize that Kash and I have been so caught up in each other that I didn't mention it. And after the pain of mentioning Lazlo Infinity's name exploded in my head and knocked me out, I'm afraid to.

"It was the warden's order," I manage to spit out. I squeeze my eyes shut, bracing for more pain, but it doesn't come. "CO Lowe told me so. He didn't find me. It was an order because—"

I screech and clutch my head as agony stabs my brain. Maddox says something I can't make out. Kash pulls me onto his lap, and Rowan gently tugs my hands down, restraining me by the wrists. Maddox splashes something across my forehead, the icy liquid cooling my skin enough to take a breath.

"Shit, her brands," Rowan says, getting me to flatten my palm against his. "They shouldn't be glowing. She's within the barrier."

"It's the magic. Nova, can you tell me anything else about the warlock?" Maddox asks.

I manage to nod my head. "He was trying to take me from here because he wants a beast like me. He wants to use me to get the High Council off his trail. He also claimed he's retaliating for me killing his brother." The words come so quietly, cautiously, that I'm not sure anyone heard me. I don't mention the fact that he knew my mother. I wish I knew more about her history and how she got so involved with all this bullshit. I can't believe this was the prison she was locked up in.

Rowan shifts and pulls a small device from his uniform belt. "I'll pull up her file and check the victims' list of next of kin to verify. We have to be absolutely sure before we proceed."

Kash stabs at a piece of what I think is browned meat with a fork and holds it up to my mouth. "Take a bite. It'll take him a minute. You need your strength."

I block him from shoving it in my mouth. "What is it?"

"Just trust me. I know you'll like it." Kash offers the fork to me again.

"Don't be stubborn. It's not cute on you. My brother went out of his way to make you a meal he didn't have to. Now try it." Maddox picks up a piece of the meat with his fingers and pops it into his mouth. "It's so overcooked that it's nearly inedible. Sounds like your taste."

I glower at Maddox. "You don't have to be such an ass—"

Kash takes advantage of my open mouth and pops the piece of meat in with his fingers instead of the fork. I snap my teeth down, locking his finger with my jaw. He laughs and pokes my side, tickling me to get me to let him go.

A burst of savory, smoky flavor explodes across my tongue, tasting a bit different than any meat I've had but still pretty good. I close my eyes while I chew, not wanting to give too much of a reaction. I can feel Maddox watching me and Kash's nearly palpable relief that I swallow his offering instead of spit it out.

"See? I told you that you would like it," Kash says, offering me another bite.

"Could be because she's starving," Rowan teases, drawing my attention to him. "Or her body knows she's going to need all the energy it can, because look at this." He holds out his device to Maddox. "See who's on it?"

Maddox groans and hands it to Kash. "I guess we won't have to worry about having such a disappointing mate for long. You killed a lot of people with powerful bloodlines."

"What does that mean?" I ask. "You know I didn't do it."

"I think you did kill at least some." Maddox flicks my knee. "And now they all will want you dead."

Kash reaches out and punches him. "Feel free to reject my brother. He's mad you chose me first and will probably never want to experience anyone else again. You weren't raised here, so you're hung up on Mortal World norms. No one would blame you."

CAGED BY HER DRAGONS

I frown, my brows pinching together.

Rowan laughs. "You just got lucky. She knows what I have to offer." He slides his hand over my thigh. "Isn't that right, Nova? Or would you like me to remind you?"

Damn him. I grab his hand, stopping him from trying to tease me. "Seriously, Rowan. Your brother just told me people are going to come after me for something I didn't do. I didn't kill anyone."

Rowan twists his lips to the side. "Actually...I think Maddox is right. You might have accidentally killed one. Gaston Infinity. He was ripped apart. No warlock can do that. It probably wasn't your intent, and he was probably trying to hurt you, but it still gives the Infinity line reason to put you through hell."

"That's impossible," I snap.

"Take a look for yourself." Maddox holds up the device and shows the severed head of a body with its innards strung out across the bar floor. "See the claw marks? We assumed you might've been a lycan, since they plague the Mortal World and it would explain how you didn't know about Magaelorum and lycans are born human, but this could also be talons. And there are burn marks on another one of the victims."

"I'd remember something like that," I say, turning my gaze away from the disgusting photo. "Right? You guys act like you know what you're doing when you go all beast-mode."

The three of them look at each other without responding right away. I inhale a few breaths through my nose, trying to recall everything that happened that night at the bar. I think about the car ride with Rhett and how he claimed my mother made it nearly impossible to find me. I also recall how he was trying to protect me. How now I know he cast some sort of magic over me. He told me to let *her* break free. Could it have meant the supposed dragon now imprisoned inside me with the brands? It's the only thing that might be plausible. If warlocks and witches are real, perhaps my mom used them to keep me away from this world. Quillon did say that my bloodline is a supposed enemy of the Drekis. My mom could've done so to protect me. If only I could ask her.

Kash's gentle hand grazes along my shoulder and trails up my neck and to my cheek, getting me to look at him. "What is it? I can feel something different and unfamiliar coming from you."

"What do you mean you can feel me?" I ask.

He shakes his head and says, "You remember something."

I lick my lips and swallow. If I speak what I now know to be the truth, it would mean that Maddox is right about me. It would mean that I do belong in this magical prison. It would mean that I can't claim innocence. But that's not even the worst of it. If I say the words out loud, it could mean that it was bad luck for the Dreki brothers to even think that I could possibly be their mate. Because I am a killer. I killed a man in my dragon form. I'm the criminal Maddox doesn't want. And suddenly, his feelings matter to me. All of theirs do.

"I—I..." I can't get my mouth to work. My heart ricochets around my ribcage, and I suddenly need to leave. I need out of here. "I think I need some rest."

Kash nuzzles his chin to my shoulder. "You sure, kitten? I can't let you sleep here."

As much as it pains me, I nod. "Will you stay close to me then?"

The three of them look at each other, and then Rowan says, "Don't worry, doe eyes. We'll never let you from our sight."

Chapter 12

Killer

I CAN'T SLEEP. If I even try to close my eyes, visions from the night at the bar swirl through my mind. So does Lazlo. His words about taking me won't leave me alone. I'm afraid that he'll get what he wants. The missing COs from duty, how CO Lowe forgot he was the one who took me to visitation, and how my brands glow every time I try to say Lazlo's name out loud proves it. I might be serving a life sentence, but my life will end up short. I can almost feel it.

The buzzer of my cell rings through the air, and I get to my feet. I stroll close to the bars as they slide open and peek at the mirror with a view of the hallway to see Maddox making his way toward my cell.

"Stand back, inmate," he calls before he even reaches the door. "Hold out your hands."

Maddox remains expressionless when he comes into view. I can't stop the frown from overtaking my face at the sight of him.

"Don't look so disappointed that it's my shift," he says, keeping his voice low. "I'm here to take you out for a bit, but behave or you'll end up in the pit again."

"Maybe you should just take me there," I quip, crossing my arms over my chest. "But don't you dare command me to stay quiet."

His stern expression breaks with a flash of fire in his eyes. I shift on my feet, the memory of him pressing me into the dirt wall to explore my body with his fingers quickly pushing away thoughts of everything else.

"We'll see," he murmurs, "but first, it's chow time."

I blink a few times. "Why? You know I won't eat anything served."

"Because putting you out in gen. pop. will hopefully stop all the fuckers here from messing with you. My brothers and I decided that it would be best not to give you special attention during meals and yard time. You will be working for us for duties." He looks at me, gauging my reaction.

"I'm not cleaning your damn toilets," I say, stepping closer.

"I could assign you to janitorial duty elsewhere." He smirks, daring me to say something.

I glare. "Whatever. As long as it ensures I don't end up alone with you."

Maddox grumbles and snatches my hand, pulling me toward the hallway. He makes me walk in front of him until he reaches the first occupied cell. The bars slide open and two older guys with gray hair both give me a once-over.

Maddox bares his teeth. "Watch Inmate D64901 during mealtime and you'll get the transfer of your choice for duties."

The old men look from Maddox to me and back to him. The taller of the two of them says, "I want stipends added to my account as well. This one has a target on her."

"Done." Maddox motions the two of them to start walking.

The tall guy leads the way before the other guy motions for me to follow behind him. I find myself sandwiched between them as Maddox ends the line and releases inmates along the way. I straighten my shoulders, trying not to react toward the stares and whispers.

"My future queen," a tatted up, buff guy says from a

CAGED BY HER DRAGONS

few places behind me. "Save me a seat. You can feed me."

"Shut it, Inmate D20733," Maddox says, whacking an iron baton against one of the bars. "I'll throw you in the pit if you say another word."

Surprisingly, the guy snaps his mouth shut, but it doesn't stop him from winking at me when the line dismantles as inmates grab trays from two rolling carts. I frown, wishing I didn't have to take one of the plates of bloody meat, but Maddox gives me a look like if I don't, he'll throw one in front of me anyway.

"This way, baby girl. You can sit with us," the taller old man says.

I only nod and let him lead the way to a round metal table on the far side of the room. The other old guy sits across from me, keeping his back to the inmates. My back faces the wall where Maddox watches from a small platform up a set of stairs. I try my best not to constantly look at him, but I can't help myself.

"Look who they let out of her cage." Quillon plops his tray down next to mine and ignores the warning look both old men give him. "Too bad you have a couple of deadweight babysitters."

"Watch it, Quillon. If you ruin this for me, I'll slit your throat." Damn. I might actually believe the tall guy.

"Easy now, Papa Jeff. Nova and I are friends." Quillon bumps his shoulder to mine. "Tell him."

I shrug. "I wouldn't exactly call us friends."

The other old man stands up. "If that's the case, get the hell out of here."

Quillon clenches his hands into fists. "You'll have to make—"

Papa Jeff launches to his feet and leans over the table, trying to reach for Quillon. He's quick to move, grabbing the back of my jumpsuit to tug me partially in front of him, using me as a shield. I stomp his foot, annoyed as hell.

Other inmates laugh and holler, telling Bastard Lou to get Quillon. And the shorter old man tries, accidentally tangling his hand in my hair in the process.

A threatening growl reverberates through the air. Bright orange flames burst over my shoulder, engulfing the table in flames. The scent of cooked meat wafts through the air, and Quillon, Papa Jeff, and Bastard Lou stop trying to fight with me in the middle.

"Anyone else want to start some bullshit?" Maddox asks, his voice rising through the silent room. "You'll get charred food for a week."

They groan like it's a bad thing, and I can't stop my damn mouth from smirking. Maddox remains expressionless, but I can tell he went unnecessarily dragon on these assholes on purpose. I doubt he'll admit it, but he charred the raw meat in an attempt to get me to eat it. And since he went through the effort...

CAGED BY HER DRAGONS

"That sounds good to me, CO," I quip, fluttering my lashes.

I pick at my plate, tearing off a piece of meat and pop it into my mouth. The others all watch me, along with a few other guys from other tables. They are bored out of their minds if me eating is so entertaining that they can't pull their attention away from me.

Maddox smacks his baton on the table, knocking my tray onto the floor. I gawk in surprise as he flexes his power. And now all it does is make me want to test him. Because, the fucker.

Turning my gaze to Quillon, I purposefully ignore Maddox's expectant stare. He obviously wants to know how I'll react to his assholeness. So I bump my shoulder to Quillon and reach over and tear off a piece of food from his plate.

"You don't mind sharing with me, do you, Quillon?" I ask, trying to keep a straight face. I know I shouldn't test my luck, but something inside me wants to keep poking Maddox. If he can be an ass, I can be a bitch and play games.

"Of course not, beautiful. I'll even feed it to you." Quillon pinches a hunk of meat and rips it off, holding it up to my mouth.

He obviously didn't get the memo about me just wanting to get under Maddox's skin with how eager he is to give me attention. I carefully bite the food from his fingers, cringing a bit because the thought of him touching my food kind of grosses me out. I've seen some of the cells and—

Maddox locks the back of his hand to my jumpsuit and drags me from the table. "Eat off the floor or don't eat at all."

"Seriously, CO?" I ask, flailing until he lets me go. "None of this was my fault."

"Yeah, man," Quillon says.

"The hell it wasn't." Maddox doesn't try to explain why and spins me around to face out.

Quillon hops to his feet. "I'll take the blame for her."

His movement sets Maddox off. Maddox jabs Quillon in the gut with his baton, knocking him back. Quillon looks ready to start something, but Bastard Lou grabs him and shakes his head. A few nearby inmates catcall toward us, egging Maddox to punish me. Someone suggests forcing me to my knees to eat from the floor and another suggests something else entirely. Pervert. A few guards enter the commons with their batons ready to back Maddox up.

"You're going in the pit, Inmate D64901," Maddox says with a growl. Turning to an unfamiliar CO, he adds, "Get them all back in their cells. They're now on lockdown. No yard privileges. Got it?"

"Yes, sir," the man says, calling order.

I struggle in Maddox's arms, thrashing to give him a

hard time just because I can. "Let me go back to my cell, dickwad."

He grumbles against my neck without a word.

"Come on, CO. She doesn't deserve the pit and you know it," Quillon calls, risking Maddox's wrath. "I'll take her place."

Maddox shoves Quillon hard enough that he stumbles back. "You can thank him for isolation."

"You really are an ass," I say, bonking my head to his chest. "You could've just let me eat instead of pulling this bullshit. Your brothers wouldn't have done this."

Maddox kicks the side door leading into the prison yard open and hauls me outside. I blink in the bright sunlight, the warmth as inviting as the heat emanating from Maddox's muscular body as he presses into me.

"I'm not my brothers." He hooks his arm across my waist and lifts me off my feet. Spinning me in his arms, he forces me to face him.

I meet his stern face with a glare. "Obviously. They know how to treat a woman. Pleasure her, too."

He releases a growl, his cinnamon breath caressing my lips. "Keep talking like that, cookie, and you'll never want away from me."

"Highly doubt it." I lean in close but keep an inch of space between our lips. "It's already you who can't stay away from me."

"Because it's impossible. I'm your keeper." He slides his hands to my ass and pulls my body to his like he can't resist testing the fabric of our clothes with his raging boner.

"Liar. You don't show this much attention to the other inmates." I squeeze him between my thighs while combing my fingers through his long hair. "Just admit it. You're only an asshole because you don't want to want me but you so want me. I bet you imagine bending me over and fucking me from behind."

Another soft growl escapes his mouth.

I smirk at him. "I bet it pissed you off that I allowed Quillon to sit with me. That I say his name when I can't say yours."

He tries to close the distance between our mouths, but I pull back, not letting him try to shut me up with a kiss. "Nova—"

Pressing my hand to his mouth, I cut him off as he says my name, my body loving way too much how it sounds like lust and need and passion rolled into a single breath of a word that leaves me wet.

"Admit it, CO. Admit to me that you know I don't belong here and that the only reason you're not already trying to overturn my sentence is because you are afraid that once I get out of here, you'll never see me again." I slowly ease my hand away from his mouth. "You feel helpless against me, and it drives your power-hungry ass crazy."

CAGED BY HER DRAGONS

Maddox kicks the metal grate of the first pit off the mouth of the hole leading down. The world falls out from under me as he drops me without warning. I hold my breath and brace for impact, my feet sinking into the soft dirt before I lose balance and topple on my ass to land on my back. A shadow blocks out the pale sunlight trying to light the pit, and a second later, Maddox lowers himself in while pulling the grate back into place.

I don't move, remaining in my spot as he drops from above and lands on top of me with his boots sinking into the ground and my sides. He tips his head down, his eyes glowing with fire, and he bends and slides his hand under my back to pull me up.

"You're wrong," Maddox says, his voice deepening even more. He sounds like a growl clings in his throat, refusing to let him sound anything other than gruff. "I'm not afraid of you getting out and never seeing you again."

He locks his fingers to the back of my neck, holding me in place. My heart pounds out of control, the heat from his fingers sparking burning desire inside me that travels through my veins to consume my good senses.

"Then what the hell is your problem? You think I like that you call me your mate and try to claim me? I don't. It's the last thing I want to be to you." I clutch the fabric of his uniform shirt in my fingers. "It's been only days, and I can tell how horrible a mate you'd be. I'd never even date you in the Mortal World."

"But you'd fuck me." His jaw twitches with his comment, his Adam's apple popping up with his swallow.

I release a gasp of a laugh. I don't know why I'm so surprised by his remark. Or how he attempts to change focus. "You wish."

"I don't wish. I know. You want me to kiss you now. You imagine what I look like under my clothes. You're pissed off that I don't show you what I have to offer you like my brothers have. Or how I won't get on my knees and beg you to accept me as your mate. How I'll never let you hold that kind of claim on me." His nostrils flare with his words. "I want you to admit how much you want me."

I shove my hands to his chest. "Fuck off, CO."

He smirks, adjusting his hard dick through his pants. I can't stop my eyes from roaming down to watch him do so. "It's why you refuse to say my name now. You know I'll make you scream it in pleasure. You're the one afraid of that. You hate how much you want me. How much you want to claim me."

Annoyance rushes over me at his cocky-ass thinking. "The only thing I hate is how you refuse to believe in my innocence."

"Because you're not, cookie." He risks my wrath and closes the space again. "Admit it."

I tighten my jaw. "Fuck off and leave me alone. I don't

give a shit if you leave me in here. I'd rather be alone than with you."

Turning away, I face the dirt wall, trying to get my anger under control. I don't know how much longer I can take this hot and cold attitude of his. It drives me insane how attracted I am to his sorry ass, and what he claims is partially true. I don't know what the hell is wrong with me. I'm waging a losing war with myself where no matter what I do, I face defeat. The last thing I want is for him to think he can pull this shit. I deserve more.

"Nova, come on. I'll take you back to your cell." His hard voice softens with his words. "My brother will come looking for you otherwise. He's probably on his way. You're projecting your feelings—calling to your mates because you're in need."

I frown. "What the hell? I'm not in need."

"You are. I can feel that the truth got to you. You still want to cling to the life you lived as a mortal." He moves closer. "It'll only hinder you."

Straightening my shoulders, I suck up my feelings and try to steel myself. "Because it's *my* life. I shouldn't be here. I'm not whoever you think I am. I'm not."

Maddox puffs a breath through his lips. "If you would just admit—"

"Admit what? That I'm a murderer?" I try to push him away from me, but he backs me against the wall, pinning me in place, so I can't fight to punch him. "No."

"Admit you killed someone. If you admit it, we can deal with it. But you have to hold yourself accountable. If you don't, I can't help you." His cinnamon breath tickles the stray strands of my hair around my face.

I close my eyes, trying to get my act together. When I flutter my lids open, Maddox leans in ultra-close, his features blurring with only the firelight in his eyes and the soft red glow of his scar across his face breaking through the shadows sharpening his face.

"I can't," I whisper, sucking my lip between my teeth.

"Why?" Lacing his fingers through mine, he tugs my hand to his chest, cradling it against his thumping heart.

"If I admit it, it'll make this real." I hate how I start to open up to him. I know better than this. He could take everything I say and use it against me. He will use it against me if he finds out my bloodline. That my name isn't Nova Noble.

"It is real, cookie," he murmurs, snaking his hand to my lower back. "You're a dragon. You killed someone. You're not of the Mortal World."

"What about being your mate?" I lock my gaze to his as I ask. "Is that real? Do you truly believe that?"

He bows his head in a sharp nod. "You will be mine."

"Maddox," I say, puffing out my lips. "I'm a dragon. I killed a man who was trying to hurt me, but I'm not a murderer."

The corner of his lip quirks up. "Now I believe you."

I sigh and rest my head on his shoulder. "You suck, you know that right? This tough-guy attitude—"

"Drives you crazy," he says, his voice lacing with something deep and velvety. "As much as you get to me."

I snap my head up to look at him. "See, it's shit like this—"

Maddox crashes his mouth to mine, shutting me up with a kiss that leaves me gasping. I don't know if it's my frustration, my sudden admission to something I want to deny, or my out of control hormones, but I can't stop myself from devouring his affection and returning his passion with my own fiery desire.

Our tongues meet in a deep caress, the taste of his kiss sweet and spicy and full of heat that I drag my fingers up his chest and around his neck. He pulls me closer by my hips, letting me feel the length of his shaft. I lift my leg up to feel the pressure where I want and moan as he guides my body to grind against his. He nips my lip, pulling it between his teeth before breaking away to trail his lips down my jaw.

I comb my fingers through his hair as he pops open the top button of my jumpsuit and sucks the skin at the top of my breast, leaving a mark. Grabbing at his collar, I test him to see if he'll let me try to undress him, but he doesn't give me the chance, hooking his fingers to his shirt to unfasten it and shrug it off.

Pulling me down, he nudges me to lie on his shirt, using it to protect me from the dirt ground. I arch my back as he adjusts himself between my legs, propping his muscular body on one hand while using the other to continue to pop open the buttons on my jumpsuit. I lift my shoulders, giving him permission to pull it down to show off the tight-fitting sports bra Rowan had given me.

Maddox doesn't waste time trying to pull it over my head and stretches the fabric so hard that it rips down the middle to expose my breasts to him. He bows down and kisses my cleavage, drawing his tongue over the supple plane of my breast to suck my nipple into his mouth. Twirling his tongue, he takes his time to familiarize himself with my body. I squirm beneath his weight, playing with his hair and massaging my fingers into his taut shoulders. My hands brush over a couple of scars, raised on his skin, and I can't help myself from tracing the edges.

Maddox works his way lower, tugging my jumpsuit down with his movements. His mouth blazes across my stomach, sending tingles exploding down my body to my groin. He moans with my movements and heavy panting, my body pleading for him to hurry.

Pushing up on his knees, Maddox tugs off my shoes and then the rest of my jumpsuit, leaving me lying in not the cutest underwear. I blush immediately, hating that I don't get the privilege to prepare for moments such as these, but his facial expression never changes. His eyes drink me in like I'm the sexiest woman he's ever laid eyes on.

He doesn't take his eyes off me, watching me watch him as he links his fingers to his belt and unfastens it, dropping it and his weapons to the ground. I swallow and rub my lips together, anticipation coursing through me. He teases me by slowly unzipping his pants. I can't stand the wait and push myself up, closing the space to him on my knees. Sliding his hand up the length of my back, he tangles his hand in my hair and tugs me to him for a kiss.

I reach between us and slip my hand in his pants to feel his thick shaft held down by his boxer-briefs. He groans a breath as I try to wrap my hand around it, my fingers unable to close completely. And damn. What am I getting myself into? Maddox doesn't seem like the gentle, love-making type. He seems like the type to destroy beds and frames and like he'd fuck me so hard and fast that I'll walk funny for days.

"You're nervous," Maddox whispers against my lips, slowing his passion to kiss me tenderly with an unexpected gentleness.

My cheeks burn and I shake my head, choosing not to answer verbally in fear that my voice might rise. Because I am a bit nervous, but it's not a bad thing. It's excitement more than anything.

"Don't be. I wouldn't have been given a mate unable to handle me." He says it so matter of fact that I can't stop an exasperated laugh from escaping my mouth. "You are tough."

Fuck. I'm going to have to be. "You can't expect me to be quiet. It'll be impossible."

"I know. I ensured to keep the yard clear."

I giggle, my voice shaking, annoying the hell out of me, but I turn my focus to his body and pull his cock free. The tip of it grazes my stomach as I stroke my hand over the length of it, taking a moment to familiarize myself with his intimidating-as-hell body now throbbing and flexing in my hand.

Maddox traces his fingers to cup my breast, pinching my nipple between his fingers. I moan at the sensation, squeezing his cock a bit harder, rubbing my hand up and down its length. He continues his exploration, spreading his fingers to warm my middle as he works his way down to my pelvis to drag my underwear off my hips, leaving them stretched at my knees, not wasting a second to dip his finger between my legs to feel the wet warmth of my body. Pleasure bursts through me, the pressure of his middle finger sliding over my clit weakening my knees. He hums under his breath, his enjoyment of touching me sounding so sexy.

"So perfect," he murmurs, using his free hand to dig into my ass cheek. "I want to taste you now."

CAGED BY HER DRAGONS

I nod my agreement, lying back so he can tug my underwear off completely. He devours the sight of my body, resting his hands on my knees, warming up my body with his closeness. He could easily lift my hips and guide himself into me, but instead he stretches my legs to fit his broad shoulders between them. I tip my head back and close my eyes, panting and squirming as he holds me in place, kissing my knee as he works his way to my thigh. He starts slow, teasing me with his tongue, and I reach down for him. Lacing his fingers through mine, Maddox holds my hand while flicking his tongue so quickly over my clit that I squeeze my thighs together, not expecting to already be on the verge of an orgasm. He moans, the heat of his breath sending tingles over me, and I call out his name, my toes curling and back arching.

He gives me a cocky-bastard smile from between my legs and pushes back up to his knees. I pant, my body buzzing, craving for him to continue. He licks his lips and grabs my ankles, stretching my legs up to drag me a few inches closer. Like he desires to test my flexibility, he spreads my legs open into the splits and aligns his body to mine. I dig my fingers into the ground, my heart thumping in anticipation. Holding me under my ass, he pulls my body to his instead of thrusting into me, slowly teasing me with his tip to watch my reaction.

I moan softly, the pressure of his massive cock sinking

deeper into me feeling like he touches every single nerve ending inside me. My skin buzzes, an unfamiliar wave of emotion swirling through my head and down to my heart, warming me from inside out.

"You're mine, Nova," Maddox says, guiding my body to his as he picks up speed. "You might not want to be, but you are."

I can't even respond to him as he bumps our bodies together, making me gasp moans every time we connect completely. A pleasure so intense courses through me that I don't even care if he stakes a claim on me or treats it as if I don't have a choice. Because right now, I choose to be with Maddox and feel the ecstasy he arouses in me. I embrace this crazy-ass experience, allowing him to screw me in a damn pit. I never imagined I'd do something like this, but I don't care. I was always a thrill-seeker, an adrenaline junkie, and Maddox gets to me so crazily that it's just a rush to be near him.

And he feels the same about me.

I don't know how I know, but it's a deep-seated feeling that grows inside me the longer I lock Maddox with my gaze. He doesn't close his eyes or look anywhere else but at me like he refuses to miss even a second of my reaction his passion evokes in me.

Leaning forward, he plants his hands at the sides of my head and bows down to kiss me. I curl my legs around him, clinging to him with his powerful thrusts that send me sliding up his shirt, getting dirt all over my hair.

His even, deep thrusting builds another intense pleasure inside me, and I feel like I'll blow up at any second in a wave of fire from the dragon locked inside me. A strange, intense need clenches my body, and my hands start to burn and smoke, something setting off my branding. I gasp, ignoring the pain, the pleasure Maddox arouses in me all-consuming until I scream a moan, my whole body trembling.

Maddox slides his hand under my neck and pulls me in for another kiss, stealing my breath to replace with his until he thrusts a few more times as he cums. Easing away, he looks into my eyes and touches my cheek, caressing my jaw. He slides his fingers through mine to hold my hand while he catches his breath, but the second the tips of his fingers touch the top of my hand, he tenses and jerks upright.

"Fuck," he whispers, running his finger over the glowing red digits. "I never logged you into the pit."

I blink a few times, the pain in my hands finally consuming my pleasure. "What's happening? Why are they glowing?"

"Fuck. Fuck. Fuck." Maddox rushes to get up, pulling me with him.

He doesn't bother to grab my jumpsuit and instead drapes his dirty uniform shirt around me before stepping into his pants. He grabs my hand, but agony burns over my skin, and I jerk away from him. My eyes swell with unwanted tears as heat unlike anything I've ever felt burns over my skin.

"Shit, hold on, Nova," Maddox says.

I don't get a chance to respond.

Red electricity bursts from the tops of my hands, shocking me. I screech in pain, my body jerking with a horrible muscle spasm. And then the electricity comes again and again.

I feel as if I'm about to die.

The red energy consumes me.

Chapter 13

Down and Dirty

"YOU RISKED HER life to claim her in the pits? Are you fucking kidding me? Our girl deserves better. She deserves lovemaking and romance." Kash's voice trickles through my mind.

"Or at least somewhere clean," Rowan adds.

Maddox growls. "I beg to differ. She loves it raw and dirty."

Keeping my eyes shut, I eavesdrop on their ludicrous conversation. Because damn it. I like how Kash thinks, but Maddox is a bit right. I cannot be making love to men I just met. Men who control the prison I'm in. It makes it sound so—so serious. The only thing I want them to be serious about is getting me out of this hellhole.

"Isn't that right, cookie? You don't mind as long as you cum." Maddox's warm hand squeezes my bare thigh. "I know this because you were pissed when I didn't let you the first time. Tell my brothers. Tell them how you like it."

Forcing my eyes to flutter open, I glare at Maddox. "No. And neither. No lovemaking or getting pounded in the pits."

A hand sneaks under my ass, pulling me from the spot where I lie on Rowan's couch. He engulfs me in a hug, squishing me to his broad chest. And then he trails his hands up my torso and slips them inside the dirty uniform shirt I wear with nothing else. He rubs his fingers over my nipples like his brothers aren't sitting close enough to touch me.

"You want to discover your third option, my sexy doe-eyed girl? I should be offended that you chose to fuck Maddox before me, but I know why you did it. You wanted to give him undeniable proof that you're our mate." Rowan slips his hands back down my stomach, stopping his hands over my pelvis. "Maybe he won't be such a dick now."

CAGED BY HER DRAGONS

I shift my gaze to Maddox. "Doubt it."

"Just wait until you bear his child," Kash says, tapping his finger to my knee. "That'll change things."

My eyes widen at his nonchalant comment, and I scramble off of Rowan's lap and dodge past Kash as he grabs at me. His fingers lock to the back of my shirt, pulling it right off me to leave me naked in front of the three of them. Rowan releases a whistle and Kash practically purrs. It's Maddox who growls and gets to his feet to come to my side.

Lacing our fingers together like it's the most normal thing, he says, "Come on. You've given my brothers enough of your time. You're still mine. I want to shower with you and make you scream in pleasure again." At least he's to the point.

I rip my hand away from his and hold my palm up. "No fucking way. Someone's going to get me some clothes so I can shower alone, and when I come out, I expect food since you ruined mine."

"Rowan will get you clothes and Kash will prepare your meal. I'm washing you. Accept it or don't take a shower, cookie." Maddox attempts to grab me again, and I arch backward out of his reach only to kick my leg up. I knock my foot right into his balls. He growls and rushes at me, looking hell-bent on capturing me to drag me like the beast he is into the bathroom.

"If you want to shower that badly with me, then knock

this shit off and ask me nicely, Maddox," I snap, swinging my hand out to slap his hip. "And then you're going to give me some answers. Like what the hell happened in the pit with my ID brandings? When are you guys going to get me out of here? What are you going to do about…the visitor?" I don't give Maddox even a second to answer as I spit out everything on my mind.

He grumbles and turns his back on me to point at the door to the bathroom. "Go take your shower."

I throw my hands up. "Seriously? Is it that difficult to be nice to me that you'd rather skip what I can assure you is another helluva good time? Or is it because you don't want to ask politely?"

"Can I shower with you, kitten?" Kash says, speaking up before Maddox can respond.

I blow out a breath. "No." I feel a bit bad telling him no, considering how sweet he asked me, but this is about Maddox.

Maddox breaks his serious expression to grin at my response to Kash. Kash lifts an eyebrow at me like he thinks I'm the crazy one for denying the opportunity, but these guys are getting out of control. I'll never get out of here if I don't stand my ground. While sex is fun, and I'm already regretting telling Kash no, I have more important things in my life—like going back to the Mortal World and taking my life back.

CAGED BY HER DRAGONS

"Can I help you bathe, Nova?" Rowan gets to his feet and extends his hand to me. "I'll be a good boy unless you ask me otherwise. I'll answer any and all of your questions too."

I purse my lips and look into his hazel eyes. Damn it. They're wearing me down, and they know it. "No sex."

His jaw twitches. I have a feeling Rowan's going to pursue the whole thing a helluva lot harder knowing that I banged both his brothers. I should feel a bit shy about how accepting they are to the idea of sharing me, but it's weirdly okay. I can't explain it. "If you insist, but I can't promise my cock won't be prepared for that sort of activity. With the minimal space in my shower, I can't be held accountable if you decide to let it slip in."

Warmth floods my face at the thought. I wish my body would chill the hell out, especially after the whole getting knocked up comment. I didn't think about it until now. Kash pulled out, not that it matters because it can still happen, but Maddox didn't. Why he wouldn't? Fuck. They're completely serious about this whole mate and procreate thing. It wasn't a joke.

"Damn, I wish I could hear what she was thinking. Fucking magic thought-block," Rowan mutters to Maddox.

"A magic what?" I cross my arms over my naked breasts. Standing nude before them should also bother me, but it doesn't.

"Nothing to worry about, cookie," Maddox says. "I'm working on it."

I frown at him, wishing there was a way to chisel through all his badass, tough-guy attitude to really figure him out. He purposely guards himself harder than he does the whole prison. If Rowan didn't start unbuttoning his uniform shirt to give me a view of his delicious muscles, I'd insist Maddox tell me. But damn it. My eyes travel along Rowan's shoulders and to the intricate glowing swirls branded into his arms.

Heat builds between my legs, my excitement uncontrollable as Rowan unbuckles his belt. I stare at the V-shape of his hips disappearing into his pants. I hold my breath in anticipation, my groin clenching, my body so turned on that I squeeze my legs together, afraid I'll drip on the floor.

Rowan releases a deep hum. "She looks ready to devour me. And she smells so good."

"Fuck. I need her to look at me like that," Kash says from a few feet away.

"Her body is ready for you, brother. Claim her." Maddox's words are like a smack across my face, snapping me out of my lust haze.

I jerk my attention to him with a gasp of a breath. "Are you joking? Just because I'm enjoying the show does not mean you can encourage your brother to fuck me, Maddox." I shiver at the thought. "And so you know, it's a bit

CAGED BY HER DRAGONS

weird. You should all be jealous or something." I was a fool to think that I could pit them against each other upon my arrival. They seem to be teaming up the longer I spend time with them together.

"Jealous? Of what? There aren't enough females for every man, so our species has evolved to share. You are ours and will bear our heirs and our females will reinforce alliances for us. We will find a new warlock to entice the fates in our favor. We will strengthen bloodlines even if yours is unheard of to us. There aren't any dragon clans in Magaelorum that go by the name Noble." Maddox cracks his knuckles. "Whoever stole you from your people ensured it would be difficult to place you. But the fates can't be stopped. You are ours. We will find out where you come from in due time."

My head spins with his info-bomb that leaves me reeling. "Uh, how about you slow down with all the childbearing, betrothing females, and stop acting as if everything you say is indeed fact, because you can't possibly know anything for sure, Maddox," I mutter without taking my eyes off Rowan. "And sharing me might seem normal to you, but it's not to me." At least not yet.

"Are you sure about that, kitten?" Kash smiles at me.

I groan. "Yes. Like I said, it's strange that you're not jealous and Maddox basically instructed Rowan to fuck me—which almost sounded like he wanted him to do so right in front of you."

Flicking my attention to Maddox, I twist my lips to the side, waiting for his response to my comment. All he does is shrug with a smile playing on his lips. And hell. He looks hot doing so. He's sexy as hell all brooding and hard-ass, but the subtle softness brought on by his smile nearly takes my breath away, making my heart flutter. Because he's smiling at me.

"I wouldn't, Nova. Not for our first time." Rowan struts forward, kicking off his pants in the process. He moves so suddenly that I stand frozen as he hooks his fingers to my hips and pulls my naked body flush against his. My heart kick-starts wildly, my damn vagina now practically throbbing with a need only his dick can cure. His warmth rolls over me in a wave, his fingers sliding around me to squeeze my ass.

"Shit," I whisper, stretching on my tiptoes. "You can't do this. You're playing dirty."

Leaning in, he brushes his lips to mine, kissing me tenderly for a second. I don't even resist. I can't help myself from wanting to accept his affection, feeling his body so close, hearing his heart bump against mine. "I'm only giving you the attention you're so set on denying, Nova. And my brother was wrong. I'm so jealous, but not of him. I'm jealous you've picked now to play coy, doe eyes. You have no idea how much I want you. I need to know if you like to be bent over or stretched up. On top. On all fours. Backwards. Mmm all of the above." His cinnamon breath tickles my lips. "I want to know if you're as adventurous as me. If you'll try anything."

I blink a few times, trying to decipher what he means by that. "I—I need a cold shower." I manage to tug myself away from Rowan and cross the room to the bathroom before any of them can stop me.

"Look at those doe eyes," Rowan says, drinking me in from across the room.

He starts to close the distance, but I wave my hand and say, "Please just give me a minute. I need to think with something other than my desire. I just—I can't believe this might be my future. I don't belong here, and I feel like you guys might not truly care if I do or not. You keep bringing up being mates and babies and sex and claiming but none of that matters to me. You can't just expect me to comply or believe you."

"Nova, I said I'd answer your questions," Rowan says. "We don't have to have sex."

"The hell you don't," Maddox snaps. "You have to claim her. We need to be absolutely certain."

I frown. "Wait so—"

An alarm screeches through the air, startling me. The Dreki brothers look to each other and then to me. Rowan jogs across the room and pushes me back into the bathroom. Fire lights his eyes as he turns toward his brothers, sharing an indecipherable look.

"What's happening?" I ask, letting Rowan nudge me farther into the bathroom.

"We're going on lockdown. Time to get showered and dressed as fast as you can," he says. "It seems something broke the magical barrier."

I follow Rowan to the shower. "What does that even mean?"

"I'm not sure. My guess is that some of the prisoners might've gotten freed."

I can't believe Rowan put me in my cell and abandoned me. I'd expect that out of Maddox, but I was pretty sure Rowan wouldn't want me out of his sight, especially after all the effort he put into bathing me in the shower.

Footsteps pound down the hallway, and I get to my feet to glance into the lookout mirror. Surprise washes over me at the sight of Quillon rushing in my direction. I link my fingers around the bars, wondering how the hell he is out during the lockdown.

"Nova, stand back," Quillon commands from a few feet away. His blue eyes flash green as they gaze around the hallway. Unbuttoning his jumpsuit, he tugs something from the waistband of his prison-issued underwear that look as sexy as mine, which is far from it.

CAGED BY HER DRAGONS

I do as he says and scramble to the back of my cell, leaning against the bunk. He slaps something on the bars and it sparks with red electricity. Flames burst across the metal with a loud pop. My mouth falls agape as Quillon slides the bars open and offers me his hand.

"Come on. We have about twenty minutes before the guards get things under control in the Fae Block." Quillon enters my cell when I'm not quick to react. "Don't be scared. I told you I'd figure out how to get you, so we gotta take advantage of this while we can."

I allow him to tug me from my spot. I think he might pick me up if I don't move otherwise. It feels strange to go with him, despite seeing him earlier. I thought he was nice before, but a deep-seated feeling screams that I shouldn't go with anyone apart from the Drekis.

"I'm sure you still have a lot of questions," he adds, searching our surroundings.

"What was that?" I point at the scorch marks on the floor instead of agreeing with his comment. I do have a lot of questions, but they're not for him. I think I'd only use Quillon's response to confirm or deny something the Drekis say. How can I trust a man behind bars? He claims to have known my parents, but what if it's the same way as Lazlo? As Rhett?

"Just a little magic I got my hands on. Nearly wiped out my stipend account, so don't let it be a waste. We still

~235~

have so much to talk about." Quillon flashes me a smile. "Though even a few minutes with you would be worth it."

I laugh and shake my head. "Laying it on a little thick."

"You like it." Quillon pulls me to a stop at the end of the hallway and presses my back to the wall. "Admit it."

Again, I giggle. I sound stupidly sweet, but it makes Quillon grin wider. "Never. I hate to break it to you, but I don't plan on staying here for much longer, so don't get attached."

Quillon's brows lower on his forehead, his smile fading. He bows slightly, closing the space. I pray he doesn't ask to kiss me or something. "Delp—Nova. What have you been up to since I've last seen you? You sound far more confident."

I cringe that he almost uses my real name. "Nothing much. It's just—"

I don't get a chance to explain my reasoning. Quillon suddenly drags me forward until I start running beside him. We dash across the main room of the block, empty of inmates. A few shouts come from within the cells as some of the guys catcall at me. Quillon growls and flips off the nearest guy at the end cell by the door leading to the prison yard.

Nerves tighten my stomach the closer we get to the exit. I can't stop thinking about how my ID brandings nearly shocked me to death when I wasn't where I was logged. If I leave with Quillon, it could happen again. It's enough to get me to slow down.

"Wait, we can't," I say, ripping my hand from his. "The brands."

Quillon jerks his gaze to my hands. "What are you talking about? They only set off if we try to leave the magic border of the prison."

I shake my head. "Not mine. I was nearly shocked to death when Mad—CO Dreki didn't log my relocation to the pit right away."

Anger hardens Quillon's features, and he scowls. "What?"

"Maybe because I'm a lifer here," I add. I honestly don't know. I doubt anyone would willingly explain. It's hard enough as it is to get answers out of the Dreki brothers.

Swinging his fist, Quillon punches the wall. "Rose's don't do that. The bastards really think they possess you. Fuck, Nova. This might be bad, especially with what I know of your parents."

I open my mouth to tell him about how the Drekis think I'm their mate and not only a possession, but a strange look crosses Quillon's face. Something dark flickers in his gaze. For a split second, I expect him to drag me through the door anyway and brace myself to fight him.

Releasing a breath, he relaxes his shoulders. "I'll figure

it out for the next time. Come on. I don't want to waste my time alone with you. If you stay pretty close to your cell, then you'll be all right. The brands will only trigger at a certain distance."

I tilt my head. "How do you know?"

"I've made it my mission to know everything about this place." Grabbing my hand, he links his fingers through mine like he does it all the time. "Now, let's go. We're running out of time. I found out some things about your family and why you were stolen."

Stolen? I consider demanding Quillon to tell me right here, but I don't think I could outmatch him in strength. Tightening his fingers, he pulls me with him in the direction of my cell but instead of running toward it, he pushes open a normal door leading into a cluster of showers only separated by flimsy curtains. I grimace at the sight and thank the fates for the Drekis' private quarters. I have no idea if they force the few women in the cell block to shower with the men, but I don't want to find out. I haven't even seen the pride of lionesses since my arrival.

"This way," Quillon says, guiding me through an open doorway. We pass what looks like a custodial storage space and finally stop in a huge laundry area with giant washing machines and dryers. "We'll be safe here. Even if the lockdown ends, no one will come in until first thing in the morning."

CAGED BY HER DRAGONS

Strolling away from me, Quillon stops in front of one of the industrial dryers and opens the hatch. He reaches in and pulls out a clean jumpsuit. I can't take my eyes off him as he unbuttons the one he wears, revealing his chiseled chest. Hair covers his pecs and fades to his rock-hard abs. I don't know if the world slows or he does, but Quillon teases me with a show, taking his time to slide the jumpsuit down his torso until it hangs on his hips. And this fucker. He grins, knowing exactly what he's doing. He's testing me, trying to see my reaction. So I don't give him one.

I twirl my finger at his body. "I thought you had something to say to me. If you had something else in mind, well, not going to happen. For one, I'm starting to think sex around here means you stake a claim on someone. Two, there are no fucking condoms, and the last thing I need is to get knocked up."

"We're incompatible, Delphia. And I'd never announce a claim on you. You don't belong to me." Quillon smirks as he drops his jumpsuit to the ground with his underwear to get naked in front of me.

My. Dumb. Eyes. They betray me, darting down to devour the sight of his dick. It also prevents me from snapping at him for using my real name. Because to my surprise, his dick is comparable to the guys I've slept with in the Mortal World. The normalcy is almost comforting. All of the Drekis have several inches on Quillon, but it doesn't mean much except that I might not gag if I gave him a blow job and could handle hours of fucking without walking funny afterwards.

What. Am. I. Thinking?

Shaking the thought of me on my knees away, I finally manage to avert my eyes to focus on Quillon's face. He lifts an eyebrow. "I know it's not dragon-sized, but I can guarantee you'd have an unforgettable time."

Heat flushes my face. "You just said I belong to someone else." Whatever the hell that means, because he's obviously not talking about the Drekis.

"Doesn't mean we can't have fun now." Again with the damn smirk.

Pressing my lips together, I shake my head. "Not happening. You said you had information about my family. If that was just a ploy to get me alone, I'm going to ensure you can't ever have that kind of fun again. I don't like these types of games. I'm not just going to fuck you when the opportunity arises."

He narrows his eyes. "What about the COs?"

I laugh in exasperation, throwing my hands up. "They're none of your business."

"So you have fucked one of them. Who? Was it Kash? It couldn't have been Maddox. I'm not sure Rowan is your type—"

"What? You know their names?" I widen my eyes.

CAGED BY HER DRAGONS

Maddox made a huge fucking deal when I said his name in one of the other cellblocks. He said if those in my block heard, it would endanger him. And here Quillon is already with the information.

"Of course I know their names, Delphia. I know a lot of things. Like who your parents were and how your mom ended up in this very prison. I know that you were promised to the Darkonian Clan to solidify an alliance with the Drakovich Clan." Quillon steps into the clean jumpsuit without taking his gaze from me. "I also know that they will come for you if you just hold tight."

My heart thrashes against my ribcage.

"You need to keep your distance from the Drekis the best you can. They will kill you, Delphia. I can't protect you like I was paid to do. They grew too possessive too quickly. That's why you must listen to me. Don't test them. Don't give them your attention. And especially don't trust them, no matter what they say." Quillon moves closer, holding his hands out. "Please. You—"

Panic floods through me as he tries to take my hands. I automatically react and punch him in the gut. "You were *paid. Paid!* I don't understand. Who the hell paid you?"

"Just calm down for a second," Quillon says.

Oh, fuck. He did not just tell me that. Anger and fear battle inside me, sending me stumbling away from him. I need to get out of here. My instincts want nothing more than to put as much space and distance between me and whoever the hell Quillon truly is.

Quillon rushes toward me. "Delphia, please. Wait. This will all work out. There is a plan in place. It was never intended for you to end up here but the Drekis arrived too soon. Rhett fucked up."

I inhale a sharp breath at his words. The way he says it almost makes it sound as if this whole thing was planned yet something went wrong.

"They will fix it. You will get out of here and home where you belong," he adds.

I don't even have to ask him to know he doesn't mean the Mortal World. And staying in Magaelorum is the last thing I want to do. It's bad enough that I'm stuck here. It won't make it any better if I'm stuck somewhere else.

Quillon holds his hands up in caution like I'll strike him at any second. "Your mates are waiting for you."

My mates? The words crash through my head, banging around instead of sinking in. Nothing has sounded more wrong in my life. How can these Darkonian dragons be my mates when the Drekis claim that I'm their mate? Are they lying? Is this some sort of game of possession? I don't understand any of this.

Spinning on my feet, I rush from the laundry room and back to the showers. A flash of red light explodes from my right, sending ruby flames across the floor. I screech in sur-

CAGED BY HER DRAGONS

prise and halt in my tracks.

"Looks like someone let you out of your cell, Delphia," the smooth, deep voice says. "This will be easier than I thought." Lazlo materializes before me, cradling a ball of electric magic in his hands. "Now don't move. I'll be fast."

I don't get a chance to react.

I don't even get a chance to scream.

Lazlo throws the magic at me.

Chapter 14

Fated Mates

SOMETHING HEAVY CRASHES into my back, knocking me off my feet. Quillon presses my body to the tiled floor and growls as the electric magic from Lazlo explodes over us. The scent of burning flesh wafts through the air, and I gag.

A deep, guttural roar reverberates through my bones, turning my blood hot. The weight of Quillon's body lifts away before a loud crash echoes through the shower room. The sleeves on my jumpsuit smoke and smolder, and I quickly rush to pat the glowing red trails of burning fabric out.

"Inmate D64901, get up. Let me take a look at you." Rowan's voice wraps around me in velvety warmth.

Something comes over me, and I can't stop myself from throwing my arms around his broad body. He has no choice but to lift me up before I climb him to securely hide in his muscular embrace. Having Quillon throw all this crazy-ass information at me is one thing, but having Lazlo appear and try to murder me or some-shit gives me an intense need to be as close as possible to one of the men who think we're fated together.

"Hey, whoa. It's okay, Nova. I got you, doe eyes." Rowan's big hand slides up and down my back in a comforting motion. And I kind of hate that I'm cowering in his arms. I should be tough and yell at him for locking me in my cell and leaving, but I'm just so tired of being on guard all the time. "Tell me what happened. What are you doing in here?"

"We were—were attacked," I manage to spit out. "The same visitor from before."

Rowan releases a low growl, and I realize it's directed at Quillon. "Attacked? But how did you get in here with this guy? Was he hurting you?"

"It's not what it looks like," I say. I regret the words immediately. Do I really care what it looks like and what Rowan thinks? Yup. I guess I fucking do. "Quillon—"

"Don't say anything, Delphia," Quillon snaps. "It's none of his business."

Rowan tenses, his muscles flexing and tightening. "What did you call her?"

My heart slides into my stomach at the realization that Quillon said my real name. Panic squeezes my chest, stealing my breath. I brace myself to be tossed to the floor, to be ripped to shreds, to die because of some feud between dragon clans I'm not a part of. But Rowan only squeezes me tighter.

"She doesn't belong to you, Dreki. Put her down," Quillon says, his voice deepening.

Another guttural growl escapes Rowan's lips, the vibration of his voice shaking my whole body. "Put your hands behind your head, inmate. Now."

Quillon laughs, the maniacal sound dragging my attention to him, so I twist in Rowan's arms to meet Quillon's glower. Something strange crosses his face, his eyes flashing a green color. His skin ripples, his body twitching. Hair sprouts from his skin, longer and darker, nothing remotely human. With cracking bones, Quillon grows taller and broader, his mouth and nose elongating into something that looks like a mutated wolf. I've never seen anything like it.

It's freaky as fuck that his eyes remain the same—human.

"Drop her, CO," Quillon commands, his voice throaty and wet coming from his beastly half-human, half-animal form. "We both know there isn't room for you to shift in here."

"How the fuck?" Rowan mutters mostly to himself.

How the fuck, indeed. Quillon shouldn't be able to transform, not with the brands.

And then I remember—Lazlo's electric magic. What if he wasn't trying to kill me? What if he was attempting to break the spell cast upon me with the brandings? It was what he was trying to do before.

Shit.

"The visitor," I say, unable to speak Lazlo's name. "The magic was intended for me. He wanted to kidnap me."

Quillon takes advantage of Rowan's sudden distraction and hauls his hulking form forward. He latches his long dagger nails to the back of my jumpsuit and rips me from Rowan's hold. I flail and fight, striking Quillon with my elbow.

"Let me go!" I yell.

The world spins around me as Quillon drops me on my ass. I groan and rush to get to my feet. Rowan tugs out his baton from his belt, preparing to fight. Every muscle on my body tenses. Without thinking, I chase after Quillon in his monster form. Launching myself from the floor, I attach myself to his back, linking my hands through his fur. It's enough of a surprise to distract him that Rowan swings his baton and slams it into Quillon's gut. I release him as he falls back and manage to flip myself over his shoulder to land on top of the beast.

Jerking my hand back for greater force, I punch Quillon in his elongated muzzle. "Don't you fucking touch him. Rowan is mine!"

My voice rings through the air, and Quillon stills.

"He's mine!" I repeat.

The alarms blare.

The whole room quivers, a strange buzzing sensation crawling over my skin. Warmth blossoms from the tops of my hands as my brandings ignite with magic. I screech at the pain, my body tensing. Quillon snatches the front of my jumpsuit and lifts me off the ground with him.

"Delphia, stop fighting me. I don't want to hurt you," he says, hooking his arm around my waist. "Let me take care of him."

I clench my teeth through the fiery pain. "Let me go."

"Delphia—"

"Stop calling me that. It's not my name!"

Quillon roars and snarls, spinning around so fast that the world blurs. My legs crash into a solid body, the quick movements knocking Rowan off his feet. He only remains on the ground for a second, launching up with fire sparking in his hands. I tense and cringe, expecting to get burned, but nothing happens when he grabs my arm in one hand while punching Quillon with the other.

"Inmate, get down!" Maddox's deep voice rumbles through the air. "If you do not comply, I will issue a death sentence."

Maddox's words are enough to stop Quillon in his tracks. Quillon inhales a few sharp breaths as he transforms back into his handsome human form. A fist imprint glows on his cheek, his flesh blistering from the heat of Rowan's punch. Slowly dropping down, Quillon lies on his stomach with his hands on his head.

"CO, get Inmate D64901 out of here. Put her on lockdown out of gen. pop. I'm taking this douche to the pits until we get things sorted out," Maddox says, glowering at Quillon.

"Remember what I told you, Delphia," Quillon says. "They're going to murder me now. Don't let my death have been in vain."

I gasp a few breaths, watching Maddox drag Quillon to his feet. A mixture of emotions course through me when our eyes meet. I can't help feeling bad that Quillon will face the Dreki wrath. I don't know exactly what his deal is, but he has answers to my questions. I need to know more. I can't just let Maddox destroy him. Because what if what Quillon says is true about the feud?

Straightening my shoulders, I turn my attention to Maddox. "Don't kill him. Please. He was trying to help me."

Rowan growls and presses into my back, his big hands hooking to my shoulders as he prepares to hold me back. I guess he doesn't trust that I won't get within arm's reach of Quillon. "He was trying to take you."

I puff out my bottom lip, lowering my voice. "He saved me from—fuck." I still can't get Lazlo's name out. It hurts to even think the warlock's name.

"Lazlo Infinity," Quillon says, despite Maddox's warning. He tips his head to look at him. "He's coming for her. If she stays here, he'll take her. There won't be anything you guys can do about it."

Ignoring him, Maddox points at Rowan. He twists his lips into a snarl, his whole body rigid with his anger. I expect him to breathe fire at any second as he lets his dragon free. "Take her somewhere safe. I'll handle him."

"Maddox, please. Don't kill him," I say, my voice growing softer. I never thought I'd beg for an almost stranger's life. A part of me feels guilty that the only reason I do is because he knows something I don't. Does it make me a bad person? Well, I guess I am in this shithole prison after all. Maybe I am more like my mom than I realized.

Maddox flares his nostrils with a sigh. His chin crinkles with his clenched jaw. "We'll see. I'll do what has to be done, Nova."

"Delphia," Rowan corrects, sliding his fingers through mine. "Her Magaelorum name is Delphia."

Maddox's brows lower on his forehead. "What? Fuck. This proves everything right."

A soft hand touches my back between my shoulders. "Delphia, relax. Nothing is going to happen to you. I'll protect you with my life."

I purse my lips, turning my gaze from the door. I've been waiting at least an hour for it to bust open. "Don't call me that. My name is Nova. I legally changed it."

Sliding his fingers to my shoulder, Rowan turns me to face him. His eyes light with his dragon fire, the heat of his gaze warming my insides. He reaches up and trails his hand over my jaw, combing my hair from my face. I find my toes pushing into the carpet to stretch my body up to close the space between us a bit more. I should be terrified that Rowan will prove Quillon right and end my life. I shouldn't allow myself to be so close to the man who holds my existence in his hands in this moment, but something inside me refuses to believe any of that is true. It's like a huge part of me is drawn to Rowan in a pull I can't and don't want to escape.

"Nova," he says, my name a whisper of a breath, almost a plea to close the space. "It doesn't matter what name you go by. I'll still protect you."

"Why?" My voice comes out just as soft as we share the same breathing space.

"I've told you already. You're mine." His lips quirk in a half-smile. "And obviously you think I belong to you. I never expected such a fierce claim from you."

I suck my bottom lip between my teeth. "Let's pretend that didn't happen. I don't know what the fuck was up with me."

"Nothing is up with you. Your dragon knows what your mind refuses to accept. We're fated. I don't know how and why Rhett didn't tell us, but I'm certain he knew." Rowan releases a breath. "And I'm sorry you got wrapped up in this bullshit. I know you didn't know any of this...except your name. Will you tell me more?"

A dozen thoughts rush through my mind. My soul feels like opening up to Rowan, telling him about my life and how I grew up, but my brain screams not to get ahead of myself. He's never been quick to give me answers. And I deserve them. More than ever.

I shake my head, easing away from him. "No."

"No?" His voice deepens in surprise.

I steel myself from his charm, sauntering away to put even more distance between us. I make my way across the room to his bed, raised on a platform. I climb the short steps and plop down, turning my back on him.

CAGED BY HER DRAGONS

"I have my own questions I want answered first. Until you can do that, then my answer will be no," I say, facing the wall. "Now, if you don't mind. My nerves are shot and I'm exhausted. I haven't had a good stretch of sleep since arriving."

"I can help with that." The bed shifts as Rowan slides in next to me without asking. I guess it is his bed after all. It's not like I mind. The heat of his body pushes away the ice left in my veins by Lazlo Infinity. "I'm an excellent cuddler. My talent has been wasting away waiting for you."

Laughter erupts from my mouth at his remark. "I'm sure that's not true."

"It is."

I turn over to face him. Lifting an eyebrow, I meet his smile. "Lies. I know you're not a virgin. No virgin would know...how to work me over like you had."

It's his turn to laugh. "Quickies are exactly that. Fast and furious. No connection and all the fun. Cuddling is for the one my soul has been yearning for. So please, don't deprive me. I've never wanted to do something besides you so badly."

This. Guy.

He steals the giggle from my lips with a kiss that sets my body buzzing. Tangling his hands in my hair, he pulls me closer, kissing me deeper, passionately, like he can't get enough of the taste of my tongue as I stroke it against his.

His cinnamon lips scorch against mine, sucking and mapping, exploring my mouth to familiarize himself. Fuck, and it's so good. My body hums with desire ignited by his kiss, sending warmth between my legs.

My hands work fervently down his sides until I tug his uniform shirt free and glide my fingers up his abs to feel each one of them. Rowan moans and returns the favor, moving his hands from my cheeks to tug the buttons on the front of my jumpsuit open. He breaks away from my mouth to kiss my jaw and neck, working his way down to my collarbone.

I trace my hands down his body again and hook my fingers to his belt, yanking it open. Rowan groans under his breath, releasing a gasp as I slip my hand into his pants to lace my fingers around his daunting dick. How things have gone from talking about cuddling to ripping at each other's clothes? I should've expected it. My attraction to him runs hotter and hotter, and I can't stop wondering if he's as good as his brothers. If he'll want to pin me and screw me from behind. If he'll give me control.

So I test him.

Shimmying lower, I kiss my way down his pecs, gliding my tongue across his nipples in hot determination to discover if every inch of him is as sweet and spicy as his mouth. Rowan gathers my hair into his hands, pulling it up and out of the way so that he can watch me lick his abs. I nudge him onto his back and climb on top of him, feeling his hard arousal between my legs. I grind against him for a minute and lean in to kiss him.

"No more touching me," I whisper against his lips. "You're mine right now to do with as I please."

He grins at my words and pinches my ass. "You really want to torture me."

I adjust myself between his legs and tug at his pants. "I don't exactly consider this torture."

Lifting his hips, Rowan helps me pull his pants off until he lies naked before me. I kneel between his legs, roving my eyes over his muscular body, memorizing every inch of him the best I can. And hell is his dick huge. I have no idea how I'm going to take it into my mouth without going throat deep, but damn it I am determined to try.

Rowan grabs his cock and strokes his hand over his throbbing shaft a few times, never taking his eyes off me. I slide my hands through my hair and push it over my shoulders. Slowly finishing unbuttoning my jumpsuit, I shrug out of it to expose myself to him. He licks his lips, fire lighting his eyes. He continues to pleasure himself while he waits to see what I do next.

"You're so beautiful, Nova. Sexy. You taste amazing," he murmurs, extending his hand to me to see if I'll come closer.

"I want to taste you too," I say, digging my fingers into

his thighs.

He hums and nods. "I'd love that. But turn around first. I want to enjoy you."

I wag my finger at him and shake my head. "I said no touching me yet."

Bending down, I smile up at him as I slowly graze my tongue over his smooth shaft, watching his face for a reaction. His bottom lip puffs with his breath, and he closes his eyes in pleasure as I hold his cock in place with my hand and lick my way up to his tip.

I suck him into my mouth, taking a deep breath as I go down as far as possible. Rowan moans at the sensation of my mouth, combing his fingers through my hair to pull it out of the way. He doesn't guide me, but cradles my head with my movements. I roll my tongue on the bottom side, adding more suction with my mouth. The taste of him turns me on, his excitement building to tease me as I work him over. Sucking him off is far better than I've ever experienced with a man from the Mortal World. It's the strangest thing to be surprised with sweetness rather than saltiness. And the way his hands travel across my body to cup my breast? I fucking love it.

He wants so badly to touch me and taste me, I can nearly feel his desire rushing over my very soul.

I've never experienced a need like it. It's like he can't enjoy himself completely unless he returns the pleasure. And

CAGED BY HER DRAGONS

I suddenly crave to give in to him. To enjoy everything he has to offer.

Like he reads my mind, Rowan touches my chin, getting me to look up at him. He gently guides me closer to brush his lips to mine, pulling me back on top of him in the process. Hooking his hands around my hips, he doesn't let me turn around and instead drags me to his face, rushing right into kissing my clit without teasing me.

A moan escapes my lips, and I brace myself on the wall, his bed lacking a headboard. I scratch my nails into the white paint as he sucks and twirls his tongue in such a way that makes my legs shake. My body warms, every inch of me blooming with pleasure. I can feel it from my toes to my fingers and zinging in my middle. I gasp and pant, squirming so much that Rowan squeezes my thighs to hold me still. An orgasm builds in my body, sending a shudder quaking through me as I tense, my muscles seizing and humming and begging for the feeling never to end.

"I want more," I gasp, sliding myself down his body as he slows. "I want you inside me."

He releases a playful growl and tries to roll over, but I lean forward and lock my fingers with his, pinning him in place. He could easily outmatch me and use his crazy strength to take over. His eyes flash with orange fire like he considers it. The only thing that stops him is that I roll my hips, sliding my wetness along the length of his dick, teasing him like crazy until I'm ready to let him in.

Aligning his body to mine, I only allow him to sink into me a few inches as I straddle him on my knees. He moans, arching his back in an attempt to feel more of me, and I lean away, tipping my head back while bracing my hands on his thighs.

Rolling my hips, I thrust myself against him, the pressure from his thick girth making me gasp again. My body molds perfectly around his, each rocking movement of my body feeling more intense, hotter, crazy-fucking-amazing than the last.

"I want you to be mine," Rowan says, arching up to sit and face me. He kisses me passionately, rubbing his big, warm hands down my back to hold me by my ass, guiding me in a rhythm that sends an explosion of ecstasy to my bones. "I need you to accept it. You belong to me as I belong to you. I won't let any other clan have you. I will prove I'm worthy."

I hum my agreement under my breath, my mind cloudy with lust and need and something feral and deep-seated like my soul awakens with Rowan's words. A strange whirlwind of foreign emotions crashes over me, and I gasp and moan, the arising pleasure more intense than I ever knew possible. And I think it belongs to Rowan, his very being merging with mine, entangling our souls with the connection of our bodies.

"You're mine, Delphia. You're my intended. You're what will save the Dreki Clan by strengthening us." Rowan uses my real name, and it sounds so utterly sexy coming from him that I'm nearly certain I'd agree to anything. "Mine."

"I'm yours," I manage to gasp, riding him harder and faster, my whole body warming with another orgasm.

Rowan smiles and kisses me deeper, moaning and panting with my bursting screams of pleasure.

My muscles tense with my orgasm, and he pulls me to him, thrusting into me a few more times until he grunts with his release.

Rolling me over, he nestles his hips between my legs without pulling out. His weight presses me into the bed, and he combs my hair from my face to kiss me a dozen more times like he can't get enough of my affection.

"You're everything I ever imagined in our mate," Rowan murmurs, shifting off me only to lie close to pull me into his arms. "I need to know everything about you. I want to understand why you've been away so long. Why you were taken from our home."

If only I could answer his questions. There's so much about my life that I don't understand. And the people who raised me? Fuck. Who were they? I'm afraid I'll never find out. It was me who left them after all. I didn't give them much of a choice. I wanted a life without the constant reminder of my parents' deaths, and Galaxy Gold and the Sky Dancers gave me the opportunity. So I left, leaving only a note behind.

I trace my finger in a circle on his chest. "I wish I knew, but I've told you everything."

"Except your Magaelorum name." Rowan sits up on his elbow. "You said you changed it, so you knew your identity before." It's not a question. "What is your dragon clan name?"

I crinkle my nose.

"Your last name."

Damn. A part of me is afraid to say it. Quillon's warning pops to the front of my mind. I swallow my nerves and shift to meet his gaze. His eyes search mine as he reaches up and caresses his fingers over my cheek.

"I already know it, doe eyes," he says, "but I want you to tell me. I need confirmation."

"And if I don't? You know, rumor has it that the Drekis are at war with...my people?" I don't even know what to call those who apparently share my bloodline. "How do I know you won't murder me?"

"Because you're the woman who will bear my children." He smirks with his words. "And we'll have lots of them."

Ah, hell. I flop back and snatch the pillow from him to smother my face with it. His matter of fact tone digs into me. I mean, come the fuck on. He's crazy to think that I'll just agree to have his babies after so few days.

"We will not," I say, poking his chest. "Not as long as I'm in this place."

He groans and rolls back on top of me. "Are you sure?"

I play-smack his shoulders. "You obviously never want to have sex with me again, now do you?"

Sinking his weight on me, he leans in and kisses me, testing my body with his hard cock to see if I'll let him proceed. I dig my nails into his back, kissing him harder, pushing away the possible consequences of letting him have his way over and over again—but it's my way too.

Neither of us gets the chance to go at it again. The door to Rowan's suite flings open, and Maddox and Kash come waltzing in, unfazed by the fact that I'm in bed with their brother. Maddox quietly clicks the door closed and struts forward, his eyes meeting mine with firelight. Kash licks his lips, devouring me with his own heated gaze.

A groan escapes my lips as Rowan rolls off me. Because damn.

I'm torn between wanting to ignore Maddox and Kash to let Rowan continue, but a strange part of me yearns to ask them to join. Whoa. My body is crazy to think I could survive being ravished by these sexy dragon men.

"Get dressed, Delphia. Rowan." Maddox's words slice right through my wandering imagination.

Rowan growls and pulls me closer. "Can't you see that our mate needs more attention?"

Grabbing the blankets, Maddox rips them away. I screech and scramble off the bed, nearly eating shit in the process. Kash catches me, pulling me into his arms to bury his face in my cleavage, inhaling a deep breath of my scent.

"Another hour won't matter," Kash says, teasing me with his mouth. "Our mate is ready for more. Just smell how good her scent is." He grins and carries me with him as he holds out his fist to Rowan. "Nice job, brother."

"The hell it won't." Maddox closes the space to me and Kash and sandwiches me between their bodies. Ah hell. I tip my head back and rest it on Maddox's shoulder. He surprises me by brushing his lips to my temple, but he doesn't look at me. "She is the last Drakovich female. We need her to confront the lycan and get the information we want."

"The lycan?" I ask, bonking my head a few times so Maddox looks at me. "Like a werewolf?"

"Closer to a Mortal World born abomination and far from the wolves of Magaelorum," Maddox says, his cinnamon breath blowing against my ear with his words. "He knows things he shouldn't. You must get them from him." It sounds like a command.

"No," Rowan says, growling under his breath. "He is fond of her. He wants her."

Kash raises his hand to stop Rowan from attempting to

snatch me away. "But she is ours. She proved it. She let us claim her. Now, we must do this. The High Council won't see things as we do. She was convicted. It's the only way."

"The only way for what?" I ask.

"To get you from Magaelorum. We're going to break you free."

Chapter 15

Last Female Drakovich

"THE PRISON YARD? Alone?" I lick my lips, staring at the open door.

"He's in the pits. You can speak to him that way. You will be safer, and that way we can all hear what he has to say." Maddox presses his hand to the small of my back, giving me a small shove. "Don't argue, cookie. This is the way it needs to be."

CAGED BY HER DRAGONS

Him telling me not to argue makes me want to complain even more.

"And you won't be alone. I'm on yard duty." Kash pushes me forward next, stopping my rant from escaping.

Rowan comes up beside me. "We'll be nearby. You've got some fight in you. I'm sure you can handle yourself until we move the twenty feet it takes to get to you."

Swinging my hand, I knock his away before he pushes me forward and out of our block. Rowan chuckles and grabs my wrist, tugging me to him. His lips meet mine for a kiss, and I slide my tongue into his mouth, giving him a reason not to make me.

"Me next." Kash spins me away from his brother and cages me by the door with his buff arms. "I've been dying to taste your sweet lips."

"Dying? That's a little much." I smile and reach my hand up to tap his lips.

"It's torture not to take you right here, Delphia," he murmurs, leaning close.

"Let it be your punishment for using a name that no longer belongs to me. And for the crackers. Don't think I forgot about that." I graze my lips to his but pull away before he can deepen our kiss. "And expect more to come."

He purrs deep in his throat. "We'll see."

Kash smiles at me and moves out of the way. Maddox stands behind him, and I half-expect for him to haul me off my feet to throw me into the prison yard. Instead, he closes the space and crashes his mouth to mine, pulling me into his arms. And damn him and his fervent kisses that steal my breath away.

I drag myself away from Maddox and press my hand to his mouth. "Punishment is definitely coming your way."

Yanking my hand from his lips, he says, "I look forward to it. Now, time to be a good inmate and get your sweet, spankable ass to the pits and find out exactly what I told you to."

The world spins, and I clench my jaw and prepare for my not so elegant landing. I catch myself in a crouch, shooting up to my feet like I took a misstep during a performance. Straightening my shoulders, I meet Maddox's gaze and give him my show smile before raising my hand to flip him off. Rowan shakes his shoulders with a laugh, and Kash steps forward and into the shade of the building. He crosses his arms and nods his head at me in encouragement.

"I can do this," I mutter to myself. "I have to do this."

Because Maddox swears that once someone has been convicted of a crime and given life without a retrial, it's nearly impossible to get the High Council to change their verdict, especially with malleable minded human witnesses and no evidence that points to anyone else, even if we have Lazlo Infinity's name.

I make it all of a foot before a shadow flickers in my peripheral vision, and I tense. Fight or flee. Fight or flee. I chant the words in my mind, wondering what would be better to do. I'm afraid if I run, some asshole will turn me into a game of predator and prey and chase me. But if I try to fight, it'll put me in close proximity to someone who might be able to overpower me and then—

"Nova Noble, have you forgotten who I am already? What have the damn COs in your block done to you?" Rose's melodic voice draws my attention from the shadow where Kash lurks. "Come on, Sky Dancer. You can hang out with me. No one will bother you since most of these assholes shiver in fear at my presence alone."

The pink-haired fairy smiles at me, skipping to close the space. I exhale a long breath. I had no idea I'd be so relieved to see Rose, but having a familiar face nearby on my first real adventure into the prison yard helps out.

"As they should be, badass killer," I say, hoping she likes the nickname, considering how proud she was to tell me.

Rose ruffles her fingers through her hair with a stunning smile. "That's right. Let's see these assholes try anything. We lifers have nothing to lose." Spinning on her feet, she points at a nearby group of men, staring in our direction. "You hear that, boys? This bitch is mine. She's under my protection."

A soft growl resonates from the shadow where Kash

remains, and I can't stop the laugh from bubbling from my throat at his reaction. Rose is clearly joking, despite the deepening of her voice. Her wink at me proves it.

"I never in my wildest dreams expected to have a fairy godmother watching my back," I quip. "Especially not one with tattoos and clipped wings."

She swings her head to look at me, rolling her sleeves up. "These are the marks of punishment from the Spring Court of the Crystal Cove Territory for killing a prince."

I stare at the blue vines wrapping around her arms. "You killed a prince?"

She wags her eyebrows. "That bastard had it coming. We were promised to wed in a union to strengthen our court, but his ass enchanted a mortal and brought her to Magaelorum in an attempt to kill me, so he could choose another. That's how I know Quillon. He was the one involved in smuggling the mortal in."

I raise my eyebrows. "Wait, you're friends with Quillon even though he brought someone in that was supposed to kill you?"

Rose smiles with a shrug. "It was in our fates to meet. Had he not been the one to deliver her, I'd have been dead. He's...not exactly sneaky. His scared-ass thought it'd be better to show up in lycan form, which I'm glad for. While the court was busy obsessing over his intrusion, it gave me the chance to deliver the mortal to the prince myself. One thing led to another, and he bowed down to me. It wasn't my fault that he couldn't handle a little rough foreplay." She bites her lip as she says it. "It was a shame the poor mortal was bound to him and faced the same fate. I liked her."

I nod my head, because I don't really know how to respond to her. It all sounds a bit fucked up and like an accident, but she also doesn't show much remorse. But maybe that's a mortal thing. I consider asking, but a growl sounds from behind me. I turn to look over my shoulder at Maddox, who now looks ready to charge out here to get my ass moving.

Clearing my throat, unwilling to test his patience, I look to Rose and say, "Since you brought up Quillon, will you take me to find him? I think he's in one of the pits."

Rose narrows her eyes. "Again? Was this because of your ass? I told him to be careful because everyone around here seems to have blue balls because of you. No man in Magaelorum would ever allow a lycan to claim a woman, no matter if she's a murderer or not or if she likes him...which, do you?"

I grimace. "I—I don't know." I don't want to start things because she's his friend.

Rose steps closer and covers my mouth. "Your automatic answer should always be no. We're being watched. You could put Quillon in danger."

I swallow, my nerves starting to get the best of me.

"Put him in danger? The asshole put me in danger. And your question caught me off guard since you're friends. I don't like him. I want to kick him in the balls. Now, will you take me to him, so I can tell him so?"

A peel of musical giggles escape Rose's lips and she hops with the movement like she tries to fly despite the rings clipping her wings together. "It would be my pleasure."

I flick my attention to Maddox and stick my tongue out at him. Juvenile? Maybe. But totally worth it seeing his snarly reaction. Rose hooks her arm through mine and together we strut across the open field of the prison yard. Some guys workout and another group surrounds some men wrestling. The rest of everyone out here, which just seems to be the shifters and fae, lounge around. The asshole who wanted to make me his prison queen waves his fingers at me and blows a kiss. I snatch the invisible kiss and press my hand to my ass.

Rose laughs again and scoops a rock from the ground, chucking it far too fast in his direction for him to catch. It collides into his forehead and knocks him off the bench he sits on with a few others and onto the ground.

"Bow down before royalty, peasant." Rose drapes her arm over my shoulders. "This doll is off limits."

I frown and glance at Rose, wondering if maybe we've had a bit of a miscommunication, because she's acting as possessive as any of the shifters around here. I try to pull myself from her arm, but she digs his nails tighter into my shoulder.

"These douches only understand like three concepts around here. Don't touch what isn't yours. Fight to make it yours. And stake a claim," she whispers. "You—and those fiery dragon COs of yours will thank me later. Perhaps enough to get me something I want."

"Oh." I don't know how I should feel. Of course she would want something. I mean, she told me as much already. I'm just afraid that she'll flip a switch and act like the other inmates who don't get their way. Quillon is a big fucking example.

"It's the same thing you want," she adds. "To go to the Mortal World."

Shit. How the hell will I pull that off? Maddox will burst a cornea if I even suggest it...which means I should ask his brothers what they think first.

"I—I can try my best. I don't even know how I'm going to pull it off." I lower my voice. "It seems impossible."

She smirks. "Just promise me that if you go, you'll take me with you."

I know I shouldn't agree, but fuck it. If a fairy wants to escape this magical prison to run away to the Mortal World, I'm all for it. I could use a magical being on my side.

"If you promise not to plot Mortal World domination,

then okay," I say.

She laughs, tipping her head back. "Damn it. I was going to offer you a position on my new court."

I shake my head. "No thanks. I already have plans."

"That's too bad. Your dragon man-servants would have made great guardians." She slows down as we near the pits.

It's my turn to bark a laugh. Because really. I can't see the Drekis bowing or serving anyone. "Yeah, they are far from my servants."

"You just have to teach them. I'll help."

I don't get a chance to respond, because a groan sounds out from one of the pits. My feet automatically start walking without my consent. Straightening my shoulders, I put on my invisible armor and close the distance to the first pit.

It's not Quillon.

The unfamiliar inmate roars and tries to jump up to get to me but falls short. I stumble back in surprise, hating myself that Rose catches my ass before I hit the ground. None of the inmates close in around us, but I'm certain whoever is watching us saw it. Now I look like someone who can be pushed around.

Rose purses her lips and whistles softly. "Quillon, you here?"

She closes her eyes and listens, her wings trying to flap against the rings. I can't hear anything, so I strut past her, determined not to get scared by those stuck in the pits. Approaching the next grate, I peer down. Another man sits cross-legged at the bottom. He tips his head back and smiles at me with flared nostrils. Then the perv whips out his dick to get a rise out of me. I scoop up a handful of dirt and chuck it at him, getting him right in the face. Before he can react, I move back.

Rose laughs. "That was ugly. Please don't tell me that hideous man-worm is the norm among shifters. It was so...tiny. And hairy. The only thing the Spring Court prince had going for him was his delicious body."

"You're right about that thing being repulsive. And absolutely not. The Dr—" I snap my mouth shut, realizing the words about to fall out of me.

"So you have had some fun with the COs. I knew it. Babycakes over there thinks he's being inconspicuous, but I can practically feel the burn of his claim on you. Smell it too. You going to let them knock you up? Is that your plan after you get out of here? I bet you're coming into season soon, too. All shifters in Magaelorum do. It's fucking nuts around here when the Woodland Shadow pride females go into heat. One of them always manages to have a litter. Their pride still expects it and waits for the young to be released." Rose bumps her shoulder to mine. "At least your offspring won't have automatic life sentences."

Shit. I couldn't imagine myself getting impregnated as a mortal, and now? Fuck. The Drekis words about bearing their children flit through my mind. They live here. I'm imprisoned here. Rose is wrong. Either way, if that crazy shit happened...I can't even think about it.

"They won't anyway." Quillon's voice sounds through the air, coming from the last pit of the line. "We won't be here much longer. Her clan is coming to retrieve her."

I hate that he supposedly knew my mom. Quillon barely looks older than me, but maybe he doesn't age since he's a lycan. Fuck. There is so much I want to know about this world and all the creatures I thought were myths. I still can't wrap my mind around the fact that I'm supposedly a dragon. Or that I tore a man apart in that form.

"Oh, this is perfect," Rose says, clapping her hands. Skipping forward, she beats me to the grate covering Quillon's pit. "Remember, you owe me. If you plan to take Nova, I expect you to take me with you."

"We're not going to the Mortal World, Rose," Quillon says.

"You owe me. You will get me there," she snaps, trying to flutter her wings. Placing her hands on her hips, she looks ready to start a fight, the vine tattoos on her arms move and twirl, coming alive in her annoyance.

"You passed my debt onto Delphia already. You can't hold me to it," Quillon mutters.

Rose spins to face me, her eyes sparkling with pink light that matches the vibrant color of her hair. "He's right.

CAGED BY HER DRAGONS

You will take me with you and demand your clan get me to the Mortal World. Either way, I'm getting there and you will ensure it."

I blink a few times at the sudden depth of her voice. Wind blows around her, wafting a floral scent in my direction, permeating the air in a fragrance far sweeter than the earthiness of the dirt pits.

"I told you I would do my best. The Drekis—"

"I need your word for the Darkonian Clan too. They will be the ones to take you regardless of the Dreki claim. Our odds are far greater with the ones opposed to the High Council and willing to wage a war. If Quillon is correct, your bond will not matter. It's more than that. You will strengthen the clan your ancestors planned for you. It is the dragon way. It's a shame they didn't find a high priestess to sever any chance of you discovering your real mates." Rose steps away from the pit and holds out her hands to me. "But perhaps if you speak up, the Darkonians will help with your transition."

It's like once I grasp one concept, someone shatters it, mixing everything up. It sounds like some witch or warlock or whatever can go against the supposed fates the Drekis believe made me their fated mate. A part of me is intrigued by the idea that someone can change destiny, but another part of me aches with despair at the thought. It's so strange how I've already accepted the possibility of a future with these three sexy beast men.

"They will do more than that," Quillon says, drawing my attention back to the pit. "The Darkonians will ensure the Drekis will cease to exist. They will not risk their mate and their future bloodlines in hopes that magic can extinguish any sort of bond, especially since she has already allowed a claim."

Anger rushes over me, and I stomp my way to the pit and glare down at Quillon. He meets me with green-flashing eyes, his lycan form half peeking through his human exterior. Whatever magic Lazlo had intended for me hasn't worn off, and Quillon can still shift into his powerful monster form.

"I thought you'd have better standards than fucking the very assholes that keep you imprisoned here, Delphia," Quillon adds.

My anger ignites into fury, and I bend down and link my fingers to the grate. It's like the strength of the caged dragon inside me breaks free, and I manage to hoist the heavy grate up and toss it aside.

Quillon's eyes widen, and he backs away from beneath the opening of the pit to take cover against the dirt wall and out of my sight.

"Inmate, no!" Kash yells from somewhere behind me.

I jump into Quillon's pit, landing in a crouch with a thump. My dumbass doesn't have time to prepare, and

CAGED BY HER DRAGONS

Quillon crashes into me, knocking me onto my back. His face morphs with his glowing eyes. Fangs push over his teeth as they spread and widen with the formation of his snout. I gasp, his weight pressing hard against me. Snarling, Quillon slobbers on my face. I cringe and buck my body, trying to summon the same strength I used to open his pit. But my rage fizzles away, cooling with my fear. Raising my arms, I protect my face. Quillon tears at my sleeves with his fangs, ripping and shredding the fabric of my jumpsuit.

"Quillon, stop. Please, you're hurting me," I say, my breath gasping. "Please."

"You do that, Dreki, and I'll give her a matching scar to yours." Quillon's guttural voice sends a shiver through me. "I have a job to do. You will not get in the way of my freedom from this fucking world."

Claws cut into the flesh of my arm, and I scream in pain, my voice reverberating through the air to vibrate in my bones. Three deep, threatening growls rumble around the pit, shaking the ground beneath me. I can't see them, but I can sense Maddox, Rowan, and Kash surrounding us like my soul cries for them to help me.

"Release her, inmate. If you release her, we'll do you one better than giving you the freedom the Darkonians promised you," Maddox says, risking to move close enough that his silhouette blocks the sun shining from above.

"Nothing is better than that, unless you promise me

time with Delphia, so we can enjoy each other." Quillon's monstrous face softens as he shifts back into his human form. Locking his fingers through my hair, he pulls my head close enough that his lips hover a centimeter above my arm. Locking me in his gaze, he adds, "Wouldn't you like that, Delphia? They might claim you, but you can still spend time with me. I'd make you—"

Kash snarls and kicks Quillon hard enough that he rolls, taking me with him. I land on top of him, straddling his waist, but he still doesn't let me go.

"If you so much as move, you will never get the one thing you desire most in the world," Rowan says, coming up to my side. He places his big hand on my back, preparing to rip me off Quillon. "The Darkonians might have offered you freedom, but they'll never be able to give you what we have."

Quillon narrows his eyes. "The only other thing I want is Delphia."

This asshole.

All three Drekis close in around us, and Maddox glowers down at Quillon. "We can get you a cure. We can release you from the lycan curse. All you have to do is get us to one of the gates."

"You're lying," Quillon growls.

"Do you want to make a deal or not?" Kash touches my shoulder. "A cure for your help. No debts owed to anyone.

CAGED BY HER DRAGONS

The High Council will wipe your record clean and send you back to the Mortal World. They won't have a choice."

Quillon inhales a few deep breaths. "How do I know you'll keep your word?"

"I'll do a magic bind. If we fail, I'll bow down to you." Kash's words send panic through me.

"A cure or a dragon guardian," Quillon says to himself. Glancing up, he meets my eyes. "If they fail, I want some of your time as well. It's the only way I'll accept a deal."

"Done," Maddox says, cutting me off before I can even breathe a response.

"What?" I say, my heart pounding in out of control beats.

Quillon smiles. "Your mate also owes Rose freedom from here and entrance into the Mortal World."

"We are aware," Rowan says, speaking up.

"Good." Quillon releases my hair, and Kash scoops me up. "You have yourself a deal, Drekis."

Chapter 16

Power Plays

"FOR THE FIFTH time, hold still, damn it." Maddox shifts on the medical cot beside me and snatches my wrist, locking my hand between his knees. "I can't heal you if you keep moving."

Swinging my other hand, I whack him upside the head. "Just give me a fucking bandage and let me go, asshole."

He growls. "This requires more than that. A lycan's

scratch is toxic to us. It won't kill you, but you'll wish someone would cut your arm off if you don't let me take care of it. Stop being stubborn. I don't want to have to call one of my brothers in here. They will leave a scar. How do you think I got mine?"

I grind my teeth at the explosion of heat flitting across my forearm. "I don't care."

"Damn it, Delphia—"

I smack his head again. "That's not my name, Maddox. Quit calling me that."

"I will call you what I fucking want to. Now keep your ass still!"

My hair blows from my face with his yell, and I once again swing my hand out to slap him, annoyed as all hell that he keeps my other hand between his knees and looks ready to skin me with the shiny scalpel on the tray next to us.

Catching my wrist, Maddox laces his fingers around it to intervene. A rumbly noise escapes my lips, the sensation tickling my throat. Did I just growl? Fuck yeah I did. Since he captures my hands, I'm about to bite too.

Throwing myself back, I attempt to break Maddox's grip on me. The bastard is relentless, refusing to let go of me. I tug my arms so hard that my body screams in pain, yet I surprise the hell out of Maddox by yanking him forward. He catches himself on one hand, letting my hand go, but my other one rests between his legs, my wrist grazing against his junk. Freezing, Maddox stiffens, probably bracing himself for me to rip his damn dick off or something. His cinnamon breath blows in my ear, his heart pounding against mine.

"Get off me, and I'll let you go," I whisper, my voice coming with my pant at the sensation of his dick hardening when I shift my hand to grab him.

"You wouldn't," he mutters, leaning in closer.

We glare at each other, me beneath him, cupping his balls through his pants while he pins my other hand over my head, so close that he could kiss me with a short bow forward. My gaze drops to his lips, and I watch his tongue dart out as he licks them.

"Try me," I say. "You're a bastard and an asshole, and this could ensure I never bear your children."

"You want my children." His eyes flicker with firelight. "You want me in you now. You love feeling my body awaken for you. You enjoy how hot I make you."

I narrow my eyes even more, shifting my fingers to adjust my hold. "I don't. All that bullshit is in your head. It's you who craves me. I don't care if we ever have sex again."

"You can't lie to me, cookie. I can feel your desire. Smell your need for me. If there wasn't a magical mental block in place, I'm sure I'd be able to hear you begging me to fuck you senseless right this second." His dick throbs under my touch, flexing to tease me through his pants.

I suck in a breath and hold it so that he can't hear or feel my breathing pick up. Because damn it. How we can go from cold to hot in a single moment...it drives me crazy. I'm still pissed off at him—and his brothers, for that matter—and the last thing I want is for Maddox to think he can have his way with me whenever the hell he wants.

But maybe this is actually me. Maybe he's getting me all hot and bothered and pretending this is all for him when a part of my very being feels how I've weakened his steely walls. With enough of a nudge, I can break through, and it'll be him giving me whatever the hell I want. Which in this case is him.

Leaning up, I close the space between us but don't give in to a kiss. If he wants one, he will have to do it first. I will not be the one to give into my heated desire for him. I will tease him until he can't stand it a moment longer. I don't care if I provoke the beast within his muscular body. I want to see exactly what I do to him.

"Nova," he murmurs, his voice going soft.

It takes everything in me not to smile because he uses my Mortal World name. It's enough to tell me that he's seconds from giving in. Maddox might act like some tough-guy asshole—well, he might actually be one—but something about the fire in his eyes lighting just for me, how his heart picks up pace, thumping against mine, seemingly wanting to be closer, and how his fingers loosen around my wrist to cradle the back of my head shows that there is more to him than this. I just have to kick—or possibly fuck—his asshole tendencies out of him.

Starting now.

Stretching even closer, I graze my lips along his cheek to his ear and whisper, "You want to know what I'm really thinking, Maddox? Because it's not how much I want you to fuck me senseless. That's what you're thinking."

He hums a throaty response, the depth of his voice vibrating against my throat. "You're lying."

I tilt my head back to meet his gaze. "I'm not. What I'm really thinking is about how you're about to be mine. All fucking mine. And there is nothing you can do about it no matter how much you try to resist. How much you want to control me. You're mine, Maddox. You belong to me. Now tell me."

His hand tightens in my hair as he locks me in place. "No."

I graze my fingers away from his dick, gliding them up to his belt. I unfasten it with one hand and unclasp the button on his uniform. Maddox twists his hand more through my hair, training his gaze to mine. We stare at each other while I blindly navigate my hand into his pants until I find exactly what I want.

I can't lace my fingers completely around his thick

shaft, but it doesn't stop me from giving him a slow stroke. "Tell me."

His nostrils flare, his chest rising and falling. "I will not."

I tighten my fingers a bit more, his dick so hard and warm that my body sizzles with my raw need to give in first. "You're mine," I repeat, leaning in closer. "Tell me."

Maddox pants against my lips, the fire in his eyes flickering to smolder across his irises. He breaks under my gaze and bows in to crash his mouth to mine. Waging a war between us with a single kiss, our mouths fight to claim control, our tongues sliding and stroking against each other's. I work my hand over his dick, pulling it free from his pants to touch the length of his shaft. Maddox drags his hand from my hair and rips at the front of my jumpsuit, sending the buttons flying off.

I gasp as Maddox shreds my sports bra, destroying the fabric with one hand. Cool air sends goosebumps over my skin. My nipples tighten with desire, and Maddox rubs his hand across my breast, gently pinching my nipple between his index and middle finger. Breaking away from his mouth, I push him away and snag the front of his shirt to pull it up. He tears the buttons in one tug, giving me a view of his delicious chest. I bow into him and kiss his shoulder, working my way up to suck his spicy skin hard enough to mark him.

He spreads his fingers, rubbing his hand from my

breasts and down my stomach, dragging away my jumpsuit. "Are you ready for me?" he asks, slipping his hand into my underwear to discover the answer without waiting for me to respond.

I moan at the sensation of his finger drawing between my legs.

"You feel so good," he says, massaging my clit.

"Doesn't mean I'm ready," I say, grazing my teeth over his bottom lip.

He takes my bait with a playful growl, the first I've ever heard from him that doesn't sound like he wants to devour me but instead humor me. Standing up, he grabs my legs and pulls my body to the edge of the medical cot. Maddox finishes undressing me and kicks off his pants to stand between my knees. I reach for him, rubbing his raging hard-on until he kneels before me.

I shut my legs, trapping him in place. "You're mine."

The look he gives me sends a shockwave through me. "And you're mine."

I guess this might be as good as it's going to be in this moment. He didn't deny my claim, but I can feel that he's accepted it as a strange wave of emotions crashes over me. I shudder at the fiery and icy sensation rippling through me, stealing my breath.

"Fuck," I whisper. "What's happening?"

"I'm yours, Delphia. That's what that is. Now stop

playing games and give in to me. I want to make you scream my name." Maddox rests his hands on my knees, his eyes searching mine, and then he eases my legs open and kisses my thigh. "I want to feel the pleasure I give you deep in my bones."

Damn it, do I want to feel it too.

Maddox digs his fingers into my hips, keeping me in place as he trails a scorching line of kisses toward the apex of my thighs. I pant and squirm, combing my fingers through his long hair to play with the tresses as he flicks his tongue over me. I moan and tip my head back, closing my eyes to enjoy the sensation cascading over every inch of me.

"How can you be so good and such an asshole at once?" I ask, shifting my legs to rest them completely on his shoulders. "You piss me off."

All he does is growl in his throat, sending tingles from my groin and up to my hips.

"How can this ever turn into anything when I hate how much I enjoy you?" I dig my fingers into his skin hard enough to leave scratch marks. "I need more than just a claim on my body."

Maddox eases his mouth from me. "I plan to give you the world, cookie. But only after you cum for me."

Gracing me with a smolder of a stare, Maddox slips his finger inside me to add pressure before kissing and sucking and licking my clit with so much passion that my mind turns to mush, and I can't think of anything other than staying like this and getting pleasured by him for the rest of my life. His determination in this moment proves he's willing to do it.

I sit up a bit, clutching his head, straddling his face. Maddox releases one of my hips to rub his dick. Excitement rushes through me, seeing such a sexy sight, and then something strange happens. My body hums with a new sensation, but it feels foreign but inviting, rolling over me with Maddox's moan between my legs.

I grip his hair in my fingers with the intense rush of my orgasm, and I throw myself back and stretch my legs, my muscles tightening. Maddox kisses his way up my hip, linking his fingers through mine as he rises from his knees and to his feet. His mouth trails kisses up my stomach and he sucks my nipple into his mouth, making me gasp. I drag my hands down the front of his body, memorizing his flexing abs, tracing my way to his dick to align it with my body.

Maddox locks his fingers onto my shoulders and pulls me to him, entering me with a thrust I can feel penetrate my soul in a way that feels like we're two beings merging into one. His eyes light with firelight, his hands tangling through my red hair as he braces me in place to ravish the hell out of me. Stretching my legs, I open my body to him completely, moaning in loud breaths every time his pelvis meets my thighs.

CAGED BY HER DRAGONS

"You are so damn beautiful. I can't think about anything else except how I want to taste every inch of you over and over until you beg me for mercy," Maddox says, rocking his body to mine. Pleasure builds inside me so intensely that my mouth refuses to do anything but call out my ecstasy.

Our eyes remain locked on each other's, and I savor the look of enjoyment and how his hard features light up under my attention. He loves me watching him. He relishes how I flick my attention to his dick entering me to watch our passionate fucking. Something shifts inside me the longer we focus on each other, and another wave of his heat warms from my core.

And then my ears pop, and I jolt in surprise.

"She's so perfect. So sexy. I need to get her away from here before this place destroys the fire burning inside her." Maddox's soft voice trickles through my mind, surprising the hell out of me. I know it's my mind, because his lips remain pressed together, his nostrils flaring with his intakes of breath.

What. The. Fuck.

Maddox's eyes widen for a split second, the irises of his dark gaze now like smoldering embers with flecks of red and orange. Gasping, he sucks in a breath and moans, his hips stopping against mine as he holds me in place while he cums.

I nearly shove him back, because damn it. What are we doing? I can't believe I just fucked him without care toward the consequences again. Maddox wants to impregnate me for some crazy-ass reason that is beyond my scope of knowledge. And my dumbass refuses to even believe such a thing is possible. He's a man-beast. A dragon. But who am I kidding? He's one of the sexiest creatures I've ever laid eyes on, and in this moment, panting beneath him, I'm nearly certain that I never stood a chance. Maddox, in all his infuriating, delicious, asshole glory could probably impregnate me with just a smoldering look.

I'm probably pregnant already.

Shit.

Why don't I even care?

"Because you're our mate. It is ingrained in our beings—a deep-seated need—to blend our bloodlines and create a powerful future for us." Again, his voice enters my mind.

But it's not scary or intrusive. It feels as intimate as sex—no, not just sex—lovemaking. This strange new connection breaks the steel wall Maddox protects himself with, and I relax beneath him, something incredibly satisfying teasing my soul.

I inhale a slow breath, studying his face to see if this is all in my head.

"It's not." Maddox finally uses his voice. Scooping me

off the medical cot, he pulls me into his arms and kisses me. He grabs the sheet and wraps it around our bodies before lying with me on top of him. He touches my cheek, vying for my attention. "It's just all coming together as it should be. Kash must've finally gotten ahold of Rhett's coven for help to bypass the magic blocking our connection. Many shifters communicate telepathically, and the High Council doesn't allow it for better control."

I lean up and rest my forehead to his shoulder to break his eye contact. "This is all so—so confusing."

"I know, cookie. And I'm sorry." Maddox tilts his head, brushing his lips to my temple. "This was far from how I imagined meeting my soul mate."

I jerk my head back. "Soul mate? Are you fucking kidding me?"

His jaw twitches. "I know you feel the bond. You strengthened it with your acceptance of me. You let me into your mind. You want me as your future."

I purse my lips. "I'm sorry, Maddox. This is fun and all but I can't possibly know that. I know nothing about you apart from how you treated me like shit and now you act like I'm just someone to fuck. Soul mates are supposed to have more than a physical connection."

"We do," he says into my mind. Propping up on his elbow, he searches my eyes again and then bows into me, kissing me softly.

And damn it. I don't mean to kiss him back, but my body automatically reacts to his gesture like we've been kissing our whole lives.

"Maddox...no. No, we don't. We can't." I press my palms into his pecs, pushing him to get him to put some space between us. He doesn't relent, and the gesture sends fire up my arms with the force of trying to move him. I wince and swear under my breath.

"Shit," Maddox says, shifting his weight to his hip. "Look what you made me do." Snatching my wrist, he pulls my arm above my head to get a better look at it. "You seduced me and made me forget about the scratches."

Annoyance rushes through me. "Me? You're blaming me? I'd have never gotten them in the first place if you hadn't made me face Quillon."

"You should've controlled yourself." Maddox stands, leaving me on the cot with the sheet slung over me. "I can't intervene all the time."

Is he serious?

"I'm very fucking serious." Maddox's voice in my mind sparks heat through me.

"Stop doing that," I snap. "Get out of my head."

With a growl, Maddox whips his attention from the metal tray of instruments and to me. He swipes a scalpel and points it at me. His gesture should scare the hell out of me, but all it does is make me jump to my feet.

"It's time to finish this shit, so I can lock you in my brother's damn closet until he gets back," Maddox says.

"Why not yours?" I dodge out of his way and rush to the other side of the cot.

"You don't want to go there. It won't be to your satisfaction." He launches onto the bed to try to just jump over it at me. "I will have something you will like in the Mortal World."

I arch away, and he lands on his stomach. Before he can move, I bolt around the cot and smack him on his tight ass. I can't help it. I already know I'm facing defeat since I can't leave this room, and I might as well get in a few moves while I can.

He jerks his head up and raises an eyebrow at me. "Don't think I won't reciprocate."

"If you even try, you'll—"

Maddox swings his arm backward and grabs onto me, pulling me to the medical cot. He flips me onto my back and pins me down, straddling my waist. My damn body loves the sudden thump of his dick landing on my stomach with his movement. I never knew that wrestling a naked man was on my list of things I needed in my life.

"Stop fighting me, and I'll give you anything you want, Nova," Maddox says, his chest puffing with his breath.

I narrow my eyes at him. "I want to see where you live."

"Not happening."

I struggle beneath him, hoping my wiggling will drive him crazy. "You said anything."

"I didn't expect your response to be something so ridiculous. You could've asked for a ten-course meal, a massage, another round of fucking with you on top. Seeing where I stay is not worth your pain." His eyes soften, the fire extinguishing.

I close my eyes, trying to think of something, anything, that could possibly be worth my pain. "I want you to take me on a date. I mean, I want you and your brothers to take me on a date, get some wine, handfeed me something delicious that has been cooked properly—and I want you to answer any and all of my questions."

"Would you like us to end your date with immense pleasure?" He smirks as he says the words. "All three of us?"

I widen my eyes. I don't even know how to respond. The idea of having sex with all of them at once is...intimidating. "Uh—"

Heat suddenly bursts over the skin of my arm. I screech at the blazing flames, my skin stinging and smoldering as Maddox blows a breath of fire from his mouth. I hadn't realized he let go of one of my hands to grab a bottle of mystery liquid. Ripping the cap open with his teeth, he dumps the liquid over my fiery skin, extinguishing his dragon fire.

A whimper escapes my lips as the scent of cinnamon

wafts around us. Maddox bends into me, resting his forehead to mine. Our breaths mingle, our hearts beating out of sync, mine frantic and erratic, his slow and melodic. He continues to pin me, locking his eyes on me as I try not to cry at the diminishing pain on my arm. Because fuck.

He burned me, and now I worry about the aftermath. I once grabbed something hot off the stove without thinking, and my hand hurt for days. But this? This might be hell.

I blink my watery eyes, wishing he'd put space between us. "Maddox, please get off of me."

"Just another second, cookie. I know it hurts, but I don't want you to look yet." His lips caress mine with his words. "It's almost over."

I groan against his mouth and kiss him to try to distract myself. He returns my affection with feather-light brushes of his lips like he doesn't want to get carried away but also doesn't want to deny me.

By the time he eases away from me, the pain fades completely and my heart slows to beat in the same rhythm as his. His tight jaw softens, and he kisses my forehead before straightening upright and sliding off of me. I shiver at the cool air blanketing my body at the absence of his heat, but it doesn't last long because he pulls me onto his lap and faces me away from him to inspect my arm from over my shoulder.

"Beautiful," he murmurs to himself. "I just need to cut

off the residue, and we'll be done. This part won't hurt."

I gawk at what looks like claw marks filled with molten lava streaking across my forearm. How the hell am I not screaming in pain? It's the strangest thing. Maddox gently traces his finger along the ridges. He kisses my shoulder, showing me an unexpected gentle side that fills me up with contentment. Who knew I'd be so comfortable with a guy who has pissed me off every other second of my imprisonment here?

"But I need you to hold still," he murmurs. "Will you do that for me? I mean it, Nova. If you move, I could scar you. If I scar you, I'll kill that inmate asshole, and he's our safest bet to putting things into motion."

Just mentioning Quillon without even saying his name makes me tense. Not exactly because of Quillon and his messing with my life, but also because the Drekis made some sort of stupid bargain that churns my stomach to think about.

I open my mouth to tell him as much, but a knock sounds on the door a second before it swings open. Kash and Rowan enter the room, locking their gazes onto me as I remain naked on Maddox's lap. Maddox brought me to the prison infirmary to tend to my scratches, not to get me naked and screw me, but it's like my desire runs rampant.

"Feeling better, kitten?" Kash says, his face lighting with a smile. "I had no idea that the procedure required the lack of clothing, though I'm not complaining."

"Our mate loves testing me," Maddox says, carefully bringing a scalpel to my arm to cut at the corner of the strange molten scratch.

I close my eyes, expecting pain to follow, but nothing happens.

The cot shifts next to me, and Rowan's warm palm rests on my naked thigh. I open my eyes and flick my attention to him, the heat he creates growing to crawl up my body to send flush over my skin.

He dangles my ripped bra in front of me. "Looks like you put up one hell of a fight."

I try to suppress my smile and narrow my eyes. "Maddox was being an asshole."

"So you made love to him, kitten?" Kash says, his voice full of amusement. "You know that will only cause him to continue to be a dickhead."

Maddox chuckles against my shoulder. His hand remains steady as he uses the scalpel to peel away the residue of the scratch, leaving behind only slightly pinkish skin. I can't stop myself from smiling at his reaction, because his laugh sounds like music, considering how rare it comes.

"And I'll just spank him again," I say, tipping my head back against Maddox's chest. "I didn't realize how fun it is to put him in place."

Rowan tips his head back and laughs. "No one can actually put Maddox in his place. I'm sure he let you."

I shrug. "Doesn't matter. I got my way."

Maddox's body ripples under my words. "We compromised."

Wiggling my ass against his naked body, I tease him a bit. "No, I got my way. You couldn't resist. Now, you must stay true to your word."

"I—" An alarm blasts through the air, cutting Maddox off.

I don't get a chance to react as he slides me off his lap, drops his instruments back to the metal tray, and grabs his discarded clothes from the floor. Maddox groans and shakes his head, smacking his hand to a glowing pad on the wall, silencing the alarm.

"Kash, give me your shirt. The two of you take Nova to my place," Maddox says, buckling his belt. "I'll be there as soon as I can."

I blink a few times, watching Kash and Maddox swap clothing. "What's going on?"

Maddox sighs a heavy breath. "The warden just arrived. The alarm is calling all head COs on duty. Something is wrong."

"What do you think it i—" The lights turn off, leaving us in utter darkness.

A bright flash of blue light explodes through the air.

I lose my vision.

Chapter 17

Waging Wars

"WE'RE FUCKED," KASH says, dragging me from the black abyss of my mind. "Fucking fucked."

"Just take her to my place. I'll meet with the warden as planned." Warm arms shift me from somewhere cold and into the familiar embrace of Kash's arms. Maddox's cinnamon scent engulfs me as he presses a kiss to my forehead. "Rowan, get Inmate D64876. Bring him with you but do not let him near Delphia." He's serious if he's using my Magaelorum name.

"Be safe, brothers," Kash says, adjusting me in his arms.

I manage to flutter my heavy eyelids open, but my voice remains stuck in my throat. My limbs hang limply, whatever the hell that power blast was messed with me.

"I will protect our mate with my life," Kash adds. Curling me up, he kisses my temple. "I got you, kitten, okay? We're leaving soon."

Rowan moves in and kisses me softly. "See you shortly, Nova."

Static zips through me, lifting my hair around my head. Kash jogs us through a different door leading to who-knows-where in the prison. I suck in my bottom lip to stop my mouth from pouting and concentrate on pulling myself together. I have no idea what is going on, but a terrible feeling swells in my chest, seizing my heart.

"Someone is messing with the magical barrier," Kash whispers into my ear. "Things are about to go to shit."

"What?" The word barely sounds from my mouth. "Is it La—"

Pain rampages through my skull, making it feel as if my brain will explode at any second. I groan and bury my face into Kash's chest. He strokes his hand up and down my side but doesn't stop to check on me. My muscles bunch with my nerves, reacting to something in the air. It makes it

CAGED BY HER DRAGONS

harder and harder to breathe.

"Slow breaths, kitten. Try not to panic. What you feel is the crack in the barrier seeping into the prison. You'll be okay in a second when it fades. As for the rest of us...I want you to be prepared." Kash slows down and stops at a huge metal door. He eases it open, his hand glowing with dragon fire. "The inmates will take advantage and wage a war against the COs."

Of course they will. If something happened to the magical barriers, the inmates will take advantage. Hell, I'd take advantage if I were them too.

Before I can say anything, Kash shoves the door open and breaks into a sprint. He speeds across an unfamiliar lot and to a chain-link gate that divides this building of the prison from another one. Wind whips through my hair at his speed, and each gate we enter clanks closed behind us. I try to peer around to take in our surroundings, wondering where the hell we're going, because the prison looms behind us as Kash runs along the electrically charged wall.

Like Kash can read my mind, he says, "My brother's place is on the outskirts of the prison. He prefers somewhere to escape in his time off. We're almost there."

Kash shifts me in his arms, turning me to face him. I cling onto him and squeeze his waist between my thighs while dangling my arms around his neck. His hazel eyes sparkle in the glow of the setting sun, igniting a different sort of blaze in their depths. A strange need cascades through me, my body begging me to close the space.

Kash beats me to it, kissing me so tenderly that I want to bask forever in the softness of his emotions. Where Maddox is hot and cold, Kash is just pure warmth like settling into the best bubble bath. But I know under his cautious care lies fiery passion waiting to burst out. He can fill the needs of whatever mood I'm in without me even having to experience such a thing. It's just something that feels like a fact, one of our truths I now desperately want to discover outside the confines of this prison. I so badly want to get to know these dragon brothers on a level beyond the intimacy our bodies crave. My soul, heart, and mind have their own needs to be fulfilled.

"And I plan to satisfy every last one of them," Kash says, his voice trickling through my mind.

I gasp at his sudden presence in my mind and kiss him harder, wanting to hear his velvety voice again. It feels as amazing as Maddox's thoughts in my mind as he let me in.

"No, kitten. You finally let him in like you're letting me in now." Kash releases his hands from me to climb up a small, steep hill where it seems the land itself attempts to escape the prison. "The magic blocking our mental link has thinned enough that if you allow us in, we can speak to you as you can do the same to us."

"I can?" I ask in my mind.

CAGED BY HER DRAGONS

Kash nuzzles his nose to mine, not even looking at the surroundings during our ascent. It's not like he has to worry about falling, and me? I feel so safe in this moment. I feel freer than I have been since arriving here.

"Right now, you're completely open to me," Kash says. "It's the most incredible thing I've ever experienced. You have no idea how hard it's going to be not to make love to you to feel the intensity of our connection. Maddox is a lucky bastard."

Kash swings on one arm hard enough to launch the two of us into the air. I squeeze him even tighter, half-expecting to fall, but he lands in a crouch in the entrance of a cave. A fucking cave. Or I guess, a dragon's lair. I don't know what I was expecting, but it wasn't this, and—now it kind of explains a lot. I'd be moody too if I had to live in a cave.

Tipping his head back, Kash roars a laugh and sets me on my feet. "I wish Maddox was here to hear this."

I flush and cover Kash's mouth. "Don't you dare tell him anything. He suspected I'd find something wrong with this, and it's why he didn't want to bring me here."

"It is completely wrong. He's the leader of our clan. We should all live in luxury like our ancestors. The Drekis had huge palaces within enormous, impenetrable mountains with only the most beautiful things nature has to offer. And this bullshit? It's inadequate for a line such as ours but it is our duty to fulfill our end of the agreement our late leader had with the High Council. It's the only reason we guard this place." Kash spins me around to get a view of the penitentiary stretching out below us. It's much larger than I expected from this view.

"I don't think I understand," I say, wiggling in Kash's arms until he sets me on my feet. "So you really are kind of prisoners here?"

Lacing his fingers through mine, he tugs me away from the opening of the cave and deeper inside. "We are free to leave the premises when we're off duty, but we have another hundred and four years on our contract."

My eyes widen. "So a life sentence."

He smirks. "Maybe a quarter life sentence. We're not mortal, Nova."

So many questions flit through my mind. I don't even know where to start, but I know if I don't ask something else, I might lose my chance to do so. "Fuck. So this is worse than I thought."

"Not for long. It was one thing for you to be here, convicted under your mortal name, but it's another thing, knowing who you really are. It's what really pissed off Maddox, thinking that some witch fucked up our fates, sending us you, a murderer and criminal." He traces his finger along my jaw. "It was a hard idea to fathom."

"And you all thought I killed Rhett," I whisper.

CAGED BY HER DRAGONS

"Which I didn't."

"I know, kitten. It's all still a bit hard to believe he's gone. Not many could ever take him out and why they'd want to? Fuck, I don't know. I don't want to think about it. I need to keep my head clear." Kash closes his eyes and inhales a breath.

Sorrow washes over me as Kash's grief trickles into me through an invisible bond I can hardly grasp. I cup his cheeks and stand on my tiptoes, kissing him in an attempt to push the sadness for his lost friend away. I've been so concerned about myself, about getting out of here and getting to Kash, Rowan, and Maddox in a way they couldn't ever deny me that I've selfishly forgotten that their attitudes and meanness upon my arrival stemmed from them thinking I was the real monster. A part of me wants to hold onto their actions to remind myself that they could make my life miserable, even if they think I'm their mate, but a bigger, louder, more urgent part of me accepts their reasoning. It accepts that they had every right to want to torment me. But even so, I'm not sure if I can let go of the fact that none of them believed me.

Kash groans and tightens his arms around me. "Delphia—Nova, I...I wish finding you would have been different, and I'm sorry. I will regret how I treated you for the rest of my existence. It is a shame that will pass to our children as they discover what you've gone through only to be stuck with a clan that might not even deserve you despite the fates."

His response touches my soul as he listens in on everything that whirls through my mind. I can't decide if I'm annoyed or relieved that he manages to break through my guard to my thoughts since I'm incapable of even uttering a breath of a word in this moment.

Resting his head to mine, he adds, "But I hope we can earn your trust, your desire for a future with us, and maybe even one day your heart."

I lick my lips. "I don't know how to respond, Kash. You say things I can't wrap my mind around, and you sound so certain."

"I am certain," he murmurs against my mouth. "But I see you need convincing. Whatever spell that trapped your true self...I'll—we'll—do everything in our power to find out answers."

"But I don't even know the questions to ask. All I want is to go back to the Mortal World. Maybe find my Aunt McKayla to confront her." I puff a breath between my lips. "If it's even possible now. I lost touch after I up and left. It's hard to explain why I did, but I just had this need to leave. I wish I understood more."

A whistle sounds through the cave, drawing Kash's attention from mine before he can respond to me. He pulls me closer and moves deeper into the shadows, sandwiching me against the rock wall. Two silhouettes appear in the mouth of the cave, and I try to peer around Kash to verify with my vision what my instincts feel.

"Stand against the wall and don't move," Rowan says, shoving Quillon away from him hard enough to make him stumble. "If you so much as move, I will tear you in half and eat you."

I crinkle my nose at the thought. Because, gross. It makes me wonder if he's actually ever eaten anyone in dragon form. With my thought, a dozen more follow, and I feel as if I'll die from my curiosity.

"Like I'm fucking going anywhere without Delphia. She's the only one who I know will assure you dickwads follow through," Quillon says, his voice rumbling through the cave. "But your brother better hurry the fuck up. The Darkonians aren't the only ones who desire to possess Delphia. You guys are dumb and dense as hell if you think this is them. Infinity is breaking every last magical barrier around this place. He'll come for his prize next."

"And we'll be ready." Rowan's fiery eyes blink yellow against his shadowed silhouette. "Maddox is on his way. Now be quiet. I don't want to hear another word from you."

Rowan struts in our direction and away from Quillon. I push against Kash's solid form in an attempt to break out of the muscular cage he creates. He finally shifts as Rowan draws closer and allows me to dart past him toward his brother. The happiness at seeing Rowan surprises me a bit, but it doesn't stop my feet from running toward him. As I slow, Rowan moves faster, closing the space to lift me off my feet.

He groans as he kisses me. "I know you didn't intend to greet me with that gorgeous smile, but I'm glad you did. It gives me hope."

I ease from his arms before he—or should I say, I—get carried away. "You can be cautiously hopeful, despite the damn move you guys pulled making the deal with Quillon. Don't think I'm just going to ignore the fact that you've taken it upon yourselves to try to alter the course of my life."

Rowan hooks his hands to my hips, not allowing anymore space to get between us. "Hey, if you want to be mad at anyone, be angry with Kash. His bargain was far worse."

I nearly forgot. Fuck.

"And speaking of bargains, you better find the little princess, Kash. It's fucking every man for himself in the prison yard right now. I suggest you change." They're talking about Rose.

Kash hooks his fingers to the hem of his shirt and drags it over his head. "I'm already on it."

My eyes devour Kash's muscles as I blatantly ogle him. Fire lights his eyes, and he moves around Rowan to come up and press his chest into my back. His heat washes over me before his lips caress my throat, silently begging for me to crane my neck to kiss his mouth.

"Behave, kitten. If you're good for my brother, I will do anything you want when I return," he murmurs. "Hopefully more than answer more of your questions."

I giggle against his lips, savoring the light tease of his voice. "We'll see."

Dropping his pants, Kash watches me watch him undress completely. It's now that it dawns on me that by Rowan's suggestion to change, he didn't mean clothes but form. And holy shit. My heart hammers in anticipation, my body smoldering and buzzing. Excitement rushes through me at the memory of Kash in his dragon form and how incredible it is to see him in such a powerful, dangerous state.

He winks at me, his body awakening at my reaction. With a quick kiss and a surprise squeeze of my ass, Kash rushes toward the mouth of the cave, his body sparking with his dragon fire before he jumps from the cave and transforms midair. I run to get a view of him flying, but Rowan cuts me off before I can get within a dozen feet of Quillon, who remains lurking in his spot where Rowan demanded he stay.

"Mmm, you want me to take you for a ride again and not in the bedroom." Kash's voice sneaks into my mind. "I think we can—"

A screeching roar echoes through the air, shaking the cave beneath my feet. Rowan swears under his breath and snatches me to lift me up. He swings me around, and I automatically cling to his broad back, my body always ready for the unexpected while off the ground. He summons fire into his hands, his arms prickling with scales as he allows a part of his dragon to break free while remaining in human form.

"Kash?" I whisper in my mind, my thought soft and nearly inaudible even to me. "Kash, what's going on?"

"Rowan, move!" Maddox's yell erupts in my head so loud that I wince.

The ground shakes again and flames explode at the mouth of the cave. A huge dragon roars and breathes fire, clawing its way inside. Rowan jogs with me deeper into the cave and out of the way.

Blue electricity sparks through the cave, sending static into the air. Quillon tumbles across the stone floor as he tries to keep his footing. Dark hair sprouts from his arms and face, his lycan form taking control. A deep growl reverberates through the cave, and if I didn't know any better, I'd think Quillon was attempting to protect me from some force I have yet to see.

"Get her out of here. Take the back." Maddox's huge head swivels in our direction, his glowing eyes meeting mine.

CAGED BY HER DRAGONS

"But her brands," Rowan says, his words mingling with Maddox's in my mind.

"All barriers are down. It'll be at least ten minutes until someone gets them back up. Now go!" Maddox blows a hot breath of fire across the floor shooting it in a circle that cuts us off from the mouth of the cave. More blue electricity zings through the air, and Maddox roars again and launches toward the sky.

I don't get a chance to see him go. My heart sinks into my stomach as Rowan yells for Quillon to move his ass, and the three of us head deeper into the cave. Firelight illuminates the dark cave, allowing me to see the vast space, sparse of basically anything. A king bed rests untouched and off to the side with a dresser and wardrobe. I think a bathroom sits nestled within another cave, but I can't be sure. Apart from those things, all I notice is a grand circular carpet. Nothing else.

"My brother prefers to sleep in his fiercest form," Rowan comments, focusing on me. "It helps him remain guarded out here."

I can't help wondering what it would be like to wake up to that. To wake up to any of them for that matter.

A rumble quakes through the cave, pushing my thoughts away. Rowan grunts and shoves Quillon out of the way as a basketball-sized rock comes crashing down from above.

With one hand, Rowan drags Quillon up, half carrying him until he regains his footing to keep up. The cave narrows the deeper we run through until soft light trickles from the purpling twilight of a large crevice in the rock wall.

It's barely big enough for one person, and Rowan and I can't fit together, so he sets me on my feet. Linking our fingers together, he squeezes my hand like he's afraid if he doesn't grip me tightly enough, I might somehow disappear. He forces Quillon out of the cave ahead of us and then slides through the crevice before me, shuffling sideways to squeeze his hulking frame through.

Fear sneaks up on me at the cool wind whipping my hair in front of my face. I thought the mouth of the cave was high up but it's nothing compared to this.

Dense forest stretches out far below, disappearing into the darkening sky. The bright moon shines above, casting silver light over Rowan's hair. I meet his gaze, his eyes flashing with blazing fire. With one hand, he starts unbuttoning his shirt. I realize he plans to transform into a dragon to fly us down.

I shift on the small ledge that drops straight down onto jagged rocks and carefully slide open Rowan's belt to speed up the process. He groans under his breath, rolling his shirt between his hands, watching me undress him.

"Next time you undress me will be for something more fun," Rowan says, his voice remaining even, light almost,

CAGED BY HER DRAGONS

like he's trying his best to assure he doesn't do or say anything to make me panic.

Quillon growls. "Hurry up already."

I glower at Quillon, letting Rowan brace on my shoulder to kick his pants into my outstretched hand. "Do you want me to knock you off this ledge?"

The ground beneath us shakes, and something explodes from our right. Quillon yells and tries to brace himself on the rocks, but the ledge crumbles beneath him. I screech at his fall, panic lashing at me. I don't even get a chance to think as Rowan slings his arm around me to jump with him.

He launches into the air, and I hold my breath for a split second before a blast of pain rips at my scalp. Rowan loses his grip on me, letting me go.

My back slams into the side of the cliff. I gasp with the force that steals the breath from my lungs. Tears blur my eyes, and I can't focus on anything except Rowan's massive form taking flight.

The world zooms around me, and I shriek in agony at the intense pain brought on by the glowing hands tangled in my hair. Someone drags me up and back to the cave. The rocks slice and scrape my back. I can't stop the tears from trickling from my eyes.

I land on the warm rock floor, and a figure materializes above me. Blue electricity flickers in Lazlo's eyes as his face sharpens in my view. A sadistic smile curves his lips. He has the gall to press his shiny shoe into my stomach hard enough to make me gag.

"Get up, Delphia. Don't make me spell you. It's far easier to transport you if you just comply. If you don't, I will stop your heart this second." Lazlo unsheathes a golden dagger, sparkling in the firelight.

I lock my fingers to his leg, trying to yank it out from under him. "Fuck off. I'm not going."

Lazlo narrows his eyes and aims the dagger at me. "Difficult like your bitch of a mother. Last chance. Stop fighting or die."

"Nova, fight!" Maddox yells, his voice ripping through my mind.

Fire explodes through the cave, sending heat through my body.

"Fight!" Kash says, his voice swirling with Maddox's.

I gasp at Kash's presence, my body reacting to realizing he's okay.

Lazlo growls and grabs the front of my shirt, hoisting me upright. I flail and punch, swinging my arms, doing whatever I can to get him to let me go.

Electricity ignites in his free hand, and he drops it onto my legs, zapping me with power. I screech and thrash as my muscles pulse and shudder. I fall to my back with a thud, the pain hard to push through.

CAGED BY HER DRAGONS

"Nova, please. Don't stop fighting," Rowan says, his voice sounding low and whispery in my mind. "Don't let him take you."

I summon my strength and launch myself forward, tackling Lazlo around his legs. He falls back under my attack, hitting the ground hard. I claw my way up his body, my veins glowing like lava. Heat cascades over me, and I feel as if my dragon will burst from me at any second.

Reaching down, I grab the front of Lazlo's shirt and prepare to punch him in his face. He intercepts my hand, his strength enough to make me scream. He squeezes my fingers, the intense pain shadowing the edges of my vision. If he doesn't stop, he'll break my hand.

"Stop fighting," Lazlo commands, his eyes glowing with blue power.

"Never," I say, gritting my teeth. "Just let me the fuck go."

"I didn't want it to be this way, but you left me no choice, Delphia." Lazlo shoves me off him, tackling me to the ground.

A roar echoes through the cave, followed by another and another as the Drekis close in on us. Heat wafts through the air, the scent of cinnamon giving me the strength to swing my arm and punch Lazlo in the throat.

But I'm too slow.

Locking his fingers to my wrist, he pins me down. I

don't have a chance to scream or plead for my life. I can't even think about the Drekis' names. I close my eyes and brace for the gold dagger to end my life.

Lazlo jabs the blade into my stomach, and I scream.

I pray for a swift death.

CHAPTER 18

Prison Break

I BLINK IN and out of consciousness, the pain coursing through every molecule on my body making it impossible to remain awake. The cool darkness of my mind is as sweet as what my death that never came was supposed to be.

A soft cry keeps me from fading away, and I roll onto my side. The deep ache in my belly forces me to curl in on myself. I breathe a deep lungful of stale air, focusing on listening to my surroundings. Water trickles from somewhere nearby, and the hum of power creates static in the air. The scent of dirt, earthy and green, leads me to believe I'm somewhere outside. Perhaps the expansive forest surrounding the prison. But I can't be sure. I'm not even sure if I'm truly alive or not. I felt the blade stab into me. I felt something inside me sever, my soul feeling as if it abandoned me to drop my body into this hell.

"We must cross now," a feminine voice says, snapping my attention away from the soft crying. "They are already on the hunt. The magical barrier around the prison has been restored. You underestimated the High Council, Lazlo. Not to mention how the sky now thunders with guardians in search of Delphia."

"I need time. Collect on every debt within those blasted walls if you have to. Create as much chaos as you can to keep the Drekis away." Lazlo's cool hand slaps my cheek. "I can't have them involved."

I try to remain still under his unwanted touch.

"It's not the Drekis circling the skies. They're not the only ones searching for the Drakovich descendant. It's another clan." The woman's voice lowers in annoyance. "Why you chose to take this one is beyond me. You should've let her rot."

"Considering she is much like her mother, I find value in her," Lazlo snaps. "And obviously there is something about her that we might find of some use since the dragons gather. We could use her to our advantage and proceed with our plan. The High Council will be far too concerned with this mess that they won't even realize what's about to come."

"I trust you, brother. Do not fail us." A strange smoky scent, followed by a burst of white light, turns my vision red. The woman vanishes, leaving my mind reeling.

Cold fingers dig into my chin as Lazlo grips my face and jerks my head toward him. "Open your mouth. I need you in better shape."

I clench my jaw, not giving into his demand.

The fucker digs his nails into my cheeks and shoves his fingers to my lips, prying at my mouth to get me to open up. I thrash under him, refusing to stop fighting just like the Drekis told me, and contort my leg to hook it around Lazlo's neck from behind, pulling him closer to me. Jerking my head up, I head-butt him in the chin. He grumbles and jams his finger into my stomach wound, sending agony through me.

I scream, only to have Lazlo shove something strangely sweet and sticky, and hot as hell, in my mouth. He slaps his hand over my lips, forcing me to swallow the gross lump of jelly-like substance.

"If you'd prefer to do things the difficult way, I could cut off those brandings and see what happens." Lazlo grabs my wrist, freaking me out. "It might give me enough time to get you through to break the barrier. The gate will not be able to withstand the interruption in power and the force of the Drakovich dragon breaking free. So what would you prefer? I don't care either way. I will get what I want from you. Now eat more."

Lazlo pinches another piece of jelly substance between his fingers and hovers it to my lips. I reluctantly open my mouth and let him place it on my tongue. I gag at the overly sweet flavor, but he's quick to cover my mouth, forcing me to swallow.

Lazlo links his fingers to the front of my jumpsuit and pops open the buttons on my middle without asking. I whack him as he tries to unfasten one over my breast, making him laugh. Pressing his hand to my chest, he pins me in place and slips his hand across my stomach. I cringe and buck my body, repulsed by his touch.

"Oh, stop it. Dragons aren't my type. I was only checking to see if your wound healed since you had to be so difficult." Lazlo locks his hand to my wrist and yanks my hand up to get a closer look. "I will barely have time to take care of these, but first..."

Tugging a collar from a bag, he wraps it around my neck before I can fight. It locks in place, scorching my skin with magic. The pain thankfully fades as quickly as it did with the brands, but my muscles tense and shudder, reacting in a way that sends panic through me.

"There. A collar to tame your beast. Now, hold still so I can deactivate your brands." Lazlo gets to his feet and waltzes a few feet away.

I turn my gaze to him, wondering if I can manage to scramble to my feet while his back is turned. A cry sounds over my heavy breathing, and I gawk at Rose, curled in on herself, blood dripping from her chest and a sparkling silver substance trickling from her un-clipped wings, the rings ripped off.

"I bet this trickster fairy regrets bargaining with you over her escape now," Lazlo says to me with a wicked grin. Rose whimpers as he drags her to her feet by her wings. "Lucky for you, Delphia, you will no longer have a debt with her. She will serve us well."

Digging his fingers into Rose's wings, he coats his hand in the glittering liquid substance. Rose glowers and fights against Lazlo, but he's far too strong for her. A part of her wing disintegrates under Lazlo's touch. My heart slides into my stomach, my whole body reacting to the pain he puts her through.

"Brekiticha vulosa mahiter explusiviton," Lazlo says, deepening his voice. His eyes light with blue electricity at the foreign words not from the Mortal World. Power hums through the air, zinging through me. In the distance, thunder claps, and a bolt of lightning crackles across the sky.

"Delphia Drakovich luminatisto fyreh nekorb."

The brands on my hands erupt in red light. My skin sizzles and smoke wafts, but I don't feel any pain.

"Eerf reh tes morf eht nogard avallisito batinitestia!" A flash of light blinds me with his words, and the world disappears for a few seconds, maybe a few minutes.

Energy hums through me, my spirit broken and seemingly spread nowhere and everywhere. Heat flourishes through me, burning from my hands and up my arms. My muscles ache with a need I've never felt before, and they clench and relax to the erratic beating of my heart.

"Delphia, you are free of the binds in which they contain you. Open your eyes, beautiful beast and let me see your dragon fire." Lazlo's voice booms through the air with another clap of thunder.

Snapping my eyes open, I stare at the world, now hazed and glowing with strange magic like I can see the life force in everything around me—from the shrubs to the trees, the bugs, the animals in the sky, everything. Confusion washes over me at the view of the world. Where I looked up at everything before, I now see into the treetops. Lazlo claps his hands from below, and fury rushes through me.

I open my mouth to scream, and with my breath explodes a stream of mesmerizing fire that swallows Lazlo whole for a second until it fades and he reappears, holding a ball of dragon fire in his hands. It's now that I realize what the fuck is going on. The world has changed because I have changed. I'm no longer Nova Noble of the Mortal World. The cage in which the High Council contained me has been shattered, allowing my dragon—my true self—free. With certainty, I now know the truth of my existence. I am a dragon. I am the last female descendant of the Drakovich Clan. I—

Something tightens around my throat, stealing the thoughts from my mind. Lazlo stands in front of me, stretching his hands out as a glowing chain made of pure magic lashes from his hands to encircle me. His form shifts with his use of power, his mouth widening with fangs intended to protrude from the jaw of a beast and not a man. Wrapping the magical chain around his arm, he yanks it, dragging me forward. My dragon body tips, my mind struggling to process how to even move, and I land on my belly, shaking the ground around us.

"Relax, my sweet beast. Obey me and you'll be fine. We will break through the gate soon." Lazlo rests his palm to my snout.

I should be scared. I should be pissed off. But a huge part of me anticipates Lazlo opening the portal to the Mortal World. Why he needs me to do this, I have no idea. All I know is that I can't wait to leave Magaelorum. Lazlo can't possibly control me forever. I will figure out how to end him and return home.

Huffing a smoky breath through my nostrils, I refrain from trying to devour Lazlo. He returns my lack of action with a smile and turns his back toward me. Extending his arms, he raises them out and over his head. Magic crackles between his glittering palms, still coated with Rose's blood. She floats to her feet, not touching the ground, locked in some sort of invisible trap. Her head lolls, and I can't stop my heart from screaming as Lazlo shoots his power at her, igniting her in electric light.

"Eaf esor springitivia proburositolorum," Lazlo says. Energy swirls through the air around us, blowing a breeze to lift Rose's hair and sending her silver blood into a magical tornado. She gasps and yells, her musical voice echoing through the air.

"Nova! Nova use your bond. Call to your mates. They will find yo—" Rose screeches with another blast of Lazlo's power that lights up her entire body. Brilliant blue light explodes from her as her form disappears into a cloud of sparkling magic.

Oh, fuck.

A roar escapes from my dragon mouth, the rumble quaking the world around us. Lazlo spins on his feet to face me, gathering more power into his hands, flicking it around me again in a chain that catches my muzzle, silencing me.

"Delphia, granto lassolioliem encantran flittin lunaromelious trecatal!" Lazlo shouts the words, yanking on the

CAGED BY HER DRAGONS

magical chain. "Your beast is mine!"

"No!" I scream the word in my mind, fighting the best I can against the restraints Lazlo drags toward the brilliant light that consumed Rose. "I'm not yours. I don't belong to you. You can't have me! I belong to the Drekis. I am theirs."

The electric chain wrapping my snout snaps free, recoiling toward Lazlo. His eyes widen, and he dodges out of the way of my wrath. A strange smoky scent wafts through the air, and thunder claps in the sky—not thunder, the wings of dragons. The ground shudders beneath me, trembling at my fury.

Jerking my neck, I break the chain from my collar, and it whips around with my movements, sending fire cutting across the ground. Lazlo's too slow to dodge it, and the buzzing chain collides into his legs. He falls off his feet and lands on his back with a thump. He howls in pain, using his arms to protect himself. A cage of power blocks my fiery breath, but I refuse to stop fighting. I'll rip him in half like he claims I did to his brother. I will ensure he never hurts anyone again, but especially not me.

My claws scratch into the ground, leaving deep crevices as I close the distance. Lazlo bares his teeth and manages to push up on an elbow. He shoots power at me, knocking me back. I shriek and thrash, whacking trees out of my way. This form is far too big to get used to. I have wings and a tail and four legs instead of two. A long neck and pearlescent red and orange scales. All of these things slow me down instead of turning me into the agile, flexible Sky Dancer of Galaxy Gold's.

Lazlo throws another blast of power at me, and then another and another. My chest tightens, my veins cooling. Ice drips through my body to replace the molten lava flowing in my soul. I try to breathe fire at him, but only steam escapes my mouth. Something's wrong. He's putting out my dragon fire, stealing every ounce of my warmth.

"Nova, fight. Get up and fight." Rowan's gruff voice hums in my mind.

Maddox growls, his presence in my head vibrating to my very soul. "Don't you fucking stop, cookie. Show him he can't tame you."

"Show him the strength and power only found in the Drekis' mate." Kash's wave of determination floods me, pushing my dragon form to straighten its shoulders and meet Lazlo's glowing eyes.

Something hot and fiery and indescribable explodes in my core, battling the cold washing through me from Lazlo's magic. Fear widens Lazlo's eyes, and his magic falters, sputtering out with my roar that blows all the leaves off the tree behind him. Smoke pours from my nostrils a second before the smoldering dragon fire inside me bursts free more powerful than I've been able to manage. Lazlo curls in on him-

CAGED BY HER DRAGONS

self, yelling through the white and yellow flames. The world trembles and he vanishes into thin air.

I drop to the ground at the exertion of summoning all of my strength. The brilliant light of the portal remains illuminating the world around me in a soft glow. Blinking the haze from my eyes, I lose myself to the magic, feeling it hum through the air. The soft voices of the Dreki brothers trickle through my mind, far quieter than they had been.

"Nova," a soft, melodic voice says. "I need your help. Please, get up. You have to get up."

Rose's voice draws me from the swirl of the Drekis' emotions coursing through my soul. Fluttering my eyes open, I stare at the moon above me and watch as a dragon speeds across the sky, breathing fire into the wind. Panic rushes through me at the sight of the unfamiliar beast, though I'm not sure he can see me now in my human form below.

"Nova, come on. It's closing. We have to hurry," Rose says, her voice drawing my attention from the sky. "It might be our only chance to leave Magaelorum."

"But the Drekis—"

Two clawed hands snatch my wrists, yanking me from the ground, cutting off my words. My world jostles, my body refusing to put up much of a fight as my back rests against a furry chest. Quillon restrains me against him, his arms resting under my naked breasts, his hairy nether region

~327~

grazing my ass, but I don't feel his dick.

"This is our only chance. We gotta move," Quillon says. "Don't fucking fight and trust me, Delphia."

I buck in his arms, jerking my head back in an attempt to break from his hold. "How the fuck are you here? Let me go, asshole."

"Not until we cross." Quillon slings me under his arm, ignoring that I slap and punch his furry leg, ripping and pinching, doing anything I can think of to get him to release me. But I'm either too weak or he can take a lot of shit in his lycan form. "Rose, give me your hand."

Rose groans from the ground, her skin as pink as her hair. She struggles to lift her arms to get help from the ground. Quillon drags her up and curls her over his shoulder. I can't stop myself from jerking to meet her gaze. Silver blood drips from her nostrils, pointy ears, tear ducts, and the corner of her mouth. A part of me aches to see her in this condition but another part of me screams that these two aren't my mates. They don't care about me and will try to use me in the Mortal World.

Reaching out her hand, Rose touches my cheek. "You'll feel better once we cross. Brace yourself, Nova. It's about to get really cold for you."

Quillon rushes us into the brilliant light, the world turning white like color and darkness no longer exist. My heart screams in pain, feeling as if it severs from my body. I

CAGED BY HER DRAGONS

gasp and yell, my muscles tensing. Something feels utterly and completely wrong. My mind and soul beg and scream and cry for me to break free from Quillon because if I don't, I think I might just die. But my body refuses to cooperate, fading with my exhaustion.

The world shifts with a wave of ice water. It swallows us whole, stealing my breath. My lungs burn with the need to breathe but if I open my mouth, I will inhale the sparkling blue water and drown. I can't even get my arms to swim. If Quillon were to let go, I'd get dragged into the blue depths of this strange body of water.

I think I pass out.

One moment, my eyes burn while my body trembles, and in the next, everything turns dark. The darkness consumes me for what feels like eternity or seconds or who the hell knows how long. Time stops in the darkness, the glow of the light now gone. Loneliness consumes me, and I wonder if this is it. If this is the true prison of my existence. I wish I knew what I did to deserve such a fate. I wasn't a bad person. All I wanted was to live my life free from things that bound me. I just wanted to live.

I still want to live.

A wave of heat cascades over my spirit, lighting the darkness threatening to imprison me forever. Warmth blossoms from my chest to flow through the rest of me. Relief and happiness and something unlike anything I've ever felt wraps me in a blanket of emotions that I know don't belong to me.

"Again," Maddox says, his voice sounding in my ears. "All together."

Bright flames light the air above me, warming the remaining ice in my veins. Three silhouettes hover around me, and feeling returns to my body. Rowan and Kash each hold one of my hands while Maddox cradles my head on his lap. Their fiery eyes rove over me, searching me from head to toe.

I squeeze my eyes shut, clearing my vision from the water still dripping from my hair. Is this real? Are Maddox, Rowan, and Kash here or am I fantasizing it?

"If you were fantasizing, kitten, it would be a lot hotter than this," Kash says, responding to my thought. He squeezes my fingers and pulls my hand to his mouth to kiss my knuckles. "You wouldn't be the only one naked."

I bolt upright, but Maddox doesn't let me get even a few inches of space between us. He pulls me close, nestling me between his legs. I sink into his embrace, my body wanting nothing more than for him to continue to hold me like this. Rowan scoots closer and drapes his big shirt across my naked body and sandwiches me to Maddox like he can't resist.

"I love your doe eyes, but I never want to see them so scared again, Nova," he whispers, easing back only to meet me for a kiss. "I'm sorry I failed you. Lazlo should've never gotten within arm's reach. Inmate D6—Quillon's ass might've survived the fall despite my intervention."

I tense at Quillon's name. "Fuck. Quillon—"

"Saved your life, Red," Quillon says. "I also kept up my end of the bargain. I got you all through. Now it's time to pay up."

My eyebrows shoot up on my forehead. "What?"

Maddox releases a growl and gets to his feet. Kash takes his spot and nuzzles his chin into the crook of my neck, snuggling me close. His cinnamon breath sends a good shiver through me, but it quickly dissipates at the sight of Maddox balling his fist.

"We owe you nothing. You didn't open the gate," Maddox says, his voice echoing through the quiet forest. It looks strangely like the one outside the prison walls, but something is off. The night seems duller, the moon doesn't shine as bright, and I can't see many stars through the sparse trees.

"But I brought her through," Quillon says. "I helped you free her. The deal stands. You owe me a cure."

Rose hums, drawing my attention to her as she leans against a tree trunk. "He's right, Drekis. If you fail to hold up your end, your brother will bow and he gets a piece of Nova."

Maddox responds with a holler, grabbing Quillon by

the front of his shirt to hoist him off his feet. A loud crack sounds through the air, startling me. Maddox drops Quillon to the ground in time to turn toward the noise coming from the trees.

Electric purple light ignites out of nowhere, spiraling in his direction.

My muscles tense and spasm at the sight of an unfamiliar man blasting his way toward us through the forest. The world shifts, an ache shuddering through my body as my dragon breaks free.

The man stops in his place and cocks his head at me.

I open my dragon mouth and engulf him in vibrant flames. My dragon craves to consume him completely and to protect the Drekis. In this moment, they feel like the most important things in the world to me—at least to my dragon.

"Delphia, stop!" Maddox rushes toward me, facing the wrath of my fire to get between me and the unfamiliar man. "Stop. It's okay. He's a gatekeeper. Rhett's coven brother."

"I felt the collapse of the shield. What the fuck, Dreki? There isn't a gate here," the man says, stepping closer.

I release a growl from deep in my throat, my dragon-self needing this guy to stay the fuck back from Maddox. My overwhelming desire to protect him surprises the hell out of me. Maddox swivels on his feet and raises his hand, backing until I shadow over him and he can rest his palm to

CAGED BY HER DRAGONS

my belly.

"Down, cookie," he says, tipping his head up to smile at me. "I have this under control. Be a good girl and try not to murder him. We just got you out of Max. I'd prefer if you didn't drag any more damn attention to us."

His scolding annoys me, so I stretch my long neck to curl my head around to face him. The fucker continues to smile and has the nerve to lean in and kiss me on the nose. I huff a steamy breath and nudge him hard enough to send him falling on his ass.

Rowan laughs. "Time for payback, brother."

The man clears his throat. "One of you get her under control before I link to the damn collar on her neck and do it for you. This area isn't protected, and the last thing I need is to deal with a mortal stumbling upon a damn dragon out here."

Kash releases a guttural noise from his throat, stomping from his place. Neither Maddox nor Rowan stop him as he swings his arm and uppercuts the man, knocking him off his feet. "Touch her and I'll rip your head off. She doesn't know how to control it yet. She didn't grow up in Magaelorum nor does she know her clan. Now get your ass up, apologize to Nova, and get that damn magical collar off her, Baker."

Kash shoves his hands into Baker's chest and pushes up. Rowan intervenes, ensuring the warlock doesn't retaliate and offers his hand to him, helping him to his feet. Strolling up next to Maddox, Kash rests his palms on the side of my face, hugging me like it's no big deal that I'm in my towering dragon form.

"I know you're on the defense, but it's going to be okay. I swear on my life that I won't let anything happen to you." His voice trickles into my mind, prodding at the imaginary steely shield protecting me. "Close your eyes, kitten. Close your eyes and just imagine the form you want to be in. It's that easy. Your dragon will listen."

I huff out a breath.

"Stop being so damn stubborn and do it," Maddox says, patting my snout. "Don't make me transform and make you."

Kash play-punches his brother. "Knock it off. She loves testing you."

Motioning for Baker to stay near Quillon and Rose, Rowan joins his brothers. He offers me a smirk and shoves between them to rest his hand on my chin. "If you transform, I'll pin Maddox down and you can punch him in the cock for his bullshit...or I'll let you pin me down and you can have your way with me."

"And I'll join," Kash says, teasingly. "But you have to transform into your sexy, mortal form or we'd risk turning this forest into fields and the hills into valleys."

Maddox groans and rests his forehead against my scaly

skin. "Close your eyes and remember that you're strong and fierce no matter what form you take. You're our mate and surely the most powerful being in the universe."

My soul swells at their closeness, my heart and mind aligning, feeling more content than I ever knew possible. Closing my eyes, I huff another breath through my nostrils and embrace the strange heat diminishing in my body. My muscles spasm with my transformation, the world shifting around me. I gasp a cool breath of air through my lips, tasting the cinnamon flavor of Kash's mouth as he steals my breath with a kiss.

He shrugs out of his undershirt and tugs it over my head to ensure no one apart from his brothers gets another look at my naked body. "That was fucking incredible. Perfect. You're a natural."

I laugh and shake my head. "Hardly, but thanks."

"All right, Baker," Maddox says, resting his hand on my shoulder while turning toward the warlock. "Time to get the collar off of her."

Baker cautiously steps forward, keeping his hands at his sides. Rowan doesn't let him get within reach and forces him to take a look at me from over his shoulder. Gathering my hair, Kash piles it in his hand, lifting it from my neck. He gently nudges me to turn around so that Baker can see the strange necklace glowing on my neck.

Baker purses his lips. "How the hell did she get that

control collar on her? The High Council banned the use of those a century ago. I thought it was one of the standard restraints or a damn CO training tool. But she's not training is she?"

"We cannot discuss such matters. Just know that Delphia is our mate." Maddox gets in front of me protectively. "If you cannot help us, then we will find someone who will." Growling, he motions to his brothers to go to Quillon and Rose.

Kash points at Baker. "You did not see us, understand? Consider it one of your debts paid. If you can help with the collar, I'll clear all debts."

Baker groans and laces his fingers behind his head. "I will need to discuss it with my high priestess. I'll need her guidance as I'm unfamiliar with this dark of magic."

Maddox dips his head in agreement. "Good. There are other matters which I need to discuss with her. Show us the way."

CHAPTER 19

Fugitives

I CAN'T STOP staring out the window, wondering how long until Maddox returns from his meeting with the Lioht High Priestess. A grand mansion glows across an expansive lawn and away from the small cottage Baker led us to. I can't blame the Drekis for wanting him to be as discrete as possible, considering they've abandoned their duties at the Maximum Magical Penitentiary to help three convicts escape.

"It could be hours, kitten," Kash says, wrapping his arms around me from behind. "Come let us give you the attention we desperately need to after everything. Rowan drew a bath, and I brought you a few things to eat from the kitchen."

"And after, maybe you'd like us to snuggle you for a bit," Rowan adds, drawing my attention away from the window to glance at him.

A smile creeps on my face as I drink in the sight of him only wearing a pair of boxer-briefs, which gives me a delicious view of his ripped body. Kash turns me around completely, and I drop my gaze to all his naked sexiness. His well-hung dick already hardens under my attention.

I reach between us and graze my fingers along his shaft. "Do you plan on joining me or something?"

"If you're inviting me. I can handfeed you anywhere you please," he says, hooking his fingers to my hip to slide them farther up my body and under the long T-shirt of his I'm wearing. "And as much as I love seeing you in something of mine, I can't wait to see you out of it."

"We could all use a bit of distracting, don't you think?" Rowan asks, opening his arms to me. "If you don't allow us, you'll be forcing us to break Maddox's orders, and you know what an asshole he is when we don't listen to him."

I bite my lip between my teeth. "So you both want my

attention?" It's something they've brought up before, but it never occurred to me that it might actually happen. How I'm going to handle such an adventure leaves my body yearning to at least try.

Kash hooks his fingers to the hem of my shirt and tests to see if I let him pull it up. I do, shivering under the sensation of his fingers grazing over my stomach. "Actually, we want to give you our attention, Nova. Seeing that asshole stab you and take your life, even if only temporary, it messed me up. A piece of me died in that moment, and I never, and I mean never, want to ever experience such pain again."

My breath catches, and I tilt my head up to lock my gaze to his, searching his face for the truth. "I-I died?" It's nearly unbelievable, but a part of me knows it's true.

Kash leans forward and groans against my bare shoulder, drawing his fingers up my ribs, leaving a trail of heat behind. "One sure way to escape Max is through death. The brands react to your life force, and if you don't have one—fuck. I can't lose you, kitten. I can't even think of that again. It makes me want to live every second giving you everything you could ever want and desire...which is hopefully us."

"Because you're all we want," Rowan says, wiggling his fingers until I come to him. "You're our mate. More mesmerizing than I ever imagined. Beyond my heart's desire.

Seeing you in your true form, Nova, made my existence feel complete."

"And if you're nervous...we'll do things how and when you want in your own time. We just want to be with you." Kash nudges me closer to Rowan. "However you please."

I step into Rowan's arms, sliding my hands up his chest and over his shoulders to play with the tousled strands of his hair. "What about Maddox?" My mind keeps drifting to him as I wonder what he's arranging with the Lioht High Priestess.

"He'd be angry if we didn't take care of your needs. He wouldn't dare want you to wait on him." Leaning in, he caresses his lips to mine, linking his fingers to my hip to tug me with him while Kash guides me forward from behind.

"Plus, he still deserves a bit of sweet retaliation for his hesitation. If you keep your thoughts open to him, it'll be the perfect brand of punishment," Kash teases.

I giggle and bump my head to his chest. "I do like to drive him crazy. Get him all hot and bothered."

Rowan kisses me again. "If that's what you want."

Warmth and excitement spark between my legs, my desire ignited by the soft candlelight illuminating the dimly lit bathroom. A floral fragrance permeates the air, and I inhale a small breath, the scent mixing with Rowan and Kash's as they both memorize my body with their hands.

Kash runs his fingers over my breasts while Rowan slips

a finger between my legs to rub my body in a way that makes me moan. I break from his mouth and kiss down his throat, letting his neck go only so I can feel the hardness of his dick in my hand. Tugging his underwear down, I lace my fingers around him and stroke him, making him moan.

He backs up until we reach a lounge chair situated in a corner of the grand bathroom where a dressing area divides the room. Sitting down, he scoots back, guiding me with him so that I rest on my knees. I kiss him again, slipping my tongue into his mouth, tasting the spicy-sweetness of his lips.

Kash lifts my long hair and brushes his lips to the back of my neck. Drawing his tongue over my sensitive skin, he licks a line down my spine before lowering himself to his back. Rowan hooks his fingers to my hips and lifts me up a few inches, and I moan so fucking loud as he lowers me onto Kash's face. My mind spins with lust and need and desire, my body exploding under so much attention I can't believe I've had to live my life without up until now.

Silencing my moan with a passionate kiss, Rowan explores my mouth with his tongue while rubbing my nipples with his fingers. I grab his dick again, sliding my hand up and down the length of his shaft, my movements desperate because of the wave of pleasure Kash ignites inside me by sucking and licking and flicking his tongue over my clit like it's his sole duty in life to make me orgasm.

"It is now," Rowan murmurs against my lips, responding to my thought.

Another wave of intense desire crashes over me, stealing my breath. Rowan and Kash open themselves to me to experience them on a level that feels like we're a shared soul between our bodies. The intensity of our emotions mingling and the pleasure rolling through my body brings me to my peak. Rowan kisses me as I orgasm from Kash's attention, holding me as I shudder through the amazing, mind-blowing sensation gripping every molecule inside me while making me squeeze Kash between my thighs.

If Rowan didn't ease me up, I don't think I'd ever move. Because fuck. I need to experience the kind of pleasure I had no idea existed until I allowed these sexy men into my life. No man before them can even compare. I've never had anyone wanting to ensure that I got what I wanted and needed first. Every man before only wanted a quick way to get off with nothing much for me.

"Now, I need to make you forget all those selfish bastards and show you what it's like being a dragon clan's mate." Kash tugs me toward him by my hips and rubs his hand up the length of my back, getting me to rest on my elbows. Sliding his hand around my waist, he adjusts my legs to tuck them beneath me.

Releasing a soft giggle, I shake my ass at him, making him hum. He kisses each of my ass cheeks and swats me

CAGED BY HER DRAGONS

playfully from behind.

I extend my arms out and caress my fingers over Rowan's thighs, getting him to move closer. He gathers my hair into his hands and twists it out of the way to watch as I lace my seemingly small hand around his astonishing girth. He moans at the sensation of my tongue gliding over him, tasting the skin of his smooth balls. Kash purrs deep in his throat from behind me, aligning his body to mine. He doesn't enter me right away but watches me pleasure Rowan. I listen to Rowan's moans, letting his voice guide me on what he likes best. He plays with my hair, his muscles flexing and rippling under the exploration of my free hand as I trace his abs.

"Ready for me, kitten?" Kash asks, slipping a finger inside me to tease and test me.

I hum my agreement, continuing to work my mouth over Rowan's raging boner, enjoying as he plays with my nipples like he can't help touching me while I pleasure him. The room fills with the melodic sounds of our passion, our pants and moans so hot and sexy it turns me on even more.

Kash enters me with only his tip, and I gasp at the building pressure with his slow thrust as he takes his time pushing into me. I scratch my nails into Rowan's legs and gasp, pulling back to moan. Rowan takes over and strokes himself, letting me focus solely on the hot, electrifying sensation of the growing power of Kash's thrusts.

A wave of raw need courses through me, drawing my attention back to Rowan. I prop up on my elbows and take back over, sucking him as far as I can into my mouth. I suck and lick and stroke him, feeling the incredible mixture of his pleasure weaving with mine and Kash's. This sort of intimacy far exceeds anything I've ever experienced and known. My very soul hums in satisfaction knowing exactly what I do to the both of them. And I know they can feel exactly what they do to me too.

Rowan tightens his fingers through my hair, his body tensing. "Nova, I'm going to cum."

In the Mortal World, the first thing I'd do with that sentence was pull away, but something deep-seated entices me to see Rowan's pleasure through until he finishes. My curiosity over tasting him, hearing his enjoyment as he cums, knowing that I'm all in, gives me a contentment that I want to savor.

Rowan braces his hand to the back of my head, letting my hair spill around me. I suck him in and out a few more times until his cum floods my mouth with his release. He moans, stroking his hands over my shoulders as I ease up and lick the strangely intoxicating flavor from my lips. A bit tangy but sweet with a hint of cinnamon and something indescribable. It makes me hungry to pleasure him again and again.

"She's so fucking beautiful and sexy. I'm so turned on

by how much she enjoys this," Kash says, rocking into me harder and faster now that I turn my focus to him.

Rowan scoots down and rests his head on his arm to smile at me. "How did we get so lucky, brother?"

I grin, words unable to form on my lips as Kash's passion steals my ability to do anything other than moan. Touching my chin, Rowan gets me to stretch my neck a bit to meet him for a kiss. I love how he doesn't care about how I was just giving him a blow job. He wants my lips on his regardless, his desire to give me his affection the most important thing for him in this moment.

Kash continues to thrust and moan, whispering my name and how he can't get enough of me, how he yearns to make love to me every moment he can. I smile through his words, continuing to kiss Rowan, watching him watch me, savoring his closeness while he shares me with his brother. The only thing missing is the fire and smoldering intensity of Maddox. My heart nearly calls for him to come to me, but another part of me wonders if I could really do this with all three of them. How I'd be willing to try it at least once.

Kash moans with my thought, pulling out of me to finish on my back. Warmth splashes across my buzzing skin, the fact that he chose not to cum inside me being the first thing to flit through my mind as I catch my breath.

Hooking his arms around me, Kash lifts me up and cradles me in his arms. "Because you desire to get to know more than my body and soul before bearing my children," he says, responding to my thought.

I blush, unable to help myself from thinking about Maddox and Rowan.

"And you've wanted my children since the moment you laid eyes on me, cookie." Maddox's voice trickles through the door. "Now, may I come in?"

"Yes, brother. Our mate called for you. You've been gone longer than she liked." Kash stands up and kisses me tenderly, combing my messy hair from my face. Rowan follows us to the grand bathtub and climbs in first to take me from Kash.

Maddox clicks open the door and hesitates without entering. "I'm sorry for that, cookie. Things have been complicated."

I frown. "What does that mean?"

Sighing, Maddox turns his gaze to the floor without responding.

Rowan grabs the shower nozzle and silently cleanses my body, knowing that I won't sit down for a soak in the tub. Maddox tightens his jaw, eyeing both his brothers, and without having to ask, I realize they're having a silent conversation and leaving me out of it.

Annoyance washes through me, and I climb out of the tub and snatch a towel from a hook. I wrap it around myself and close the space to Maddox, not even caring if I drip soapy water all over the floor.

"Tell me what's so complicated. Maybe I can help. I know the Mortal World and many people here." I grab the front of his shirt and shake him. "I don't care where we go or what we do as long as I don't ever go back to Magaelorum."

"How sweet of her to say such a thing," a feminine voice calls, drawing my attention to the living room. "Come out here, dear. I need to take a look at the mate of the Dreki Dragons."

I startle at the sight of the woman, her familiarity sending panic through me. "Aunt McKayla?" I know it's not her the second her name escapes my lips, but the woman looks identical to my aunt.

The woman steps forward, a grimace marring her beautiful face. "No, dear. That would be my wretched, banished sister. She nearly ruined our good standing with the High Council with her treachery. And now I see why."

Stepping closer, the woman holds out a few garments to me and motions for me to get dressed. She returns to her spot on the couch and watches me until I turn my back on her and head into the bathroom.

"We need to leave," I whisper to Maddox, Kash, and Rowan as they surround me. "Something feels off. What if she turns me in?"

"McKenzie gave me her word. The Liohts have given

us such a courtesy because it's what Rhett desired. He ensured that his coven would look out for us if something were to happen. And I told her the truth about what happened and how he was searching for you." Maddox runs his hands over my arms, using the towel to dry me off.

"Trust our brother, kitten. He knows what he's doing. Now let's hurry. It's rude to keep the High Priestess waiting, especially with the favor we need from her." He touches the band of now puckered skin wrapping my throat.

Taking a deep breath, I follow the Drekis from the bathroom and plop down into the loveseat across from McKenzie. She lifts the lid of a covered tray to show a collection of cookies and small sandwiches that probably wouldn't satiate the hunger still roaring within me.

"Please, help yourselves," she says, motioning to the table.

I can't stop staring at McKayla's twin adding milk to a cup of tea. It's hard to fathom the information, because I always thought the woman who raised me was my mom's sister, but she wasn't. She isn't even related to me, nor is she a dragon but a witch. Holy fucking shit.

"I don't understand any of this," I say, bowing forward to rest my elbows on my knees, covering my face with my hands. It's the only thought to cross my mind. "Are my parents even dead? Why would my aunt—why would McKayla kidnap me and cast a spell to lock my very nature away?"

CAGED BY HER DRAGONS

"If I had even an ounce of an idea of why my shameful sister does what she does, I'd have been able to stop her from getting thrown out of our coven," McKenzie says, pouting her bottom lip. "I could have prevented her from helping a blasted prisoner escape the Maximum Magical Penitentiary all those years ago. I partially blame Rhett for even allowing her to follow in his footsteps to help secure that place."

I blink a few times. "Wait, she worked at the prison. Rhett, too? How many years ago?" I recall Lazlo mentioning my mom was in the same prison. Was it McKayla that helped her escape? Why was she even in there?

So many questions swirl through my mind. Rhett mentioned how difficult my mother made it for him to find me, and I wonder what she offered to McKayla to do so. That would make better sense than some random witch stealing the last female of the Drakovich Clan.

"Longer than we've all been alive. Rhett was there since the first day we started to fulfill our bloodline's debt, Delphia. He was a CO before he was promoted to a gatekeeper." Maddox slides his arm around me to pull me onto his lap, hugging me close. "It's also how he knew your name. We've spoken of the Drakovich line before."

But it can't be. He knew of my mother. There is more to it.

McKenzie straightens her shoulders, her posture turning rigid. "A Drakovich? You're the child of Delilah Drakovich?" A shock of purple light flickers in her eyes.

Fuck. She doesn't have to say anything for me to know that I was right about McKayla helping my mom escape the prison.

"This all makes sense," McKenzie continues. A smile pulls across her lips. "That clever, clever sister of mine." Ice travels down my back from the cold hardness of her stare.

"What makes sense?" Maddox asks. "You cannot hold such a thing as sibling treachery against our mate. That was her mother's wrongdoings. Your sister's. Now please, High Priestess, do as you promised, and we can leave."

McKenzie stands with a flourish, her hair and long skirt flowing with her movements. I tense as she closes the space to me and grabs onto my hair, yanking it with malice away from my neck. All three Drekis growl, but McKenzie raises a hand, gathering purple power on her palm.

"Uncanto draconi Delphia. Graulot momensi trevistitato." Static swirls through the air with McKenzie's spell. Her eyes grow brighter and brighter until a lash of burning agony laces around my neck.

I clutch my throat, unable to scream as my airway cuts off. Panic consumes me. This isn't right. She's not helping me. She's killing me.

"McKenzie, stop!" Maddox roars, gathering fire in his hand.

CAGED BY HER DRAGONS

"Graulot momensi trevistitato!" she yells, chucking power at me.

Maddox unleashes his flames, intercepting her. Screeching, McKenzie flies across the small living room and crashes into the wall. Rowan and Kash get between the witch and me, summoning their dragon fire.

"Get her out of here! We'll handle it!" Rowan says, his eyes smoldering with fire.

"There is no need, Drekis. If you want to ruin your lives for someone who can never belong to you, then so be it. Consider this a warning. Her freedom—and yours—won't ever last."

McKenzie blinks from existence, leaving behind an earthy, floral fragrance in the air. I gasp a breath, my chest heaving as the magical rope suffocating me vanishes with her disappearance. Adjusting me in his arms, Maddox turns me to face him, resting his forehead to mine.

"Take a slow breath, Delphia. This isn't over. We don't need them, okay?" Maddox says, getting me to breathe with him. "We are Drekis. You are our mate. The fates proved it. Our souls have aligned."

I close my eyes, letting his words sink in. I never expected such words to feel so utterly and irrevocably true. "You're right."

"We will get through this," Rowan says, caging me to Maddox with a hug.

"Together." Kash engulfs us in his arms, adding to his brothers' delicious warmth. "And then maybe you'll have our babies."

I laugh. "Knock it off."

"Never," Maddox says, kissing my temple. "Our future, our freedom, our fulfilling lives together are what we need to remember. Because all of that—that's what we're truly fighting for."

Damn it. I'll never admit it to his face and give him that sort of satisfaction, but Maddox is right. My dragon heart knows it. The thought alone makes the beautiful beast within me roar.

I've never felt so powerful.

EPILOGUE

Break Free

"HOME, SWEET HOME," Rowan says, uncovering my eyes in the front yard of a surprisingly impressive house with a view overlooking the Pacific Ocean. "What do you think? Will this do?"

I blink in awe and turn to face him. He offers me a small smile and shifts on his feet to glance at his brothers. Maddox remains stone-faced, and Kash keeps his gaze to the sky like he thinks it might fill with all the dragon clans of Magaelorum.

"Well?" Rowan asks when I'm not quick to respond.

I twist my lips and turn to the house again. Their anticipation for my reaction and response nearly swallows me whole. They've been on edge since we left the Lioht Coven's Mortal World property days ago, and now all I want is to lighten the mood. So I decide to tease Maddox.

"Well," I sigh, letting out a breath.

"I told you it was a fucking bad idea. This place is substandard." Maddox balls his hands into fists.

My eyes widen as he doesn't allow me to get to my joke. Rushing to him, I grab the front of his T-shirt, a strange sight to see because I'm still so used to him wearing a uniform, and stop him from charging his brother.

"It's perfect," I say. "I was kidding. It just...wasn't what I was expecting."

"What were you expecting, kitten?" Kash asks, speaking up for the first time since our arrival at the open gate of the block wall surrounding the property.

I narrow my eyes at Maddox. "A cave. Somewhere for this beast to sleep."

Rowan laughs from behind me and steals me away before Maddox can pick me up. I squeal at their sudden game of keep away. Throwing me into the air high enough to flip, I brace myself for one of them to catch me, knowing they'd never let me hit the ground. Kash beats both his brothers, engulfing me in his hot arms. My kiss is enough to finally make him smile.

A whistle cuts through the air, turning Kash's smile into a hard line. Wiggling in his arms, I wait for him to put me on my feet to see who comes out of the house. Quillon crosses his arms, leaning on the doorframe. Behind him, I spot Rose grinning like our arrival is the best thing she's ever experienced.

"What took you assholes so long?" Quillon asks. "You were supposed to be here yesterday."

I swing my attention to Rowan. "You better be fucking kidding me. He is not staying here. I thought we were done with him." With Rose for that matter too, but I don't say the words out loud.

Quillon barks a laugh, his deep rumbly voice tensing my muscles. "Who do you think this house belongs to, Red?"

Fuck. Fuck. Fuck.

I turn to Maddox. "Go pick out a cave."

"That's not how this is going to work," Quillon says. "A deal's a deal."

Kash groans and spins me around to face him again. Reaching up, he combs his fingers through my messy tresses to push them behind my ear. A wave of disappointment collides into me, but the emotion belongs to Kash. I knew something had been bothering him, and now I know exactly what it is.

Fury rushes over me, and I break away from Kash and dodge past Rowan and Maddox. Quillon's smile widens into a leer, and his eyes flash green in preparation for my attack.

But I don't get within a foot of him.

Tackling me, Maddox pins me to the ground, straddling my ass. He locks his fingers around my wrists and stops me from fighting. "Calm down, Delphia. This is only temporary. As soon as we get the cure, we can rid him from our lives forever."

I growl and kick my legs, trying to get Maddox off me. I don't care if it looks as if I'm throwing a tantrum. I fucking am.

"You can't make me spend time with that creep!" I yell. "I won't do it."

"If you don't fulfill your end, I'll ensure that your mate never turns human again. He has already bowed to me. I control him." Quillon bares his teeth and looks past me at Kash. "Isn't that right, Kash? Should I prove it?"

"That won't be necessary," Maddox growls.

"Oh, but I think it is. Delphia needs to see that I'm being a nice guy. She needs to see that this could be a lot worse." Quillon flares his nostrils. "Now, Kash. Transform. Transform and take a bow."

CAGED BY HER DRAGONS

Kash yells out, his clothes splitting and ripping as his body contorts with the uncontrollable change into his dragon form by Quillon's demand. My heart sinks into my stomach, watching Kash hunch forward until his big head rests on the ground.

"Stop! Okay! Let him change back," I cry, my heart feeling as if Quillon squeezes a piece of it with his control over Kash. "I'll do what you want."

Quillon grins. "Good, gorgeous girl. Now come inside and go down the hallway to the first door on the left. That's our room together."

"You can't expect me to fuck you," I exclaim, anger shadowing my vision red.

Licking his lips, he drinks me in as I remain on the ground even as Maddox gets up. "I don't. But you will serve me as if I am your mate. And when I'm through with you, you will beg me to claim you. You will love getting down on your knees. You're mine, Delphia. Mine."

I inhale a few breaths, trying my best to remain composed. Because fuck that. Quillon will learn the games he's playing now will only be his end. I'm more determined than ever to break the restraints that bind me.

I will break free.

To be continued...

GINNA MORAN

Thank you so much for reading *Caged by Her Dragons*! I hope you enjoyed Nova and the Dreki brothers! Don't forget to check out *the Freed by Her Dragons!*

If you love the *Mates of Magaelorum World* and haven't read *The She-Wolf Games*, you will definitely want to! The Lunar Crest pack is waiting.

Other Reverse Harem Novels by Ginna Moran

THE VAMPIRE HEIRS WORLD

La Vega Vampire Showstoppers
Vampire Nights

The Divine Vampire Heirs
Blood Match
Blood Rebel
Blood Debt
Blood Feud
Blood Loss
Blood Vows

The Royale Vampire Heirs Series:
Rebel Vampires
Rebel Dhampir
Rebel Match
Rebel Heir
Rebel Fight

Academy of Vampire Heirs Series:
Dhampirs 101
Blood Sources 102
Coven Bonds 103
Personal Donors 104
Blood Wars 105

THE MATES OF MAGAELORUM WORLD

The Pack Mates of Lunar Crest:
The She-Wolf Games
The Wolf-Mate Trials
The Omega Hunt
The Witch Chase
Winter Wolf Games

Fated Mate of the Dragon Clans
Caged by Her Dragons
Freed by Her Dragons
Saved by Her Dragons

SEVEN SINNERS WORLD

The Seven Sinners of Hell's Kingdom
Her Personal Demons
Her Deadly Angels
Her Darkest Devils
Her Sinful Saints

ABOUT GINNA MORAN

GINNA MORAN IS the author of over seventy novels including the popular La Vega Vampire Showstoppers, The Pack Mates of Lunar Crest, The Seven Sinners of Hell's Kingdom Academy of Vampire Heirs, The Divine Vampire Heirs, and The Royale Vampire Heirs WhyChoose novels.

She always carried a fascination for all things paranormal and wrote her first unpublished manuscript at age eighteen. Her love of the supernatural grew stronger through her adult life, and she now spends her days with different creatures of the night. Whether it's vampires,

GINNA MORAN

werewolves, dragons, fae, angels, demons, or mermaids, Ginna loves creating and living in worlds from her dreams.

Aside from Ginna's professional life, she enjoys binge watching TV, crafting and design, playing pretend with her daughter, and cuddling with her dogs. Some of her favorite things include chocolate, mermaids, anything that glitters, learning new things, cheesy jokes, and organizing her bookshelf.

Ginna is currently hard at work on her next novel and the one after, and the one after that.

Made in United States
Orlando, FL
03 December 2023